THE PRIDE LIST

EDITED BY SANDIP ROY AND BISHAN SAMADDAR

The Pride List presents works of queer literature to the world.
An eclectic collection of books of queer stories, poems, plays,
biographies, histories, thoughts, ideas, experiences and explorations,
the Pride List does not focus on any specific region, nor on any
specific genre, but celebrates the great diversity of LGBTQ+ lives
across countries, languages, centuries and identities, with the
conviction that queer pride comes from its unabashed expression.

Jacob Israël de Haan

Pathologies

The Downfall of Johan van Vere de With

Translated from the Dutch by
Brian Doyle-Du Breuil

LONDON NEW YORK CALCUTTA

N ederlands
letterenfonds
dutch foundation
for literature

The publisher gratefully acknowledges the
support of the Dutch Foundation for Literature

Seagull Books, 2024

First published in Dutch as *Pathologieën. De ondergang van Johan van
Vere de With* by Jacob Israël de Haan in 1908

First published in English translation by Seagull Books, 2024

English translation © Brian Doyle-Du Breuil, 2024

This translation is based on the 1975 edition of *Pathologieën*, published by
Kruseman's Uitgeversmaatschappij, The Hague, available in the public domain
through the Digital Library for Dutch Literature (DBNL). The Dutch edition
includes an essay by Wim J. Simons (1926–2005), reproduced here as 'Epilogue
to *Pathologies*' in Brian Doyle-Du Breuil's English translation.

Every effort was made to identify the heirs to Mr Simons's estate but
without success. Please contact the publisher if you can provide information
in this regard: info@seagullbooks.org

ISBN 978 1 8030 9 346 8

British Library Cataloguing-in-Publication Data
A catalogue record for this book is available from the British Library

Typeset at seagull Books, Calcutta, india
Printed and bound in USA by Integrated Books International

Contents

Foreword

GEORGES EEKHOUD

This is a very important document. Its author, Jacob Israël de Haan, an exceptional literary artist and a profoundly intuitive psychologist, has penned a unique account of deviant emotional inclinations, namely, uranism.

De Haan already explored the subject in an earlier novel entitled *Pipelines*, set in one of the most unique neighbourhoods of Amsterdam. With poignant veracity, exceptional literary skill, and an abundance of tact and moderation, *Pipelines* opens a window into the life of two emotionally challenged young men. Both share company with a much rejected and unloved segment of society, towards whom public opinion, preceded by science and, in particular, literature, is now, finally, exhibiting a degree of fairness.

I am reminded here of a gallant endeavour in the French press to support the remarkable English writer Oscar Wilde, who was sentenced by 'biblical' judges to a dreadful fate for deeds that had impinged on no one's freedom, deeds that were far from morally inferior, that had in no way disadvantaged his self-opinionated accusers. I am reminded in particular of the articles penned by Octave Mirbeau, Henri Fouquier, and especially Paul Adam and Henri de Regnier in *la Revue Blanche* and Hugues Rebell in *Mercure de France*.

In the scientific world, Professor Richard Freiherr von Krafft-Ebing, a leading authority in the domain of psychiatry at the University of Vienna, has been instrumental in expanding our horizons in this regard, exposing the true moral and physical nature of countless individuals who have been rejected and marginalized by society through no fault of their own.

In the preface to a French edition of a publication by Dr Albert Moll—also a renowned physician—dedicated to deviant emotional inclinations, Von Krafft-Ebing writes:

> The law and public opinion must acknowledge that such deviant emotional inclinations are not *perversité* but *perversion*, i.e. they require a specific predisposition, and are often symptomatic of illness. This scientifically established fact must ultimately put an end to any enduring prejudice that judges and despises people whose only wrong is to have been allotted homosexual feelings and inclinations by impartial destiny. Advocates of justice and humanity will be deeply satisfied to learn that those who experience deviation in the object of their affections may often be ill-fated, but they are not criminals. They are not abusers, but rather disadvantaged victims of negligent mother nature. They deserve no more to be despised than someone born with a physical deformity.
>
> The facts of history and my own clinical observations are sufficient to convince me that many such individuals make a valuable contribution to society and are deserving of every respect. Their only misfortune is that some of their feelings are irregular.

Literary artists, novelists, poets and playwrights are at liberty to base their work on these unfortunate individuals and the lives they live.

This, and no more than this, is what Jacob Israël De Haan has done. And yet, the publication of his book *Pipelines* generated such unexpected hostility from many of his former political allies: the socialists. They registered more irritation than the dullest of do-gooders, and the pettiest puritans. The devotees of biblical morality felt obliged to betray and vilify their former companion with such contempt that he found himself in severe difficulties. Indeed, their behaviour threatened to rob him of his livelihood.

At this juncture, one of socialism's champions, and one of its most principled advocates, Ferdinand Lassalle, demonstrated particular decency of character.

When a leading socialist by the name of Dr. Schweizer was condemned for allegedly immoral behaviour, the Workers Association in Frankfurt am Main quickly moved to have him struck from their membership list. Lassalle knew Schweizer well and wrote a letter to the executive of the said association rejecting their intolerant narrow-mindedness in no uncertain terms. He went on to express both esteem and affection for his friend, a man now burdened by undeserved inequity.

'Such treatment of a man of your intellect and standing,' Lassalle wrote to his comrade, 'is evidence, if it were needed, that our people are prone to pettiness and duplicity when politics are involved.'

De Haan's new book *Pathologies* focuses on the life and circumstances of two homosexuals. While one of the two might be difficult to describe as belonging to the elite of his sort in every respect—what has been called a 'superior uranist'—he remains a refined and artistic young man, affectionate and dedicated to those he loves. While his inclinations are overpowering, they are nonetheless pure.

His homosexual tendencies and affections lead him slowly but inescapably into complete dependence on a second homosexual. While René is a great artist, he is nevertheless wicked to the core and forever in search of new pleasures, as one often finds among those whose romantic inclinations depart from the norm. René's desires are foul and vulgar, intensified by cruelties of the most sadistic nature and expression.

In the end, Johan is no longer able to live with the suffering, the abuse and sophisticated torments, the fears and anxieties. His once resilient nature falls apart and he takes his own life.

De Haan's depiction of the gradual downfall of this unfortunate young man clearly demonstrates that his literary skills have strengthened significantly since he wrote *Pipelines*. He has avoided the kind of material that would attract the scandalmongers and their smut-driven pens. He writes with sensitivity and restraint about the relationship between Johan and his father, and later his relationship with René Richell. He relates Johan's sacrifices, his selfless affections, his efforts to steer his friend towards less tortured forms of love, his inability to end their relationship. We witness the demise of Johan's artistic talents, his strength of will, his mental health, and ultimately his suicide.

Pathologies is more a psychological tragedy than a portrayal of distorted desires. As a result, this extraordinary work radiates the authentic, excruciating magnificence of hidden misfortune that marks a genuine masterpiece.

The primary scenes are surrounded by more serene accounts. And besides Johan and René, the book's characters are portrayed with exceptional precision, especially Johan's father. In the best of prose, De Haan recounts Johan's childhood, his extraordinary home life with his father, his school years and the boys he encounters there, and his life as a lodger with an elderly couple in Harlem, where he meets the purebred demon who will be his ultimate downfall. These skilful portrayals often serve to soothe the strong emotions stirred by the intense passions at the core of the author's tragic narrative.

In short: *Pathologies* will serve as an enduring confirmation of its author's literary skills.

Georges Eekhoud wrote this foreword in Brussels. Jacob Israël de Haan translated the French original into Dutch in Amsterdam.

Preface

The publication of my novel *Pathologies* provides me with an opportunity to clarify a misunderstanding concerning my earlier book, *Pipelines*.

Let it be clear: *Pipelines* was never seized by the courts or the police, nor was its publication halted for any other reason.

As a literary artist, I stand by my work. *Pipelines* was a joy to write, although my life as a member of a certain community has become much more difficult as a result.

I have already completed part two of *Pipelines*, which will be published as soon as circumstances beyond my control permit.

PART ONE

FOR GEORGE EEKHOUD

Quoi dono lepidum novom libellum?
Amico, tibi, namque tu solebas
Meas esse aliquid putare nugas.

To whom should I dedicate this amiable book?
To you, my friend, because you tend
to think that my trifles are meaningful.

***

Vivamus [. . .] *atque amemus*
Rumoresque senum severiorum
Omnes unius aestimemus assis.

Let us live [. . .] and let us love
and treat the senile moralists
and their nonsense as worthless.

***

Lugete, o Veneres, Cupidinesque
Et quantumst hominum venustiorum.

Mourn, O Venuses and Cupids,
and pleasing people one and all.

CATULLUS

Amo e il segreto mio non posso dir.

I love, and my secret I cannot tell.

LORENZO STECHETTI

Chapter One

1

What follows is a measured description, although written with great anxiety, of the pathologies that occasioned the downfall of Johan van Vere de With.

2

Cuilemburg is more a village than a town; its market square is elongated and rectangular, serving the town as a sort of interior courtyard. A house is nestled in the middle of one of the long sides, an old house.

On the outside it appears to be a double house consisting of two stepped gables on either side of a broad door, broader than two regular doors. But on the inside, it is in fact a single house, occupied by three people: a boy named Johan, his father, and a very elderly woman named Sien. Given the size of the house and the conspicuously quiet life led by its inhabitants, it often seemed uninhabited.

Johan's mother had passed away many years earlier, before Johan and his father settled in Cuilemburg. As a result, she had never graced any of the rooms with her presence, a fact that did not displease Johan's father. But the house, nevertheless, was full of her things. To Johan these were odd and of little value, but to his father they were precious, irreplaceable treasures.

3

Johan occupied two rooms at the back of the house, both of which looked out onto a mature, dark and overgrown garden, reminiscent of a sprawling and mysterious forest. But the darkness did not reach the house. Between it and the garden there was a narrow lane and a meadow filled in season with a multicoloured array of flowers. In the evenings, Johan would work at his window, the floor lamp casting a frail haze outside, like a golden sun-spurred mist that transformed and refined the colour of the flowers, recasting them in a strange, fragile tale. The light of the lamp was unable to penetrate the dark, dense, forest-like garden. The trees were aligned in a rampart of black, behind which was the other world.

3

The finest objects in their well-appointed house were the doorbell and the hall clock. The bell was attached to the back of the front door. It wasn't made of silver, but of an unknown metal that sounded much sharper than silver, and more stirring. It was a joy to hear it echo through the high, hushed corridors, then thin to nothing as silence enveloped the house once more. It saddened Johan that this delightful and majestic bell was rarely heard. Most people didn't use their distinguished front door, preferring instead the garden entrance at the back of the house, across the meadow and the lane. When Johan busied himself in the evening without his father, and his thinly whispering lamp misted white, he often longed for someone to ring the bell in the silence and for something unusual to follow. But that never happened, because they lived such a quiet life.

The clock, which Johan loved dearly, stood in the bright, high-ceilinged hallway. Its tick was dark and solemn, like the voice of an elderly man. But when it struck, there was light and laughter, like the laughter of a boy, a grown-up boy. At night, when Johan lay awake, he couldn't hear the clock ticking, but he heard it strike every single hour.

Opposite their house was a brown-stone church with a sonorous bell suspended high above the rooftops, which rang for a full quarter hour until ten o'clock. Johan never forgot to hurry downstairs to the lofty white hallway to see if the hall clock and the church clock agreed.

4

When Johan's father was eighteen he moved to Amsterdam to study law. He met a much older woman there, a doctor, and they married shortly thereafter. They wasted little time in having a child, the older woman fearing that her chances of having a healthy pregnancy were limited. The birth of the child brought great joy to the young father and his older wife.

Shortly after the birth of her son, the mother succumbed to mental illness. Its most severe manifestations were the many and harsh reproaches she hurled at herself—that she should never have had a child at her age, that she couldn't give such a child the care it deserved. In the course of time, her self-reproach evolved into profound self-deprecation and perpetual confessions of guilt. She then declared that she was completely unfit to continue living with her husband and her son and had decided to die by suicide. She repeatedly inflicted deep and bloody wounds on herself, and the only way to preserve her life was to keep a close guard on her day and night and pay no attention to her actions. After maintaining this arduous duty for several months, it seemed that her desire to die had diminished. She realized that it was a result of her illness and her self-reproach changed: she should never have longed to die. Her body, alas, remained weak, while her still-faltering mind struggled to recover its equilibrium.

One night her guilt and death wish unexpectedly returned, something no one could have anticipated. Her husband and child were asleep in the next room. She got up and went to them, her pale feet silent in the night. She gazed at her husband and child for a long time. She listened to her husband's deep nocturnal breathing, the man she loved so dearly. She turned to her child and repeated word for word in her thoughts: 'Hans is such a beautiful child . . . his father will be happy with him when he grows up. But I must die, because the guilt I bear is too heavy, giving birth to a child at my age, unable even to feed him.'

She was calm enough, in spite of her insanity. She returned to her own room, in search of death. But how would she do it? She had nothing with which to cut or strangle herself, and she didn't dare move or make a noise for fear of waking her husband.

Her hair was long and abundant, reaching far below her waist. She untied it and plaited it with slender nimble fingers into two long and sturdy cords, like braided silk. She then strangled herself, silent and motionless, her plaited hair, fierce and alive, tightening around her gasping throat.

5

Her horrified husband found her lifeless body the following morning.

After the funeral, the young man and his exceptionally handsome son set up home in the old house, on one of the long sides of the market square that serves the town of Cuilemburg as sort of interior courtyard. It's more a village than a town.

He completed the requirements of his legal studies with calm despair and then continued his research into the criminal mind. He did not start a legal practice and he had little contact with his family or that of his deceased wife, or indeed the people of Cuilemburg. His only acquaintances were academics, a few Italian and French colleagues, with whom he never discussed his house or his stifled marriage.

Johan was aware that his mother had taken her own life and that his father preferred not to talk about her.

Johan had a picture of her in his room and he was intent on keeping it. Not so much because it was of a mother he had never known but because it was exceptionally beautiful.

The portrait had been printed around the time of their marriage and was now seventeen years old. Years of silent exposure had left its black ink and white paper grey and drab. The face was full of hair-fine cracks, like the crazing on delicate bone china, a costly piece of which was among Johan's most prized possessions. Looking at the portrait always cheered him, knowing that his mother had been so serene and distinguished. Her forehead was high, her eyes penetrating, her nose straight, and her lips firmly sealed.

6

Sien took care of the family's household needs. She was an elderly spinster, diminutive, always modestly dressed. Her delicate face, framed tight by her white bonnet, was often prone to nervous twitching around the eyes, nose and mouth.

She didn't do much in terms of physical labour. She had a maid to make up the beds in the morning and a cleaning lady for the heavier work. But she did what she was able, and often complained to Johan—who listened—about how lazy domestic staff tended to be these days. When her maids were finished with their work in the early afternoon, she would sit for hours in silence in a room on the street side by the garden with the door to the corridor open to be sure she didn't miss a sound in the house. But with her failing hearing, even the resounding doorbell was a struggle to hear. They lived a quiet and independent life and visitors were few and far between, so the elderly spinster was rarely disturbed. She spent much of her time with her Bible, reading passage after passage although she knew most of them by heart. When Johan returned home in the late afternoon and emerged from the dark garden, she would speak to him about God's great miracles, which many didn't believe until they witnessed them in person. The boy listened, calm and ever polite, as he and his father always were.

7

Johan's father, like his mother, was born into well-to-do and highly civilized social circumstances. Their world was cultured and sophisticated, unfamiliar with hard, physical labour. Johan was like both his parents. He had enjoyed exceptional good looks since early childhood, and his disposition had always been composed and temperate, until his life was dramatically disrupted. By the age of sixteen he was an adult, with the appearance of a well-groomed twenty-year-old with youthful features.

He was slender and delicate of stature, and always immaculately dressed. Johan had blue eyes, like blue roses should be when they fill our gardens.

His father thought it best not to send him to school until he turned eight. Johan was a deeply sensitive boy, but he was also insecure and home was better for his emotional tranquillity. While his intellect was strong, his father preferred to protect it from undue stress. As a result, sixteen-year-old Johan went to school with boys two years his younger. It wasn't an unpleasant experience, and since Johan was far from stupid it was easy for him to rise to the top of the class and stay there. He didn't mix much with the other boys, partly because of his age, and partly because of his different disposition and nature.

In the previous two years, as he matured into adulthood, he started to notice occasional yet intense affections towards young, well-dressed and gentle boys at his school. He didn't understand, aware as he was that making friends was not something he found easy. But he also sensed that these affections were dangerous, of such a nature that he could not discuss them with his father. As his body matured, these dangerous affections increased in frequency and intensity. He dreamed at night of certain boys and did indecent things with them in his dreams, which they reciprocated. What they did was both pleasant and emotionally stimulating. In the morning he noticed that his nightclothes were damp and stained. He often felt both helpless and hopeless, and melancholy would fill his day.

While he knew that these things happened in a person's life and every boy experienced them as he matured into manhood, he felt ashamed nonetheless and it left him deeply unhappy. He was certain he didn't want to talk to his father about it, and indeed he didn't dare, but he also knew it would bring him comfort and relief if he were to do so. Often the desire to speak to his father was so intense it hurt him that he was unable to satisfy it.

8

Johan had never imagined the slightest difficulty with his father. In his early years it never even crossed his mind. When he heard about other families and restless discontent between fathers and sons, he would think about his own father and it brought him deep joy. He later realized that there was nothing about their relationship that needed to change. Mutual affection ensured that calm, spontaneous resolution was the result of their every interaction.

9

But of late, Johan's life had been disrupted in a most distressing manner. His beloved and much-respected father had now started to feature in his indecent dreams. His father engaged in indecent acts with him and he with his father, and both took great pleasure in it.

Johan was left speechless and ashamed by these dreams, staggered by the very thought of them. He stared at his father, his blushing blue eyes wide with shame, anxiety and disbelief. He struggled to remain calm and amiable, terrified he would do something untoward. He appeared withdrawn and out of sorts, the effort to behave normally was so immense. His father noticed, of course, and asked tenderly if anything was wrong. This threw Johan into the depths of despair and misery.

The dreams continued and now focused exclusively on his father, tormenting him night after night. He was plagued with nerves and stony pale. His glossy blue eyes faded; once silken, now lacklustre and dull, their bright whites now grey. Johan could see that his father was aware of his deterioration and it only made things worse. At the end of his tether, his voice calm nonetheless and his words carefully chosen, Johan spoke to his father: 'Father, I'm in great distress and it's affecting my health as you can see. I can't tell you why . . . and that makes it all the more painful . . . but perhaps things will improve now that I've told you . . .'

Their eyes met, but the emotion in their gaze unsettled Johan, breaking his resolve. All at once he started to sob. He threw his arms around his father and kissed him on the eyes and open lips as he had done when he was a little boy. But then the same wicked yet pleasurable sensations that plagued his sullied and indecent dreams engulfed him and his clothes felt defiled and damp. His wretched body stiffened in his father's arms and he crawled upstairs to the bathroom where he showered his agitated limbs with cold, gushing water. His father could hear the water gush and splash and was deeply troubled, unable to comprehend his dear son's sudden inhibitions and strange behaviour. He remembered his wife's insanity and the night she took her own life in such an unusual way when everyone was sure she no longer suffered from suicidal inclinations. His thoughts returned to his son and a shiver ran down his spine. Johan was careful with his words and always weighed what he said, so emotional outbursts like this were exceptional. Now he had spoken, after suffering in silence for so long. His cautious words seemed written not spoken. He had revealed the depths of his wretchedness, what it was doing to his health, that he didn't dare speak about it.

At table that same afternoon, Johan raised the subject again. Their table was always handsomely set with the finest things. The boy took rare and subtle delight in their many beautiful possessions. Surrounded by such sophistication, he spoke to his father, his bright blue eyes flickering in the thin lamplight: 'My sadness won't last, I'm sure . . . then we can be content with each other once more.' As he spoke he was anxiously aware of his body. But it remained calm, without the slightest depraved agitation. This hugely delighted Johan and he enjoyed the rest of the evening with his father as he had before.

10

But the torment got worse. During the day, when he spent time with his father, he was overcome by a desire to embrace him, kiss his kindly eyes, his ruddy lips. When he tried to suppress this temptation, all he could do was picture himself lying in his father's arms, both of them naked. The very thought disgusted and terrified him. Johan's body became so acutely tense at such moments that he often lost control, so overpowering was his love for his father. He would throw his arms around him, kiss his eyes and lips, groaning from deep within: 'Darling . . .'

His father was at a complete loss to understand the nature of these unrestrained and passionate episodes, or the fatigue and weakness that followed them. Johan was unaware that his exceptional feelings were not new to the world of science, but he hated them with such a vengeance that it pained him physically.

At one point, after enduring yet another frantic outburst, he thought: 'Perhaps it would be better if my father and I no longer shared the same roof.' But moments later he was completely distraught: 'I can't leave my father . . . if I had to leave him I'd kill myself . . . like my mother . . . I love my father so much . . . that's why this is so distressing . . . it's so awful I *want* to kill myself.'

It became impossible to spend a quiet evening alone with his father in the same room. He struggled with all his might to suppress the endless emotional outbursts, but he often succumbed to them.

He decided to tell his father that he preferred to spend more time alone. After that he withdrew to his own room in the evenings, separated from his dearly beloved father. But his inability to satisfy the overpowering desire to be with his father completely exhausted him. He was subject to bouts of loud and tearful melancholy that weakened him even more, often leaving him in the depths of despair for days on end.

Contact with his father was reduced over time to the dining table. But the stress of longing for him day and night weakened Johan's self-control and outbursts of desire and despair plagued him almost every day.

He neglected his regular schoolwork, to his great disadvantage. In the past his teachers had treated him with unusual respect, much like an adult among minors. He was always measured and pleasant in what he did, and his schoolwork was always highly legible and consistently without error. But things had changed, and Johan had to endure unwelcome remarks and critique of the kind most often reserved for foolish, witless schoolboys. Attending school thus became an unbearable burden. But if he stayed home from school, he would have to tell his father he was sick and his father would want to be at his side as much as possible. Johan knew for sure that this would be intolerable.

Before long, it became impossible to go to school, but staying at home was also unbearable. Johan then decided to pretend he was going to school, but he did not go. Instead he spent his day wandering around the open fields outside the town and along the river. He knew he couldn't keep up this pretence for long, and it tortured him immensely when he sent notes to the head teacher saying he was sick and hoped to be well again soon. He had never lied before.

11

The school deceit was exposed after a while. From then on, the headmaster, his staff and the younger boys saw Johan as a liar, pretending to go to school while spending his days roaming around in the countryside. It broke his heart to think he might have to leave school. It was the only school in town and there was no better option. The boy was at a complete loss: 'Must I leave my father? . . . But I love him so much.' His thoughts were a muddle: 'If my love for my father wasn't tarnished by such terrible things, how happy we would be together, as happy as we have always been.'

His father was convinced that Johan was unhappy because he had to share the same classroom with younger boys and follow the same lessons, while he was at least two years older than most of them. He suggested Johan stay at home and prepare himself to go to secondary school in Utrecht or Bommel at the beginning of the next school year. If Johan was unable to work by himself, his father would help him, give him lessons, and set aside his own much-cherished criminal studies. Johan was overwhelmed by his father's offer and became even more deeply aware of his love for him. He responded, anxious and trembling, that he preferred to return to school after all, right away and every day, although the very thought of it made him blush with shame.

12

But Johan's overtaxed constitution took a serious turn for the worse and he was forced to stay home, to rest and recover his senses. The boy's suffering was intense. His father was at his side every moment of the day, taking care of him with great affection. But these fond attentions only served to intensify Johan's love for his father and amplify the abhorred assaults.

Late one evening as Johan was resting on the couch and the muted lamplight softly caressed his glistening blue eyes, leaving him awake yet adrift in a delightful dream, a sudden and profound insight into the essence of his life brought him back to reality with a jolt. He thought to himself, sentence by sentence, word for word, as if he was writing everything down: 'If I didn't have these wretched feelings for my father, our life together would be perfectly happy, just as it was before. But I do have these wretched feelings and we can never be happy together. If I say something sweet to my father, my body reacts and it leaves me desperately unhappy. And if I'm unkind to him, *he* is desperately unhappy. If it continues like this, we'll have to go our separate ways, live in different homes, in different cities. But that would be unimaginable. We need each other.'

Shortly thereafter, as nocturnal silence engulfed the house and his father came to say goodnight, Johan said to him unperturbed: 'This strange and terrible melancholy is to blame for everything, Father, and I can't explain it. I know it pains you deeply that there's something I can't tell you, but I know it would pain you even more if I did.'

Johan chose his words with care, as if he was writing an essay but with clear resolve. His father didn't respond, so Johan continued: 'So, I won't tell you . . . but I'm determined to get better, and then we'll be happy together as before . . . I know what I'm about to ask will be difficult for you, but if you don't approve I will have to leave home, go my own way. I want to spend some time alone, without you . . . here at home, if you can agree. And elsewhere if you can't . . . don't ask me why . . . I simply can't tell you.'

His father was visibly shaken, but his thoughts were swift and sure: 'The boy has lost his mind . . . I have failed him . . . he should have had more people in his life . . . experienced more.'

Johan's father said: 'If that's what you want . . . if you think that will help you get better, then so be it . . . it might be good if we have the doctor visit . . . '

He got to his feet.

'I hope you're better soon, Hannie . . . I really hope so.'

Johan sensed the emotion in his father's voice.

He wanted to run to him, tell him he couldn't imagine them living apart, that it would be impossible. But at that very moment his body intervened and overwhelmed him. The boy was empty, hollow, alone: 'For now we're sharing the same home . . . before long we'll go our separate ways . . . and I can never tell my father why.'

13

Johan persevered for days on end, living in the same house as the father he loved so much without seeing him or touching him. But the constant struggle and the energy it demanded left him irritable and fragile. His mind was so fatigued he couldn't even read, and without distraction his desire for his father was undiminished. It was all he could do to stop himself from running to his father when he imagined touching him in such a disgusting and perverse manner.

When Johan heard his father move around the house, he suffered more than when there was only silence. He was tempted to ask his father to leave the place or at least to give him permission to move to another house in a different town. But the very thought of leaving the father he loved so much filled the ailing boy with dread.

No one visited Johan in his depressed state except their aged housekeeper Sien. She had little time for Johan's father, convinced as she was that Johan's mother had taken her own life in such a dreadful manner on account of her marriage. The pious elderly spinster was also irked by the thoroughly irreligious household in which she lived, where her employer neither knew nor served her dear Lord. But she had time for Johan. He would often listen at length and with much patience to her words about God and his service. She hoped in her heart that the seed she had sown in his young heart would not fall on stony ground but on good soil, where it would take root and bear ample fruit.

Sien didn't really understand what was going on between Johan and his father. Such sensitivity wasn't in her nature. She thought they had simply fallen out over something and would soon forget about it.

After a while, Sien grew troubled by the amount of time Johan was spending alone in his room. It was completely out of character. She also noticed that his physical condition had deteriorated and she feared he might die before she could pass on to him the spiritual goods that were more precious than anything on earth.

14

The elderly spinster asked Johan if he wouldn't mind her spending time with him, speaking to him about priceless treasures, and perhaps reading for him from the Bible. Johan said if that's what she wanted, he didn't mind.

From then on Sien came often to his room and told him about the goodness of God, who tries his children sorely to know their hearts. But in their greatest need he is always at their side. He would appear to his saints and his prophets in dreams and miraculous visions, showing them what to do.

The old spinster's words had a strange effect on Johan's tired, pliable mind. She tended to use expressions and sayings she remembered from holy books, leaving Johan with the impression that he was listening to someone more erudite and sophisticated. In those days—and nights—he too had divine visions and dreams, in vivid colours, like the devotional Italian prints his father had bought for him, which he loved so much.

One night an angel of the Lord descended from the heavenly throne. He approached Johan barefoot and silent, kissed him and called him 'darling'.

The next day Johan thought: 'If it's all true . . . everything Sien has to say about God in his high sunlit heavens . . . and if God were to set me free of this terrible evil, how grateful I would surely be.'

So, he started to look forward to Sien's stories and recitations, and he invited her to come and read to him more often. Sien in turn thought the seed she had sown had now fallen on fertile soil. Johan felt good when he saw how pleased she was, that he could make someone happy. He now longed for God more than his father.

15

The contradiction was painful. 'Here I am living in the same house as my father,' he thought, 'and I'm willing to spend time with the maid, but not with him . . . What must he think? This can only be deeply hurtful.' He decided to tell Sien that the readings and discussions had to stop, that they didn't really interest him after all and were very tiring. Johan could see that the elderly spinster was startled and saddened by his words and at being dismissed in this way. Grieving her pained him deeply. He also missed her stories and recitations. The spectacular and vivid visions subsided. 'But this is for father,' he thought.

Isolation and suffering had left Johan's body weak and listless. But upsetting dreams no longer haunted his sleep. His desire for his father now reminded him of his childhood feelings and no longer triggered unwanted physical urges. Johan was gratified at this improvement and he began to think he had conquered his dreadful desires and the despair they instilled. Before long he started to ask after his father. Their life together resumed, and there was touch, without Johan sensing anything untoward.

After a while they returned to their usual routine. But life with his father wasn't the same, because Johan had a secret that pained him deeply, a secret he could not share.

When Johan's health improved and his physique strengthened, the attacks returned. His constitution was still weak, and his disgust at these renewed emotions and desires was deeply disturbing. This helped him to control his behaviour towards his father, but it drained him to such a degree that the thought of complete separation seemed the only solution, in different cities, in different countries.

16

In those days, Johan was able to consult certain documents that described the emotional life of people who differed from the majority as he did. He came upon the first essay on the subject by accident, but it took his interest and he started to explore his father's extensive library in search of books on the same divergent condition of mind and body he recognized as his own. He had always enjoyed free access to his father's books and his father never asked what he was reading or indeed what he wasn't reading. Some of the feelings that haunted his earlier years were explained to some degree by what he read, including his bizarre yet swiftly passing attraction for young boys dressed smartly in sailor suits. But much of the specialized language of medicine and law remained a mystery to him. He used to ask his father about everything, but now he didn't dare. The pain of hiding so much from his father was often overwhelming. 'My feelings for my father,' he thought dejectedly, 'have confused our relationship. With someone else I could indulge my feelings, but not with my father. Still, I love my father so much I cannot bear to leave him.'

Chapter Two

1

Johan and his father spent a number of pleasant days together in the autumn, and to all intents and purposes their situation seemed to have returned to normal.

One Monday morning, after an excellent Sunday with his father, Johan lay awake in bed thinking about how enjoyable it had been.

The darkness of night's last vestiges slowly made way for the hushed light of dawn. Johan always loved watching night turn to day. There wasn't a sound in the house. Johan stayed in bed, indulging thoughts of his father now that their relationship had improved so much. And it also struck him that there was nothing unusual about a boy keeping his inner life to himself and not telling his father everything.

Johan heard nothing, but he could see that it was raining outside and that a delicate grey mist separated the hanging clouds and the dark earth. But the garden, the pathway and the meadow beyond looked as if the night had been less kind and less quiet, as if it had stormed loud and hard. Strong gusts of wind had shaken the trees and branches the day before, and now the night seemed to have stripped them of their leaves.

The nocturnal wind and rain had left the little pear tree just below Johan's window without a single leaf. Its wet branches seemed wretched in the dismal morning light.

2

Johan's room opened onto an upstairs hallway that was even darker than the room itself. Its walls were oak-panelled halfway up. Johan took great pleasure in the traditional opulence that characterized every corner of their house.

The daylight increased as he descended the stairs to the ground floor, its bright, whitewashed walls banishing the last traces of sleep and leaving Johan with a smile on his face in spite of the rain.

The breakfast room was awash with light. He sipped tea from an antique French teacup in pale-grey-and-matt-gold porcelain. His breakfast plate was of rare Italian earthenware from Faenza's golden days. Owning and using such unique objects pleased him so much it sometimes sent a shiver down his spine. He remembered asking his father once why it was that he was so emotionally attached to certain objects. His father responded that having strong feelings for people and things could actually be quite pleasant.

After breakfast in the delightful breakfast room, he made his way along the downstairs corridor, past his exquisite clock with its earnest and mature tick, out onto the market square. The square was enclosed on four sides, making it look to all intents and purposes like a large room. The sun was low in the morning sky. Johan found the market square magnificent, just as he found fine porcelain and exquisitely decorated earthenware magnificent. On the short sides of the square, the town's finely fashioned inner gate stood opposite the town hall with its steep stately stairwells and stepped gable. Johan was more attracted to the town hall than the inner gate that morning so that was the route he chose on his way to school.

3

Johan greeted the other boys politely as he passed them. He didn't linger with them outside since he rarely had anything to do with them. Instead, he made his way directly to the pale blandness of their classroom to wait for lessons to begin.

At nine o'clock a boy tugged wildly on the school bell, which was worthless compared with the precious bell that graced the ground floor of Johan's home. He knew well enough that everything at home was better than at school, but he simply didn't dare spend entire days with his father.

Johan's class had a bad reputation. While the teachers were in charge, without question, they struggled to keep order and frequently lost control. As a result, they were inclined to dole out punishment for the slightest offence. Johan never took part in the classroom disturbances, partly because he did not consider himself the equal of so many of the other boys and partly because he was determined to recover his untarnished reputation among the teachers, which had suffered so badly from his deceitful absences from school. He handed in his homework free of error, his results improved significantly, and critical remarks were now few and far between.

That morning Johan was plagued with questions. Why did he have such disgusting affection for his father? Why was he so unduly attracted to certain boys, as long as they were young? Why was he so drawn to certain buildings: their house, the town hall, the inner gate? What attracted him so much to certain parts of their house more than others: the dark wood-panelled upstairs hallway, the doorbell, the fine porcelain tableware?

In the pale blandness of the classroom, with far too little sunlight for Johan's liking, the morning seemed depressingly long.

4

But then, oh then, he turned his back on the dismal school at midday and walked outside. The sky above both town and field had shed its rain and been cleared by the wind. For the first time after days of rain, the towers and tall houses, trees and everything around glistened proudly in the hazy sunlight. At the sight of it, Johan knew he couldn't go home right away. He wanted to see what the river was doing in the headwinds and currents, and he wanted to explore the town's many tiny houses and its few larger edifices. The countryside along the river on the outskirts of town was also incredibly beautiful. It was windy, but it wasn't raining. The sun-filled sky arched high and blue above the silent town. The air was fragrant and glimmering gold. A corner of the market square was bathed in light, a couple of slated roofs aglow in the sun.

Johan stood in silence, embracing the view. There was sunlight in front of him, but the sky behind him was still heavy with rain, still fighting its aerial battle with the sun, high in the blue vast-vaulted sky above the town. The beam of light on the market square had already thinned to nothing. Johan suddenly felt chilled, weary, sad that he was so far from home, that it was such a long walk back. It also saddened him that he had kept his father waiting for one of their meals.

He thus joined his father in the dining room, hushed and dejected.

5

His father didn't ask why he was late. This vexed Johan and he thought: 'The good in our relationship is no more, and it's only dawning on me how good it was now that it's lost.'

That afternoon Johan used a coffee cup of the same pale grey porcelain as the one he used for tea. Both were gilded with matt gold, but the coffee cup was prettier. Johan thought on a whim that he might give this almost irreplaceable cup away to some ordinary boy, as he had done before with a number of much-treasured objects in moments of spontaneous affection. When his father found out, he told him that he was free to do what he wanted with his own things, but he didn't consider such impulsive generosity to be a laudable trait. On the contrary, it was a habit generally associated with people of poor morals and weak, unstable emotions.

When Johan reflected on his father's words that Monday afternoon, he deeply regretted what he had become. He looked at his now silent father and said calmly, and with restrained affection: 'Do you know why I was so late today? I took a long walk outside the town. I would love to spend Wednesday afternoons with you, but I don't want to miss school. Could we go for a walk in the country after four? Will you collect me from school?'

Johan could see that his father was genuinely pleased at his suggestion and that made him happy, tremulously happy, a happiness that stayed with him when he returned to school that afternoon.

6

It was a struggle to pay attention in all three classes that afternoon. Johan longed for his father so much, he remained calm and without melancholy.

They headed off together at the stroke of four. They crossed the market square. Johan found its light and architecture particularly beautiful that day and at that hour. They then passed under the impressive inner gate towards the outskirts of town and finally reached the surrounding open countryside. Johan could hardly believe he was able to live so intimately with his father once more without the shameful feelings. They walked hand in hand, like a boy and a girl. His father's left hand felt extremely soft. As dusk fell, they walked at their leisure under a heavy autumn sky towards the river. The rising wind was audible in the trees below the dike, and Johan was determined to see what the magnificent river looked like in the wind and evening light.

'Father,' he said, when they reached the river, 'I love you so very much . . . it feels just like it used to feel, when we were at our best.'

The sky was almost completely dark when they got back to town. Night-time had already started for most of the houses; those with shops were illuminated, the others dark.

When they arrived at their own house, Johan said, 'Let's not use the garden door at the back . . . let's ring the doorbell. I rarely hear the bell on the corridor and it's such a delight.'

His father smiled. This was the first he had ever heard about Johan's love for the bell. Johan also smiled, but his words were serious: 'I'm sure it's strange, but I can't deny it. I'm really attached to the sound of the doorbell . . . I often hope that someone will visit of an evening and ring it into life.'

Johan then rang the bell and listened intently to the purity of its timbre.

7

Johan made tea for both his father and himself. It was something he did often but he always enjoyed it. Making tea involved the use of a number of objects for which he had a special fondness. The prettiest of the things Johan employed that afternoon were an antique Dutch copper burner, both tasteful and elaborately designed, a French earthenware teacup for his father, and a coffee-brown porcelain beaker with an inner glaze of white and blue for himself.

He left the room unlit. The gold-glistening flame of the copper burner scattered bands of light across the walls and ceiling. Some of them illuminated his father's face with soft light. The boy gazed at his father's cherished face, hushed and tranquil in the golden radiance. He knew that life with his father had not been serene and undisturbed in recent years. He thought unruffled: 'Perhaps now is the time to tell my father about what has troubled me so deeply.' But he quickly changed his mind: 'Don't do it . . . don't do it . . . once you've told him there's no way back . . . and Father might be disgusted with you if he knows?'

Johan's sense of well-being had disappeared, to be replaced by a sense of dread. The tempting serenity of that day had almost led him to tell his father about his terrible secret.

Unease at the very idea of confessing took hold of him, and he understood how dangerous it still was to spend so much time with his father. His thoughts were crystal clear: 'Such are the consequences of my deviant emotional life.' He got to his feet and said without agitation, as if writing each carefully considered word: 'Father, I am so content and happy with you I could even share my secret, tell you what used to make me so unwell . . . but I'm also certain that if I did we would both be deeply miserable. I think the time has come for me to return to my rooms and live alone . . . at least that way I would feel safe.'

8

As the evening passed, Johan lost the dreaded urge to tell his father about the terrible scourge that saddened him so deeply. He was happy for both their sakes that he had not succumbed to the reckless disclosure of such a dangerous secret. If Johan's father knew about it he would hate him forever.

The boy's mind was at rest. He worked undisturbed late into the evening. The table lamp whispered warm and soft beside his head. Outside he could see the road and the meadow between the house and the garden, bathed in bright lamplight. The garden and trees beyond were dark, like a forest full of secrets.

The shrill drone of the church bells tolling on the hour until ten didn't bother him. And the sound of his beloved clock chiming ten in the whitewashed corridors downstairs even thrilled him. Moments later the sonorous peal of the doorbell filled the house. That was the postman, who didn't dare cross their deep and dark garden late at night for fear of dangerous ghosts. Johan thought the man's conviction deserved the fullest respect, especially as it afforded him more frequent opportunities to hear the bell's resonant tones.

When the downstairs bell had rung its last, Johan got up and made his way to the front door to collect the letters and other printed matter for his father.

His father was working in one of his libraries, lit by two lamps and warmed by firewood burning in an open hearth. Johan sensed a satisfying desire to spend some time with his father and said, 'Father, our relationship is no longer as simple as it was . . . but it would please me immensely if I could spend an hour with you . . . '

The boy flattered his father with his voice, and both were very happy at that moment. Johan lay down on a rug in front of the fire, content in its warm glow, reading a simple book at his leisure. He noticed his father looking at him from time to time, but he didn't reciprocate, afraid of unsettling his father's smiling face.

When the downstairs clock heralded eleven, a sound that moved Johan deeply, he asked: 'Father, why is it that the sound of that clock is so blissful? I love it so much.'

Chapter Three

1

It seemed to take forever that year for the wind and rain of autumn to make way for solid, unbroken winter. In the autumn Johan longed for winter with its softer shades of light and open, clearer skies. On many a winter afternoon, the town hall's handsomely decorated facade stood out in particularly sharp relief.

When autumn finally surrendered to winter, the weather quickly changed and stabilized. It froze every night, and when Johan made his way to school in the morning, the frost-covered fields on the outskirts of town seemed decked with snow.

White days and white nights followed.

One fine morning, the market square was solid white and silent. The splendour didn't last, of course, as the whiteness of the snow was quickly trampled away, but beyond the streets, in the cold air on the town's virgin fringes, the snow survived much longer. In those days, Johan and his father spent many an hour outside the town's gates. Their life together had returned to its familiar rhythm, with a hint of melancholy.

In the early winter, Johan developed a strong attraction for a boy in his class after seeing him for the first time dressed in a new winter coat and black, tightly curled fur hat. But Johan had learned by now from his father's scientific journals how dangerous such emotions could be and he was wary. He was able to keep them to himself because his feelings for the boy were only a fraction of his feelings for his father. So, he cautiously enjoyed the attraction without giving expression to it. He thought: 'If this is the nature of my emotional life then I must learn to accept it as best I can, and be careful above all that my good name does not become a byword among the common folk, as I've often read in Father's journals.'

Johan noticed that his affection for the other boy, with whom he had no relationship whatsoever, seemed at times to replace the abysmal desire he had for his father.

But his special appreciation for the boy came to an end when he overheard him—improperly clothed moreover—say unpleasant things to another boy Johan had always disliked. Johan was disgusted, and his admiration for the boy quickly faded.

After that, his sensitive constitution remained free of passions and affections for quite some time.

2

Later that winter, a boy from overseas started to attend Johan's school on Mondays. They ended up in the same class and he was assigned a bench in the row to Johan's right. The boy was clearly too big for the bench and instead of sitting properly and facing the front, he was forced to sit sideways. This meant that Johan could easily keep an eye on him without the teacher noticing or having reason to reprimand him for not paying attention.

The boy was from the Indies and half Dutch. He wasn't quite fully mature, but rather of an age that Johan found most attractive in boys. His hair was bluish black, thick and trimmed short. His face was flat and his cheeks blushed, but their glow was muted by the subtle brownness of his skin, which Johan found splendid. His eyes were a deep blackish blue. The boy was a stranger to the school and to the class and wasn't at his ease. He also had trouble understanding what the teacher had to say and that made him timid and withdrawn.

Johan found the entire spectacle pleasant and amusing. The boy preoccupied him all morning, but he was careful not to miss anything of the lesson and made sure no one noticed.

He learned during the last lesson that morning that the boy's name was Paul Mansfeld and it cheered him greatly. It brought him closer to his boy.

3

Johan's emotions made it impossible for him to go home to his father at noon.

The academic journals he had been reading of late were strongly inclined to justify the feelings he now knew for certain were his own. Johan had grown to respect himself deeply, and it would have been a struggle for him to recognize a feeling he had embraced as something unworthy and repugnant. But while he was delighted to read what he found in his father's journals, it saddened him immensely that these same feelings could be so dangerously strong towards his father.

Shortly after noon that Monday, Johan headed out of town, away from their house, along open country roads, to the low grassland by the river. The sky was bright and high, and his heart was light and happy, but his blue eyes betrayed a trace of tension. He longed for his father.

As he passed along the tall white corridors on the ground floor of their house, Johan reflected that his desire for Paul Mansfeld was similar to the desire he had experienced for his father and equally strong. But in the gloomy dining room with his father, he was completely calm and unperturbed.

In the afternoon, before school recommenced, Johan left the house, sensing a need for fresh air and rest in his otherwise turbulent existence. He was in the best of spirits, but anxious nonetheless. His good spirits lasted until the first lesson that afternoon, which he spent staring at the new boy from overseas. He thought: 'What would the teachers and the other boys say if they knew I was so attracted to Paul Mansfeld?'

During the second lesson, however, Johan's cheerful mood changed dramatically. He felt sluggish, limp, as if he had eaten something his trembling body wanted to eject. He decided then and there to go home, to his father. But he realized he would have to tell the teacher that he felt ill and wanted to go home and that was something he didn't want to do because it would draw the unwanted attention of certain boys in the class. So, he spent most of his time weighing the pros and cons of speaking to the teacher until it dawned on him that it was quarter to four and it no longer made any sense.

The fading day and the evening that followed were relatively peaceful. He did his homework with the necessary diligence and rarely thought about the overseas boy. After that he spent some time reading a book, something simple in both content and style. His mind drifted frequently that evening. He sat with his head close to the lamp, its thin vapours full of golden light reflected in the gleaming mirrors of his eyes. His thoughts blossomed like flowers, quivering in the lamp's sunny brilliance. Most of the time he thought about his father, whom he now loved without a trace of physical attraction. He also thought a lot about himself, and how long he and his father would continue to live together in the same house.

Later that evening he spent some moments with his father and listened to the magnificent clock strike ten. Johan waited to see if the superstitious postman had letters to deliver, hoping the sonorous doorbell would echo through the white downstairs corridors. But the postman didn't pass by that evening and Johan started to ready himself for bed when the time came. He rested his contented head on his pale folded hands and without further ado he fell asleep.

That night Johan's dreams were brilliant and golden. His father was involved but without unwelcome agitation. Paul Mansfeld also featured. Johan felt happy for once, and his happiness continued beyond the morning.

4

The morning was intensely bright and aglow with early sunshine. Spring was still a time away, yet the sky was awash with the crispest white and blue, stirred gently by the wind. 'What a beautiful morning,' Johan thought.

He also thought about Paul Mansfeld. He wondered if he hadn't been polite enough. Should he have said something to Paul? He resolved to speak to him that very morning. Then he would hear the boy's voice for the first time. The desire to hear his voice was very strong, so Johan left early for school that day. His heart pounded as he crossed the market square, which was bathed in glorious light. His anxious desire to hear the voice of a boy he barely knew didn't please him at all. But when he spotted Paul Mansfeld with other boys near the school, the sight filled him with such delight it took him by surprise. The effect the boy had on him was reason enough to avoid him, but he couldn't stop himself. Johan approached Paul, trembling and afraid his voice would betray him. He spoke timidly, in a voice that left the other boys speechless:

'Forgive me,' he said, 'for not introducing myself yesterday . . . I want to make up for it . . . my name's Van Vere de With.'

'I'm Paul . . . they call me Pauken at home, and at school too.'

'I'm Johan.'

He felt calm enough now with the boy at his side. They walked together away from the other boys. Johan was determined not to let anyone know he had irregular affections for Paul, but when he tried to appear unruffled, his words instead seemed smug and haughty: 'Your family must be recent arrivals?'

'I'm on my own . . . my father and mother stayed home in the Indies . . . I'm staying with an uncle on Goilberdinger Street.'

'That's not far from us . . . we live on the market square, in the grey house . . . it's old, but really beautiful . . . old houses are much more beautiful than new ones.'

The half-Dutch boy stared at Johan with his blue-black eyes. He found him strange. Only yesterday, other boys in the town had told him much the same: Johan's father had nothing to do with the other men in Cuilemburg and Johan with none of the boys.

'If you like,' Johan said, 'you can come to our house for a visit and see our garden. I have lots of beautiful things . . . I'd love to show them to you . . . and if there's something that catches your eye, I'll give it to you.'

It was time for school.

5

That morning, Johan did the same as he had done the day before. He angled himself in his chair to be sure he had a good view of Paul and could look at him whenever he felt the need. He thought about their conversation. Johan had said two things, both of which were unusual in themselves. He had invited Pauken to visit him at home and even come up to his rooms, and that was something he had never done before. He had also offered Paul a small share of his favourite artistic objects. This was strange behaviour on his part and he recognized how dangerous it could be. What would he say to his father, he thought, if he asked why he had suddenly decided to bring a strange boy back to the house? And what had inspired him to offer the boy something of his prized collection. Johan knew well enough that he would be able to refuse Paul nothing in his present emotional state. Even without answer or explanation, his father would probably guess that Johan's feelings for Paul Mansfeld reflected some kind of deviant disposition.

Johan had always trusted his father in everything, and knowing that he was concealing something of great importance from him pained him sorely. He often had the urge to tell his father all about his unusual affections, and even about the ghastly desire he had experienced for his father himself. Johan knew that his father suffered greatly because of the secret that had made his son so sick, and that he would probably welcome a proper explanation, but fear held him back, because he had no idea where his father stood on the matter. Some writers Johan had read were inclined to respect such feelings, but broadly speaking they tended to be condemned. Johan had also read biographies stating plainly that many men in his position had been hated and despised to such a degree that they took their own lives.

Johan couldn't predict how his father would react to a similar revelation about his son. He didn't even know if his father was aware that he had been reading books and journals on the matter in their library.

<h1 style="text-align:center">6</h1>

Johan left for home that day at noon. He had been feeling particularly delicate all morning, and couldn't stop blaming himself for the suffering he had put his father through by talking about a dreadful secret without revealing what that secret was. But then he wondered whether his father might be even worse off if he were to learn about the kind of things that had preoccupied his son for such a long time and governed his life. Respect for his father made him want to confess everything that had transpired in both body and mind. But fear of the unknown and the unpredictable results of such a confession held him back.

He remained silent for a while and then said: 'Father, there's a new boy at school . . . just arrived.'

Johan's father was surprised that his son had raised the topic of what was going on at school, since he only ever talked about it by extreme exception.

'Is there something special about the boy?' asked Johan's father.

'Yes,' said Johan, and for a moment he thought: 'I love my father so much, I should tell him everything.' He continued without a breath: 'He's just an ordinary boy, really, but I sense something unusual about him. He arrived only yesterday, and I've already asked him to come and visit our house. I surprised myself a little . . . what do you think?'

'Surprising indeed . . . and not very pleasant if you ask me . . . I'm not fond of impulsive decisions . . . but you should do what *you* see fit and not what *I* see fit. It's your life.'

His father's voice sounded severe. He thought: 'Does he suspect something, or does he know already?' He spoke softly and deliberately: 'I told him that our house was beautiful and that we had lots of beautiful things . . . and that I was willing to give him something . . . '

His voice was unassuming, as if he was confessing guilt for something humiliating. He looked at this father and decided to say nothing more.

'Why are you telling me this, Hans? Is it important for you?'

Johan's voice regained its composure: 'It's strange, I agree, since you and I are generally not so friendly and generous with strangers. There are strange things that I can't tell you about although I want to very badly . . . but it would make us both sad . . . when strange things happen I always want to tell you about it . . . but this would tear us apart, you understand?'

'Now you speak of it . . . there are indeed things that happen . . . things I fear that we can do nothing about . . . and you become a different person . . . when the years of change have passed.'

'What should I do about the boy at school? Invite him home?'

'You should do what *you* want and not what *I* want . . . I've told you that more than once . . . but if you want my advice, sudden affections can be dangerous and tend to be worthless. And giving away money and possessions without thinking about it is not a virtue but a trait associated more with those of lesser morals.'

'Father,' said Johan, his voice now deep with sorrow. 'I love you very much . . . if I loved you less our relationship would probably be less troubled . . . is that possible?'

His father replied that strong affections were a heavy burden that was difficult to bear.

Johan's special interest in the half-Dutch boy Paul continued unabated. He often experienced a powerful desire to be with him, especially because of his eyes and his voice, and he regularly satisfied that desire, although frequently with complete revulsion. In the end, Johan never brought the boy home, thus avoiding the opportunity and temptation to show him his possessions and give him something he liked as a gift.

Chapter Four

In the winter, Johan's afternoon lessons at school lasted two hours without the freedom of a fifteen-minute break. In the spring the break was reinstated, but then the afternoon lasted until half past four, half an hour longer than usual. The afternoon break and extra half hour were intended to help the boys who were preparing for admissions exams, mostly for the third year or more advanced classes at the Senior Secondary Schools in Utrecht and Bommel, or for the Cadet School in Alkmaar and the Naval College in Willemsoord.

Spring arrived early that year with an abundance of crisp and sunny days and as a result the school's summer planning also started early. Between four and four thirty, the lamps in the classroom often had to be lit. There were three of them hanging above the centre aisle and their pale yellow light illumined the room at the end of the afternoon.

Some boys in the class made plans to have a little fun with the lamps one afternoon. It had to happen during the French lesson because their French teacher was young and often nervous and distracted and had trouble keeping control of the class. The same young teacher was also in the head teacher's bad books and he didn't mind disorder in the classroom because it gave him reason to dismiss the man. The same boys had caused havoc in the class in previous years by playing with the lamps.

One of the boys would ask if the lamps could be turned up or turned down, which meant they had to be lowered from the ceiling. Then the same boy would run his wetted fingers over one of the glass shades causing it to crack and burst into pieces. The other boys would have the time of their lives at this, in spite of all the dangers.

2

There was more than enough daylight in the open, high-ceilinged classroom when the French lesson started. But Kor Koster, the naughty-boy ringleader, lit the lamps of his own accord without asking the young teacher's permission. The man didn't dare say a word about it.

After a few moments of unusual quiet, Koster got to his feet and asked if the rear lamp could be dimmed a little because it was whining like a dog, then he stuck out his tongue at the innocent young teacher. The young man sensed that the class was ganging up on him yet again. He wanted to respond, but the words stuck in his tightening throat.

Then the first lampshade shattered, crashing to the ground in hot thin shards over the rear benches. A larger shard fell on top of the flame and the room started to fill with dirty yellow and black smoke. At this point the boys shrieked that the lamp might cause a fire, that they could be injured in the head and eyes. But then Kor Koster smothered the smouldering lamp.

'You're such an infant,' he said to his chum Geo Geertsma . . . 'You've no idea how to interrupt the class . . . admit it.'

Koster sat down at that point, but some of the other boys continued to harass the teacher. They didn't want to sit on the back benches until the dangerous shards of glass had been cleared up.

They lit matches and searched loudly and excitedly for fragments of glass, and when they found one they held it up between thumb and middle finger as they brought it to the bin, pretending to take it all very seriously.

The young teacher struggled to get the class under control and back to reading French. He had to keep an eye on every corner of the room and it left him tired and dizzy.

Then the second lampshade shattered. The boys shrieked all the louder, that their lives were in danger, they were certain of it. Two boys who were usually inseparable started to argue as if they were arch enemies. Kor Koster got involved. Holding up an entire class, he said, was an absolute scandal. He also said that French was an essential part of the exams and an important subject. Their teacher was in terrible distress. In short: they should calm down.

The young teacher said nothing. He was terrified the head teacher would storm into the classroom and restore order in an instant. If the head teacher had been a friend and willing to lend a helping hand, as friends do, to a young teacher who had trouble with a class full of very difficult boys, he would have welcomed his intervention. But the French teacher knew well and good that the head teacher was simply waiting to gather enough evidence to dismiss him. He was dizzy with fear and the storm raging inside him made his eyes bulge.

3

In spite of the French teacher's muted powerlessness, the clamour subsided. The third lamp was extinguished and quiet returned to the classroom. The teacher wanted to continue. His thoughts turned to pedagogical theory, which he tried to implement: 'May I first insist on some elementary respect? It amazes me that I still have to ask . . . whosever turn it is can continue.'

It was Kor Koster's turn, and he read the French text they were translating with skill and agreeable clarity. Johan thought: 'what a fine voice he has.' He was taken aback by its beauty and surprised at his own reaction.

The young teacher's blood boiled as he listened. Oh, that boy Kor Koster! He hated him with a profound yet impotent hate. He was always correct, but it was an annoying correctness. Wicked stubbornness was manifest in his steel-blue eyes. He rarely did anything obviously punishable, but he ruined lesson after lesson with his stupid questions, which he posed with devilish politeness or by feigning mental sloth. But his true nature was otherwise.

While the commotion had calmed, silence hadn't completely returned to the class. The young teacher was still terrified of the headmaster. What would he do if he lost his job yet again? Teaching was his living, and he needed it badly.

4

Kor Koster raised his loud but handsome voice:

'Sir,' he said, 'I just had a thought . . . do you mind if I ask you a question? It's not about the lesson.'

'Not about the lesson? No, I'm afraid not . . . if you ask me, we've wasted enough time already. If you have a question, save it for after school.'

'That would be my pleasure,' said Koster politely. 'You know from experience how much I enjoy spending a little time with you after school . . . but my brother's arriving today from Delft . . . you remember my brother . . . the one studying in Delft? . . . what a place, Delft. What do you think, boys? What a place!'

He continued, still quite composed, with an entire speech to the whole class. Everyone was in hysterics at his cool yet risky arrogance. The young teacher was at the end of his tether. How dare they mistreat him like this? He yelled at the top of his voice:

'Shut up . . . shut up . . . shut up . . . get on with the translation!'

Kor Koster pretended to be taken aback:

'Of course, I'll continue . . . at your command I would be happy to translate from now until the end of time, amen . . . all I want to know is: can I ask my question or not? By tomorrow I might have forgotten . . . it's very, very important . . . do you mind, sir?'

'Oh, get on with it then . . . as long as you're quick . . . '

'So, I can ask my question?'

'I said: if you get on with it, and we don't waste any more time.'

Kor Koster's voice changed. He now sounded sad and deadly serious:

'I don't understand . . . first my question wasn't welcome and now it is . . . does anyone here understand? If you do please explain . . . but only in French, of course, since we're supposed to be studying French . . . pay attention Geo Geertsma, we're supposed to be studying French . . . '

He turned to the entire class again, all of them laughing their heads off at this point. The teacher yelled, close to breaking point:

'Get out of here, Koster . . . get out! And no, leave your books . . . leave your books!'

'No,' said the blond, cocksure troublemaker, 'I can't do that . . . shall I report to the headmaster?'

'Yes . . . on the double.'

'Fine by me . . . getting kicked out of your class is actually an honour . . . but first I wanted to ask if you've read the article in *Eigen Haard* about unbreakable lampshades?'

Immediately after the boy had politely posed his question, the entire class exploded with uncontrollable laughter. But Kor Koster wasn't laughing. He sat back down on the bench and completely forgot about reporting to the headmaster. This was much more fun. And if the French teacher were to lay a finger on him, he would throw him head first against the benches. He continued with a straight face:

'Such idiots, those boys, don't you think? They'll laugh at anything . . . Geo Geertsma, control yourself. The teacher is trying to get on with his lesson . . . shall I continue with the translation, sir?'

'No thank you. Do me a favour and leave the room . . . Nico van Neerrijnen, read the last segment.'

'Nico van Neerrijnen would be happy to read, sir,' Koster responded. 'But Nico can't see a thing. It's too dark and he's sitting in the corner.'

Before the class had a chance to explode with laughter yet again, the overworked and badly mistreated teacher roared at the top of his voice:

'Silence! This instant! If I hear another word from anyone you can all expect detention. Kor Koster, just shut up or leave the room . . . Silence! All of you! I mean it! The first person to open his mouth can translate the entire text from beginning to end . . . Van Vere de With, continue reading.'

5

Johan started to read with fluency. There was plenty of light through the windows on the left and obviously enough to read by. Johan wasn't impressed with spineless Kor Koster and his wayward sidekicks. Everyone knew that the teacher was a hopeless case and easy to upset. Picking on him was cowardly. But while he wasn't very impressed with the teacher either or his inability to control the class, he was pleased to be able to help him out.

The laughter and chaos had subsided by this time, though the classroom was anything but quiet. The boys leaned over their books, seemingly concentrated, yet each of them was humming, quietly but provocatively, their lips tight shut. None of them hummed continually. When one stopped, another took over, making it impossible to tell who was involved. The French teacher was at a complete loss and had more or less given up. His goal was to get to five o'clock without further conflict. He took his revenge later by handing out extensive written revision, conjugating highly complex and irregular verbs. He also marked low and gave holiday assignments.

Johan read his part of the French text followed by a flawless Dutch translation. Johan and his father had translated the text together the previous evening and had been careful to find appropriate Dutch words to match the French original. As he repeated the words out loud, he couldn't help thinking with stifled emotion about his father at home. The French teacher was amazed at Johan van Vere de With's sensitive choice of words and exceptional translation. It also pleased him to think that Johan's skill and proficiency were evidence of the qualities of his French lessons. 'If they want to, they can learn as much from me as any other, even more,' he thought to himself.

Silence had returned to the classroom, a calm that gave the teacher a sense of victory and self-confidence. When Johan had finished reading, the teacher was clearly relieved and enriched by what he had heard.

'Thank you, Van Vere . . . your translation was very good . . . take note Van Neerrijnen, there was more than enough light to read by.'

Kor Koster piped up once again with his admirable and unruffled voice:

'Excuse me, sir . . . Hans van Vere doesn't count . . . his father is an aristocrat and his mother committed suicide.'

Only one boy laughed, and even then, it sounded fake. The blood drained from Johan's face, leaving him deathly pale. His mind was a muddle, but he quickly regained control of himself.

He closed his books and jotter and started work of his own accord on another subject. As far as he was concerned the French lesson was over. The teacher noticed what he had done but said nothing. He respected Johan, especially for his evident self-control.

6

Kor Koster was silent for once. In fact, he was feeling out of sorts and regretted what he had said about Johan's father and mother. The lesson continued. It was now too dark to read, but the teacher refused to light the lamps. He was convinced that the class was now in a state of shock, disgraced, powerless to resist. Paul Mansfeld was sitting by a window with a little light and the teacher asked him to read. Reading French was a struggle for the half-Indo boy because he was inclined to swallow all the vowels. That day his reading was unbearably bad. The harassed teacher trembled with rage and snapped:

'Spare me, boy . . . what kind of fish-market French is that . . . you clearly haven't been studying.'

'I have, sir, but that's the best I can do.'

'You have not! You never study . . . never . . . '

Paul opened his mouth to respond, but the teacher roared:

'Shut up, boy. You haven't studied . . . not a single word.'

'But I did study, sir,' said Paul, his voice deep and fragile.

The class was furious with Mansfeld. The boy lived with a strict uncle who knew the French teacher and wasn't afraid of confronting him. But the boys didn't dare do anything at this point, not even raise their voices. So much had already happened that crazy afternoon and they were tired. They had also noticed the headmaster passing the glass door to their classroom a few times and peering inside. The teacher was standing menacingly close to Paul. He too was exhausted and was already sorry he had attacked the boy who was far from difficult. But now he was determined to buckle the obstinate Indo, if not break him. Tired, dejected and crippled with anger, he barked:

'Is Mister Mansfeld going to read, or is Mister Mansfeld not going to read?'

The boy didn't answer.

'Then you can report to the headmaster! His room's next door.'

When Paul refused to budge, the teacher leaned over him as if about to pick the boy up and throw him out of the room.

'If he dares,' thought Kor Koster on edge, 'I'll throw him head first into the benches.'

Johan's inhibitions dissolved. 'I really like Paul . . . it's time to get involved.'

7

Johan stood up and readied himself to leave the classroom, announcing loudly but with restraint:

'I'm very sorry to interfere, but I'm afraid I simply cannot remain in class under circumstances like this . . . I'm going home.'

The tension dissolved in an instant as the entire class collapsed into fits of laughter and loud cheers. Van Vere was a dark horse, much more defiant than anyone had thought. The teacher turned his attention from Paul Mansfeld and said, in despair, with a voice intended to sound sarcastic:

'What do we have here . . . is Johan van Vere siding with the class reprobates?'

'I'm going home,' said Johan.

'If you want to join this posturing bunch of reprobates that's up to you, just be aware of this: if you dare to leave the class now, you'll never be welcome in my lessons again.'

'Fine,' said Johan, 'I was planning to ask for an exemption from your lessons, and if it's refused I'll leave the school completely.'

Then the headmaster walked in.

'What's going on, Van Vere?' he asked, ignoring the young teacher who was now anxious and ashamed. Johan pretended not to notice that the headmaster had ignored the teacher and asked him a question. He didn't answer, left the classroom and hurried home.

8

By the time Johan had settled back at home with his father in their familiar surroundings, he was calm again. And although he wasn't happy about what had happened at school that afternoon and had trouble putting it out of his mind, he didn't mention it to his father. His unrestrained affection for Paul had driven him to get involved at school in a way that was completely out of character. He thought about his father's words of caution: affection can be a danger and a source of instability in a person's life, and a single unrestrained deed can ruin the work of years.

Johan decided to have a word with his father late that evening when things were quiet and ask his advice: should he stay away from school and work at home, or should he go back after the problems with the French teacher had more or less settled down? Johan was sure that the teacher could easily be persuaded to come to some sort of arrangement. He had little if any authority or respect in the classroom and didn't have much of a reputation with the headmaster either. The last thing he would want was to have one of the best pupils leave the school because his French lessons were a complete chaos. Johan preferred to come to an agreement. If he didn't go back to school he would have to put the feelings he experienced around Paul Mansfeld behind him for good. He was terrified that the ghastly feelings he had for his father would then return. Staying away from school meant working at home. His father would want to help him with his homework, both written and oral, and while he was deeply grateful for the man's kindness and willingness, he feared that being so close to him would quickly trigger the passions he feared so much. He was also terrified that naive affection for his father might one day move him to confess his still-secret attraction to certain types of boys. And what about the dreadful passions he had for his father? The terrible yet still-concealed truth. What if he blurted it all out? There was no one Johan loved more than his father, and no one he desired to liberate more from the burden of his secret.

9

Johan retired to the privacy of his room after lunch, lit the lamp, and did his best to order the thoughts that were running through his mind. He decided not to mention the worthless incident to his father. He thought it better rather to pay a visit to the French teacher in person that same evening. He was sure the man wouldn't be difficult, and might even be delighted that Johan had come to seek resolution, given his considerable influence at school.

Johan thought: 'If I didn't suffer from such irregular affections, I wouldn't mind having to miss Paul Mansfeld, and I could stay at home with my father.'

He started to realize just how much his strange desires dominated and complicated his life. It pained him deeply and he thought to himself: 'Why am I so different, Father?'

10

Johan had asked for tea in the red china cup, a gift from his father. Sien had poured the tea.

Johan listened as her aged feet quietly descended the stairs and he knew that the house would remain silent from then until the bells sounded ten o'clock.

But moments later the silence was broken by the sonorous bell in the white downstairs hallway. It was two hours too early for the superstitious postman. The last time someone unexpected rang the doorbell was weeks ago, Johan thought. He heard Sien climb the stairs.

'Hans, there's a boy for you.'

'Is it Paul?'

Sien handed over Paul Mansfeld's visitor card, and Johan hurried downstairs to the white hallway where the boy was waiting on a bench next to the clock.

Johan's heart was racing and pounding all at once and his voice was unsteady. He tried to calm himself, searching for words he couldn't find, not wanting to appear unpleasant. He spluttered:

'Shall we go upstairs, Paul? To my room? Follow me.'

Climbing the handsome, well-appointed staircase to his rooms gave him time to compose himself. He was calm and content, confident that everything was under control and he was not about to do or say anything dangerous.

Paul came straight to the point:

'I came to warn you, Johan. You can expect serious trouble. The teachers are furious with you . . . La Mar and Smid too . . . because you didn't answer them this afternoon.'

'Thanks for the warning, Paul, but detention or anything like it is out of the question . . . and the same goes for a roasting . . . I was just thinking about whether I should go back to school . . . I can work at home just as easily.'

'That's what you said this afternoon, but I thought you didn't really mean it. What would your father say? Would he mind if you stayed away from school?'

'Not at all . . . if it's better for me . . . I always ask him what he thinks, of course, when it's something important . . . but usually we're of the same mind. And even if we disagree he always tells me to do what I think best and not what he would prefer.'

'That's easy.'

'Yes, indeed. Father says that it's better for everyone to follow their own opinions . . . your father lives in the Indies, doesn't he?'

'Yes . . . on Serdang . . . I wish I could swap with you.'

'So . . . you're expected to be cadet or midshipman of the year?'

'Yes, that's what my father wants . . . preferably cadet, but if I don't make the grade then midshipman is also good . . . I'm not expecting to make either grade . . . the French is too much for me . . . and they expect a lot more than we've done so far . . . '

'The language questions aren't that bad. And your English is good . . . and your geometry.'

'I know, but French counts the most.'

'I'm not so sure . . . if your maths and science are good you're pretty safe . . . ask Kor Koster . . . his oldest brother is a lieutenant . . . by the way, did they hand out extra homework?'

'Yes, the whole text, from beginning to end . . . Kor Koster, Geo, and me.'

'And are you going to do it?'

'Yes, of course . . . I have no choice . . . my uncle makes all the decisions . . . and if I don't, they won't allow me back into French class . . . I'll just do it . . . then it's done.'

11

Johan took great pleasure in having Paul in his room. Meeting him at school was one thing, but a personal visit was quite another. Johan felt confident that he wouldn't do or say anything untoward. He was tired, yes, but pleasantly tired.

Johan thought the midshipman's uniform was much more handsome than that of a cadet, so he secretly hoped Pauken would fail for cadet but then pass for midshipman.

They continued to chat about everyday things. Johan boasted about his house and the objects he had collected. He showed some of them to Paul but wasn't tempted to give him anything as a gift and that pleased him immensely.

Paul then said it was time to go home. In addition to his regular homework, he still had to write down the entire translation of the French text they had been reading.

'Of course,' said Johan. 'It's easier through the back garden . . . you're closer to home that way. Let me show you.' Johan lit a costly Chinese ceremonial lamp from an important dynasty to guide the way. 'Paul probably isn't even aware of this beautiful object,' he thought, 'and he certainly doesn't know I'm using it especially for him.'

Johan carried the delicate lamp with its delicate light along the timber-framed upstairs corridor. He shivered with joy in the presence of Paul, without the slightest hint of pain. The weather outside was deathly calm, but he insisted nevertheless:

'My lamp isn't up to this wind . . . hold my hand . . . I know the way, and there's enough light.'

Paul and Johan walked hand in hand through the deep dark forest of a garden. Holding Paul's hand was simply wonderful. Paul moved with caution and stopped suddenly a couple of times as if he had almost walked into a tree, in spite of the fact that they were on a pathway.

'That's what's so strange about the dark,' said Johan, 'the feeling that you're about to bump into something, but we're following a path and here's the gate . . . goodnight, Paul.'

Johan watched as Paul passed through the gate and he followed him until he disappeared beyond the circles of yellow lamplight. He gazed upward at the thin blue sky filled with golden stars. For a moment his thoughts were empty, and when they returned to Paul he took his valuable Chinese lamp in his pale white hand and made his way up the dark stairwell to his father's rooms.

12

Johan decided to tell his father what had happened at school that afternoon. He also mentioned that Paul Mansfeld had paid a brief visit earlier in the evening and that he had shown him several of his beautiful possessions without succumbing to the urge to give anything valuable away.

'I should probably have minded my own business,' said Johan. 'It makes no difference as far as Paul's concerned, but now I'm in trouble. It isn't easy to manage my urges, Father. But what should I do now?'

'Do whatever you think is best . . . if you want to work at home until September I can help you find a routine, as if I were your teacher.'

'And what about your own work?'

'You're more important, Hans.'

Johan now knew just how much his father was willing to invest in his studies and was sure he would help him at regular intervals whenever he asked. Then he thought . . . 'How wonderful it would be to live and work in our beautiful home with my father at my side every day . . . but I love my father too much . . . it's too dangerous.'

'You know what, Father?' he continued. 'It's not so late. I'll pay a visit to Mr La Mar, right away. If he doesn't make a fuss I'll go back to school tomorrow, but if he's unpleasant and gives me extra homework then I'll stay at home and you can be my teacher.'

13

The young French teacher was at home that evening and welcomed Johan into his room. Johan had expected the teacher's quarters to be dull and petit bourgeoise, but they were surprisingly well appointed, even tasteful. He noticed after a few moments that the teacher had a collection of French literary artists, which he and his father both knew and admired. The young teacher was pleasant and welcoming, and the atmosphere was relaxed. He admitted that events at school that afternoon had been regrettable and added that he understood Johan's behaviour during his classes. He was ready to forgive him without insisting on any kind of punishment. And there was no need for further unpleasantness.

The teacher then changed the subject, giving Johan the opportunity to tell him a little about himself and his life. Johan shared that he wasn't really interested in the other boys at school and that life with his dear father was enough for him.

The teacher also inquired about their house, which he knew from the outside and greatly admired. Johan described the interior, loudly praising the sonorous doorbell, the clock in the white downstairs hallway, and paying particular attention to the wooden stairwell that led to the upper corridor.

Johan made his way home, pleased that he would be returning to school the next day without any issues to deal with, and pleased he wouldn't have to miss a day in Paul Mansfeld's company. He was also aware that spending every day with his father was far too dangerous for his emotional life.

14

As Johan crossed the market square, he was stopped in his tracks by a sudden and deep sensation.

The shops and houses were void of light in the late evening. The blue night air was free of mist and the moon was high and motionless in the sky. For a few short seconds Johan felt as if the whole world had come to a standstill forever. He turned to the city hall with its perfect step-gable facade and then to the house he shared with his father, broad and double-fronted, grey and still in the white moonlight.

Johan continued on his way and arrived home in just a few seconds. He didn't use the garden entrance at the back but decided rather to ring the sonorous front-door bell, just to hear its echo in the white, downstairs hallway.

15

Johan left the house for school early next morning. As he closed the front door behind him, he spotted Kor Koster waiting on the market square. The boy approached him and said humbly:

'I'm sorry for what I said about your mother at school yesterday, Van Vere . . . I'm really sorry I offended you like that . . . '

Johan was disgusted by Kor Koster's voice, although he hadn't forgotten how surprised he had been at its beauty only the day before. He responded as if he didn't care:

'I don't actually remember what you said about my mother . . . but it's not important . . . please feel free to offend me whenever and however you want.'

Johan then continued on his way to school as if Kor Koster wasn't with him, as if he was on his own. This made Kor Koster's blood boil and he felt humiliated. There were no side streets on the way to school and Koster didn't have the guts to turn on his tracks and walk away.

16

Every detail of what happened in that couple of days was engraved in Johan's mind. He remembered what everyone had said and done. He also remembered precisely how the light had been at the time, inside and outside. His favourite memory was of the market square, empty and motionless against the dark blue sky.

Spring and summer passed for Johan without exceptional excitements.

Chapter Five

1

In the middle of a magnificent summer, Johan took exams for the Senior Secondary School in Zalt-Bommel and was admitted to the third year, starting after the holidays.

His father asked if the time wasn't right for them to take a long vacation together. Paris was a possibility, with its French literary artists. Or Italy, where Johan could visit silent white monasteries and witness their exquisitely coloured wall paintings. Tuscany was a region replete with small towns, each of them bursting with artistic treasures.

But Johan preferred to avoid hectic travel. There was no place like home, and nowhere more beautiful. It would also be impossible to take his precious yet brittle porcelain objects with him. Their absence would certainly spoil the pleasure of even the most handsome treasures.

So, they stayed home and delighted in each other's company, enjoying the long summer days that filled the orchards with ripening fruit.

2

Paul Mansfeld spent the summer with various family members in different major cities. He passed his exams with flying colours and was assigned as a cadet in the East Indian Service in Alkmaar. Johan was disappointed that Paul no longer had midshipman ambitions. Boys in midshipman uniforms were much better looking than boys in cadet uniforms.

While Johan missed Paul's company and now spent most of his time close to his father, the dreaded desire for physical intimacy with his father did not return. Johan approached physical adulthood in those days without paying much attention to his body and its development. Arousing dreams were few and far between, and those he had never featured his father. Their relationship was just as simple and uneventful as it had been before he became an adult.

But the secret he could not share with his father, the secret his father knew he could not share, still disturbed him deeply. Johan was frequently tempted to tell his father everything, but he resisted the temptation at every turn.

One day his father asked about the secret with caution and modesty.

'Hans,' said Johan's father, 'is it still impossible for you to tell me about that secret of yours? Maybe I can help . . . it often worries me, not knowing, not understanding.'

'Father,' Johan replied, his voice trembling with anxiety, 'I can't tell you because I love you so much . . . it saddens me too that I have a secret I can't share with you . . . but I simply don't dare . . . I'm afraid that telling you will be worse than silence.'

Johan's father thought: 'Hans never exaggerates . . . his secret must be something truly dreadful.'

His father didn't pursue the matter. But Johan knew well and good that he was suffering in spite of his efforts to hide it, and that knowledge disturbed him profoundly.

3

Summer turned to autumn and Johan started in his third year at the Senior Secondary School. As an older, intellectually gifted pupil, he quickly excelled in knowledge and insight, far beyond the other boys. And with his distinguished character and pleasant manners, he soon rose to prominence in the school, a position of influence he had enjoyed throughout his time in Cuilemburg, with some occasional disruptions.

Several boys from Cuilemburg were now attending Den Bommel and they travelled together to school. But Johan opted for more expensive transport to be able to travel alone.

His new life wasn't unpleasant. He had to be up and ready earlier than before, but the city and the country roads were sometimes exceptionally beautiful at that time of the morning, as autumn set in and the days grew shorter and darker.

Johan was now spending more of his day away from his father, but the longer absence and return from another town made their daily reunion all the more joyful and important. Johan's affection for Zalt-Bommel deepened daily. The expansive wash of the river Waal, the serenely shaded waterways, the deep canals and gullies, lined on either side by reddish-brown houses, mostly old, with shades of dark grey from wind and weather.

The school in Bommel was more striking than the school in Cuilemburg. It was once a stately residence occupied by nobility and it had changed little over the years. Its luxurious wood-panelled corridors were just as striking as the dark upstairs hallway in Johan's house. There was a paved courtyard at the back of the school. It was rarely used and the grass was left to grow, covering the flagstones like a green blanket.

The generous stairwell coiled upwards to the floors above, its handsome balustrades of white wrought iron, its dark wooden banisters smoothed by the years. The white ironwork depicted leaves and flowers, a miracle of craftsmanship.

Johan used the stairwell many times a day. It was a thrill to let his hand glide over the banister, familiar as he had become with every delicate bend and curve. It often made him shiver with mild gratification. 'Strange,' he thought. 'Why do I find some objects so exceptionally attractive?'

4

In those days, Johan didn't sense a special attraction to any of the boys at school and this pleased him enormously. He was now convinced that his deviant emotional attractions had been part of the instability of growing up, in spite of their frequency. The only person he loved was his father. But that made the temptation to tell his father about his secret all the stronger and more pressing. He resisted out of fear, which had grown so strong that he didn't dare spend time with him and he avoided him for days on end. They each had different quarters in the house. Much to his dismay, Johan's father feared that his son's troubling problem had now returned. Johan's incessant longing for his father left him sick and uneasy, such that he didn't dare approach him.

Johan had to stay home from school at the time. His father would come to his room and spend time with him, but this made his suffering all the more intense. The desire to tell his father everything was formidable and deep.

One night he had an amazing dream. As he slept, he saw a deep waterway with embankments on either side. Shadows and

62 / JACOB ISRAËL DE HAAN

reflections of townhouses, centuries old, shimmered on the surface. It was autumn and the light was golden. The water in the deep canal was stationary and the golden autumn air was lazy and tranquil. The shadows and reflections of the old houses were motionless.

When Johan woke the next morning, he thought: 'I dreamt of light, and when I dream of light I know I'm on the mend. Today I'll go back to school, and return to spending time with my father.'

That evening Johan wrote down exactly what he had dreamt about houses and light. He had no particular reason to do so beyond his own personal curiosity, but as he wrote he experienced an extraordinary sense of pleasure. When he reread what he had written, he thought: 'Peculiar prose, indeed, and nothing like the work of the Dutch literary artists father and I know.'

Johan's first encounter with the joys of writing prose inspired him to write more. Besides portraying many of his inner experiences in exceptionally fine detail, he also composed elaborate descriptions of his favourite objects.

5

It was late winter, clear skies, almost spring. The city and the surrounding landscape awoke to an unexpected and deep layer of white snow.

In the middle of the night, struggling to fall asleep, Johan watched the first snowflakes whirl in the dull-white moonlight. They covered the lamplit lane between their house and their garden with a layer of grey snow that deepened and turned white in the course of the night.

By morning the countryside was covered in deep snow, filling the air between heaven and earth with a delicate, white snow-light.

The sky was suddenly empty of snow and had turned a thin blue, wispily frozen, windy and dry. The temperature dropped and the snow on the surrounding windblown fields remained smooth and pristine for days on end. The dark ground then started to thaw, leaving loose clumps of snow scattered behind steep icy verges, soft and melting. The arable land surrounding the town shivered back to life and Johan sensed that spring had arrived.

Day after day he described how the climate was evolving and how spring was spreading its beauty all around.

Writing prose was quite satisfying.

But around that time, Johan's determination to trust his father in all things and tell him about his secret intensified.

6

One Wednesday, travelling home from school in the middle of the day, Johan decided that the time had come to talk with his father about everything. For the first time, the thought of such an encounter did not fill him with fear. For once, trusting his father seemed completely easy and simple.

The afternoon was free of anxiety, spent admiring the objects he needed and used. For Johan this was evidence that he was calm enough.

Johan descended the stairs to his father's library.

7

'Father,' he said, with quiet satisfaction in his voice, 'I've always been determined to share everything with you . . . it's been terribly difficult to keep part of my life a secret from you, and I know you too have suffered because of it . . . but up to now I haven't had the courage to talk about it . . . and even now I don't know why, but the time has come for me to tell you everything.'

Johan then told his father everything about his attraction to certain boys and even about the time he felt the same about his father.

He told him how he hadn't understood his feelings at first, but after thinking about it long and hard and reading books and articles he found in his father's rooms, it had slowly dawned on him. He hadn't dared say a word about his deviant affections or his reading, not because of some undefined anxiety, and not because, as he later learned, the majority of people in his situation denied the very existence of such attractions, but because of an overpowering sense of contempt.

Johan also told his father about how he had deeply despised himself when he entertained immoral thoughts about him, and that the effort to control these passionate urges had often been indescribably difficult. He loved his father so very much, but that was the reason for the long periods of enforced separation while sharing the same roof.

Johan spoke deliberately, his sentences carefully formed, and his words chosen with caution. He was different from other boys, even in the way he spoke.

His father listened motionless, crushed. What Johan had told him was so indescribably horrible that it left him dizzy and he struggled to breathe.

Johan stared at his father and a deathly chill overcame him. What had he done?

'Papa!' he cried, 'I shouldn't have told you . . . '

8

The tension between Johan and his father was unbearable. Knowledge of Johan's true nature and deepest inclinations had left his father unwell. Johan himself felt lifeless . . . he wanted to go to his father, to console him, wrap his arms around him, kiss his eyes and anxious, trembling lips.

Johan's father then emerged from his intense dejection and spoke without emotion, his words, nonetheless, chosen with caution, and his sentences carefully formed:

'Johan, what you told me is so overwhelming I don't know what to do . . . I did indeed find it unpleasant that you felt compelled to keep something so serious a secret from me, but knowing about it is even worse. I know affection motivated you . . . and that you have suffered too . . . I know that. Hans, you need to leave me alone for now . . . I have to think things over, decide what to do . . . go to your rooms . . . I'll make up my mind soon . . . no, say nothing, our happiness is done, you'll see that soon enough.'

9

Johan returned to his rooms, pale and petrified. In deep dismay he asked himself why he had spoken to his father. The very thought of what he had said didn't bear repeating. Elbows bent, his head in his hands, his father now knew exactly who and what he was. His rooms were impossibly suffocating, but he had nowhere else to go and no one to turn to. He felt abandoned in the middle of a catastrophe.

He tried to be strong but failed.

He sobbed and whined: 'Father . . . Father . . . '

He didn't see his father again that day.

10

The next day he knew he couldn't stay at home, but school was also impossible. So, he set off on an unfamiliar route, crossing the rivers Waal and Maas, until he arrived in 's-Hertogenbosch, where he wandered shiftlessly in a city he did not know. He and his father, the man he loved so much, had to go their separate ways. He knew his father was disgusted with him, and he knew he would have to live without him and leave the home they shared.

He returned to Cuilemburg that evening bent and broken. Living in the house in the evenings that followed was horrendous. Johan heard nothing more from his father.

The elderly housekeeper Sien asked Johan why he and his father were living apart in the same house. Johan responded condescendingly, vexing her small pious face and saddening her as she turned away.

Johan lay awake and ailing deep into the night. Books no longer interested him and he couldn't even bear the light of the lamp. But the darkness was also unbearable, because it filled him with irrational fear as it shifted and abused him.

He longed for his father, who was also alone in the house with no one to help him. Everything in him wanted to go to his father, but he resisted, knowing that he despised him because his feelings were different.

Johan fell into a short and restless sleep.

11

The morning was miserable. He awoke to a dull uncertainty that quickly made way for the same desperate desolation that had overcome him the day before. Johan knew he was too battered and bruised to go to school that day, and too tired even to leave his rooms, so he stayed inside, lifeless and forsaken.

Exhausted in both mind and body, his thoughts that day were cloudy, vague and unsure. He briefly considered the possibility of seeking a way back to the way it was before, but quickly realized that this was just a pipedream. He could no longer live with his father. Every move, every touch would be tainted and suspect.

But the status quo was also out of the question. Living in the same house with his father without the least contact was nothing short of a nightmare.

He struggled to see a way forward, but there was nothing he could do. All of his woes had but one source: his deviant emotional life. 'Why me?'

12

That afternoon, Sien handed Johan a piece of paper. 'Hans, a letter from your father,' she grunted disapprovingly.

His father's handwriting was meticulous, his sentences well-formed and his words well chosen.

Dear Hans, I love you dearly and I appreciate that what you told me yesterday was out of love and your desire to alleviate my suffering. But you made the wrong decision, although you could not have known in advance. Had I remained ignorant, I would have been a tolerant father, but what you chose to tell me can no longer be undone.

You seem to have read and understood a great deal about your deviant emotions. I was unaware of this and I would not have recommended it. But it has one advantage: you now clearly understand my situation. I am also familiar with the articles you read, of course, and

I know that there are highly respected authors who are inclined to justify your kind of love. I do not. I despise such sentiments to the very depths of my being.

Now that I know you are frequently prone to such feelings and that I am even involved in them, I can no longer associate with you, precisely because I am your father. As much as I love you, and you love me, every form of personal interaction between us has become impossible. From now on, the best way to show your affection for me will be to respect this reality to the letter.

Our life can no longer continue as it was. To facilitate change I am offering you three options. You are completely free to choose. I for my part prefer to conceal any personal preference.

First: you stay here in our house in Cuilemburg. I then move elsewhere, with the right to take whatever I need with me for my personal use.

Second: we share the house in Cuilemburg, but we promise in good faith to have no personal contact with one another.

Third: I stay in the house and you move elsewhere. You will be free to take with you whatever you would otherwise miss. You can then organize your life as you see fit and consider safe.

The choice is yours.

To conclude: pandering to uncontrolled passions is always a mistake. But if you in particular should ever dare to indulge your attractions without inhibition, it will be the end of you. Your inclinations are intolerable, so do not think for one minute, Hans, that they will be tolerated.

Now you can see the vigour of my response. I have no reservations.

13

Johan read the letter twice, slowly and carefully. He was now certain that his father had cut him off forever. He also knew that this was a source of indescribable distress for his father, and it pained him that the man he loved so dearly had to suffer so much on account of his intolerable inclinations. Johan cursed the day he was born.

To his surprise, however, he felt more at ease in the afternoon than he was before he had received the letter.

Johan reflected on the three options that would change their lives. He didn't want his father to have to leave the house on his account, but the very thought of leaving himself made him shiver. Where would he go, and how could he live without the home he had known for so long?

Johan opted for his father's second proposal. They would share the house, but be sure to avoid the slightest contact. He did not base his choice on the hope that their life together might return to what it was, but because he believed they would both suffer the least this way. He wrote to his father agreeing to the second option:

My dearest father, I write to inform you that I have accepted the second option. Any further written communication on my part would only sadden us both.

Unhappiness is our lot.

Hans.

14

They continued to live together in the same house, separated, in a way their elderly maid Sien described in conversations—which Johan indulged—as ungodly. She claimed piously that their house had become an ungodly house, where the deity and his good commandments were no longer obeyed. She added that while she was a servant in the house, she nevertheless felt obliged to bear witness to the faith that inspired her in no uncertain terms. She hoped that Johan would save his soul from its steep decline. Salvation was otherwise no longer possible.

She spoke, as before, in the words of a more sophisticated woman, a woman of greater eminence, but they fell on deaf ears. It had been a long time since Johan dreamt about the heavens opening with God and all his angels in attendance. He often longed for such beautiful dreams in the depths of his present despair.

He had also lost the desire to write pages of fine prose, a desire that had once pleased him greatly when he was able to indulge it.

School and study went remarkably well under the circumstances, so well that he rarely if ever received criticism or a negative comment. He excelled in languages and sometimes discussed his interests with the teachers. People seemed to think he lived a tranquil and happy life. 'If only they knew,' he thought embittered, 'that my life is devoid of happiness and tranquillity.'

Johan and his father did not meet each other all this time. They knew each other's ways so well that they managed to avoid accidental encounters outside their rooms. But Johan's desire to be with his father did not disappear, and his inability to satisfy it was deeply painful.

15

One evening, Johan was sitting in one of his rooms, the one with a view of the garden, weary from the misery of the day, his idle mind crowded with dismal thoughts. The lamp was unlit. He sipped his carefully prepared tea, breathing in its temple aromas. This evening, he thought, he had never been so deeply conscious of his misfortune. His treasured copper burner glowed a delicate gold in its own light. Its elaborate upper edge had a diamond-shaped pattern that scattered tiny shafts of light all around. Johan stared at the lights. Then he heard a bird outside the house, whistling for a few seconds. The whistler whistled again as it took flight, its fast-fluttering wings carrying it upwards into the darkness between the trees and their house.

'A bird,' thought Johan, 'a bird . . . spring is coming.'

He set about his activities, but later that evening, shivering with pleasure, he penned a page of prose about the bird, which had whistled and flown away. After this moment of indulgence had subsided he thought to himself: 'What if I write to my father and tell him that the inclinations he finds so depraved have not troubled me for quite some time? Could we perhaps return to our former life? We are both so unhappy. I can also promise that I will leave the house immediately and definitively should my vile desires prove to be permanent and recurring and not simply passing.'

But Johan did not write to his father, fearing that the man would refuse his request and that his suffering would only get worse.

16

During the Easter holidays, Johan's sense of desolation was deeper and more wretched than before. The emptiness of the days exaggerated his yearning to be with his unhappy father to such a degree that he could not stay in the house they shared or even in the same town. He thus spent many a day wandering aimlessly in unfamiliar towns where he knew no one.

But it dawned on Johan at one point that staying away from home all day long was a bad idea. His father might notice his lengthy absences and start to worry about his whereabouts in addition to all his other burdens.

So, Johan stayed at home in his room, yearning, feverish, wretched.

Chapter Six

1

Johan was happy when school resumed and his days were busier. He was gratified to see the old school building again, both inside and out. Faintly moist in the mild spring air, bare-branched trees lined the paved, grassy courtyard behind the school, their budding leaves a translucent yellow-green, growing darker and denser day by day. At noon, as Johan made his daily journey home along the canals, the white sun stood ever higher in the sky, glistening on the deep, clear water's mirror surface. The fields surrounding Bommel and Cuilemburg were a hive of activity, after months of frozen winter idleness.

2

Bouts of desire for his father plagued Johan with particular intensity during the days of spring. He thought: 'Father must surely share my unhappiness. My depraved nature is to blame for everything . . . Am I doomed to this misery for ever, to be rejected by everyone as my father has rejected me?'

Anxiety engulfed him at the very thought that he might lose control one quiet night, go to his father's rooms and pray, beg for pity, to be relieved of this life of despair, that it was no longer worth living.

And when such restless urges took hold in the past, Johan almost always gave in to them, his heart in his throat. He knew himself, and this made his fear all the greater.

As time passed, the only way Johan was able to subdue his desire for his father was to imagine that they had come to a better arrangement together. His imagination was almost as convincing as reality, and when his fantasy took over it was as if his father was really with him.

But his mind was unable to endure these fantasies for long, and they were often followed by periods of unspeakable wretchedness.

3

The dreams that so tormented Johan returned, confirming to his horror that his vile desires were far from transitory. The dreams were intense and passionate, populated by a multitude of men, often strangers, including some of the boys in the junior classes at school . . . and his father.

Johan was at his wit's end and was tempted to end it all. But one thing prevented him from departing his miserable existence: the thought that his father would be left thinking he had driven him to do it by continuing to reject him.

Johan later decided to leave the home and the town he shared with his father for want of a better solution. He wrote:

My dear Father, I realize as time passes that it is too difficult for me to share a home with you while living in complete separation. You once gave me the freedom to choose from three different options intended to change our life together, but I now believe I made the wrong choice.

With your approval, I would now prefer to leave our house and city, to put some distance between us in the hope that I might regain a sense of calm. Ideally, I would like to find a welcoming household. But it's a shame looking back that we know so few people. I am at a complete loss to think of a potential host. Perhaps you can think of someone? If so, please write to me and let me know.

Our lives are now marked by deep unhappiness and are no longer what they used to be. I am doing well nonetheless.

Hans.

Johan wasn't sure whether he should mention that he was doing well without his father, fearing it might hurt him. But it was also possible that positive news from his son might also cheer him up.

4

Johan's father replied to his son's letter. But when Johan saw that a letter had arrived from his father he was disappointed. He realized then that he had hoped his father would pay him a visit. He thought: 'My situation must be worse than my imagination can comprehend since my father has clearly rejected me for ever.'

His father had written:

My dear Hans, if you wish to leave our house and city please do not let me stop you. The relationship between us remains the same, however. I have taken note of your request and will try to find appropriate lodgings for you.

Thank you for letting me know that you are doing well.

I agree that our lives are deeply unhappy and no longer what they were. But I can accept no blame. Your completely immoral and socially intolerable inclinations are to blame and they cannot be justified. You

will surely understand this if you ever try to seek their justification.
Do not!

I do not know if we will ever see each other again. Perhaps, if we
both grow old without accident or misfortune. Do not ask for a per-
sonal farewell. I cannot give it.

The letter did not upset him. Rather, for this first time in his life,
he disagreed with his father's opinion. He thought: 'I was born this
way, and it's not my fault that we are so deeply unhappy.'

5

Johan's father later wrote:

My dear boy, I believe I have found something for you in Haarlem
with the Riemersma family.

Haarlem is a fine city with beautiful surroundings. It has broad
and narrow canals, just like the ones you admire so much in Bommel.
There are plenty of fine buildings too: a city hall much nicer than ours,
a gatehouse opening onto the road to Amsterdam, which you are sure
to appreciate as much as our inner gate.

The Riemersma family is made up of two individuals, husband
and wife. I knew them well in the past but we haven't met in years.
Mr Riemersma, a former doctor, is now blind, almost seventy if I'm
not mistaken, and his wife is close to sixty. I opted for a quiet, elderly
family because you are used to a quiet life without the company of
young people.

If you have no objections against a family like the Riemersmas
and a city like Haarlem, I would be happy to pay them a visit and
learn a little more about them and their home.

So, let me know what you think about the city and the family.

After reading the letter, Johan was convinced that his father had made up his mind and truly wanted him to leave. Until now he had cherished an albeit vague hope that they might continue to live together, that his father, in the end, would not be able to live without him. But now it was clear that he was more determined than ever for them to separate. He replied:

My dearest father, thank you for going to the trouble. I'm open to the idea of moving to Haarlem. I also think the idea of moving in with an elderly and quiet family is for the best, so I have no objections to the Riemersmas. I have one question, however. Are they the kind of people who rent rooms to all comers, to whoever responds to their rental notice?

It's kind of you to go to Haarlem in advance. Be sure to take good note of the house, the street, the garden, and the rooms they are planning to rent.

Now that our miserable existence has finally forced our separation, I think I should move out as quickly as possible, certainly before the summer holidays.

Kind regards.

Hans.

6

After receiving Johan's reply, his father visited Haarlem. Johan came home from school that day and saw that his father was not home. He thought: 'Now is my chance to take a look at his rooms . . . I'm curious all of a sudden, and I'm sure he won't mind.'

Johan made his way to a part of the house he hadn't visited since the beginning of their troubled existence. 'How miserable we are,' he thought despairingly.

He tried then to open the doors to his father's rooms but they were locked. The sense of rejection and estrangement left him dizzy at first and then fraught with fear and self-loathing.

7

Johan's father returned from Haarlem and wrote to his son:

My dear boy, today I visited the Riemersma family in Haarlem. They have aged since we last met but their affection for me was evidently still considerable. They also knew your mother well. As a result, they are looking forward to your arrival and ready to welcome you with the kindest intentions. This is more than you would be able to expect from a random landlord. In that sense the Riemersmas are ideal.

They do not rent rooms. I tell you this because I sensed a little anxiety in your question and I also wanted to ensure that you would treat them as your equals at the very least. Dr Riemersma's years of blindness have left them with little money.

They live in the Lange Veerstraat, in the middle of the old part of the city. They have the upper part of the house, so there is no garden, and the property is small, with only one spare room. The room itself is large and sunny, at the back of the house, where you'll be spared the noise of the street.

They presently have one lodger, an artist by the name of René Richel. His work is familiar to me. Do you have any objections? I didn't meet the young man, and I thought at first that his presence would be a problem for you. Nevertheless, you are surrounded by young people at school, and one way or another you will have to keep your intolerable inclinations under control and without conditions.

If you think the limited space and lack of a garden are too much of a disadvantage, you can always stay here or look for something better yourself. But if you agree to move to Haarlem, you should do so as soon as possible.

The Riemersmas asked why we had decided to live separately. I couldn't tell them the truth, of course, knowing that they would simply refuse to allow you anywhere near them. Necessity thus obliged me to lie. I told them that my research into prison life would require me to travel abroad, and we both thought it best not to leave you alone in the house with only Sientje, given her advanced age. I'm telling you this so that you can respond appropriately should the opportunity require it. It made sense to offer this explanation, since I do in fact plan a number of research trips out of the country.

Now you can see how deep our misfortune has become, Johan, when we are forced to resort to lies. Let this be a warning. You must live the rest of your life in prudence and modesty.

8

After reading his father's letter Johan decided not to stay. Living in the old house only intensified his longing for him and this pained Johan all the more. So, he made up his mind to move to Haarlem, aware of the city's beauty and its proximity to the dunes and the sea, which he had never seen before. His host family was also elderly and kind.

Johan wrote to Mrs Riemersma:

Dear Mrs Riemersma, today I learned from my father that you are willing to offer me lodgings. I would like to make the move to Haarlem as quickly as possible, as I'm sure my father has already informed you. Would you be kind enough to let me know when it would be convenient for you to receive me? The earlier the better.

My father also told me that your husband once knew both my parents well. It is thus a delight to know that we are not complete strangers.

With courteous and cordial best wishes to you and your husband.

Johan van Vere de With.

The finished letter lay open on his desk. Johan started into the light of his lamp's thin flame. He thought about the far-reaching changes his father had made to their life. He was now about to move to a house and a city where he was a complete stranger. He would have a room in the upper part of a house on a noisy street. He would no longer go to school in Zalt-Bommel, in a residence that was once home to nobility, a place he loved as if it were his own home. He would never see the courtyard at the back of the school again, with its paved terrace and grass growing between the decaying tiles, covering them like a blanket.

9

Johan left the house to bring his letter to the post office. On the way he passed his little pear tree, already out of blossom, thin and black in the white moonlight. By the garden gate he passed two tall chestnut trees, both still in bloom, with lantern-like clusters of white nestled between their dark green leaves.

Johan followed a modest lane named after the *Vier Heemskinderen* or the *Four Sons of Aymon* leading to the market square. It was already late, and most of the residences were boarded up for the night, the occasional shop left lit in-between. Johan was taken by the beauty of the square, and his sadness at having to leave their home and their city was grave indeed.

He stayed up late that night, in a room without light, half-listening to the gusts of wind rustling in the branches of the trees in the garden. It sounded like rain.

10

Mrs Riemersma replied to Johan's letter as quickly as she could. Her response was long and hospitable. She told him he was welcome to come at his leisure and that his room was ready and waiting. There was only one room available, but it was spacious, quiet, light and sunny. Richell likewise had only one room at his disposal, although he also had his own little house on Koudenhorn Street. She had considered moving out to make way for Hans, but she wasn't sure how long he was planning to stay and if he later found alternative lodgings she would be left with the burden of a house that was too big and too expensive. Moving out was also a problem for her blind husband who was able to find his way around with his hands in their present circumstances but would have trouble adjusting to a new home. She concluded with greetings from her husband. He had indeed known Hans' mother well when they were studying medicine together. But he hadn't stayed in touch with Hans' parents as time passed, and in the end, he lost track of them. She asked Johan to let her know when he planned to arrive at the station. It wasn't far from the Lange Veerstraat, but it was always nicer to be met from the train, especially for the first time in a strange city. She would be waiting under the clock in the middle of the platform.

Johan took his time to read the letter. The idea of moving to Haarlem and lodging with Mrs Riemersma was now beginning to please him. 'She's very precise in the way she describes her thoughts and considerations,' he thought.

Johan then sent a note to his father, with little reference to himself:

My dear Father, this coming Sunday I will leave for Haarlem on the seven minutes to eleven train. Our unhappiness remains profound.
Hans.

11

Johan suffered greatly in the days that followed. The pain was such a burden that he often thought of ending his own life, but his love for his father stopped him. His infirmity made it difficult for him to contemplate travel or returning to school, but staying at home was equally taxing. The house itself was an obstacle. At home and alone, restless and deeply unhappy, all he could think about were the horrendous changes that had disrupted their life.

Johan paid a visit to the head of his school to discuss his departure. He was left waiting for a while outside his office, in a room that opened onto the quiet, tree-lined courtyard with its well-trodden flagstones. Intense distress at the thought of having to leave took hold at that moment, but he composed himself, aware that he was about to face the headmaster.

He reported that life in their house in Cuilemburg had changed completely, that he and his father were separating, that his father was planning to travel extensively. He himself was moving to Haarlem and would be leaving on Sunday. Saturday would be his last day at school.

Johan asked the headmaster to write a letter on his behalf for the headmaster of the school in Haarlem. Without a letter or evaluation of some kind, he would be assigned to the third year. The man promised to write, adding that Johan would certainly need time to get used to life without his father. He asked if Johan could stay until the end of the school year to make the transition to a new school easier.

Johan was confronted once again with his unfortunate life and its disintegration. He responded politely but haughtily: 'Father and I have decided that Saturday will be my last day at school.'

The headmaster was slightly miffed at Johan's response. Johan was clearly aloof and lacking emotion, he thought, and he never mixed with the other boys as an equal. They took their leave with seeming indifference.

In the time that remained before afternoon lessons resumed, Johan wandered in silence along the opulent canals in the centre of Bommel. But he was anxious, plagued by stormy thoughts. He blamed himself for his father's unhappiness and asked himself if this was how a normal person felt just before going insane. He groaned with pain, the pain of being alive.

Afternoon lessons were dour and laborious. The stormy thoughts in Johan's mind were a complete distraction. He longed desperately for his father, but he also knew he would never be able to satisfy his longing.

12

In the days that followed, as his departure came closer, Johan spent his time packing books and other useful objects that belonged to him, planning to send them well in advance to their new destination. Once they were packed, Johan suddenly missed them, realizing he would have to use things that were unfamiliar. His delicate disposition left him trembling, his soul and his senses scorched by everything new.

Sien helped Johan prepare for the journey. She told him he was right to put an end to his ungodly coexistence with his father. In her mind it was sinful and could never be granted God's blessing. She concluded by insisting that she was only a maid and had no right to meddle in her master's affairs. Johan was a child she had known and attended since the day he was born, but she felt she had the right to speak when her heart demanded. She also told him that the house in Haarlem was equally ungodly, a place in which God's commandments were not obeyed. She was old and did not have long to live. All she could do was wait for the giver of all to grant her a better future in the world to come. All she could do was pray that the seed she had sown in Johan's heart would not be the seed that fell on stony ground.

Johan was always polite with her when she talked a lot about things he didn't consider important. 'I shouldn't make Sien sad by ignoring her,' he thought. 'I'm already to blame for my father's sadness and that is more than enough.'

13

Johan made his way to school in Bommel on the last Saturday before his departure. He was exhausted, physically and mentally. During the day he longed for the night and at night he longed for daybreak. His stormy thoughts kept him from falling asleep and getting the rest he needed. He indulged in an excess of sleeping potions, which made him drowsy and caused the skin on his face to erupt.

The sky was white and motionless the entire morning, without the shifting colours of the sun. And with few at work, the countryside was also quiet.

Johan had decided to go to school and not stay at home, afraid to get too close to his father. This was his last chance to thank the teachers for their lessons and the Saturday assembly was the ideal opportunity. He pictured them sitting in a row, each according to their grade, with the headmaster in the middle.

But by the time he had arrived at school, Johan had completely lost interest in seeing anyone, convinced he would have a breakdown if he had to endure this torture any longer.

He was unable to resist the temptation to rush back to the train station and take the next train to Cuilemburg and home. He didn't have long to wait.

14

Johan dragged himself through the day in a state of complete misery. His longing for his father took hold of him in feverish bouts, leaving him trembling and deathly cold. He asked himself why his father had not left the house immediately when he learned the truth. He must have understood that his son's longing for him was unsustainable. In his frenzied anxiety he managed to convince himself that his father wanted to see him again in person.

He succeeded in putting the idea out of his head, but as soon as he did, his mind was flooded with thoughts about his present reality. He knew that he was about the leave the house without seeing his father, but the paralysis of despair somehow calmed his nerves.

So, he left the house in the twilight, through the garden and the *Vier Heemskinderen* lane to the market square. He paused to admire that fine city hall then made his way out of the city.

Johan followed the dike, tired, without thinking, eastwards towards the darkness of the evening. The river had swollen to its winter embankments. Dense clouds shifted slowly across the sky, casting dark shadows on the shimmering river.

Johan arrived at a trail that would bring him back to the city. Before descending the dark side of the dike, he turned to look west, to the setting sun, which had turned the clouds orange and red. Behind the intricate arches of the railway bridge, he could see ribbons of dull red cloud. A train was crossing the bridge, slowly and without a sound.

15

Johan's carriage was stationed at the front door of the house. It was an exceptional vehicle, unique in Holland, a gift from his father in happier days. Instead of two doors on either side, it had a single door at the back with a roll-down window. It also had windows on either side, but none at the front. The passengers thus never saw the back of the man steering the carriage or the boy sitting motionless at his side. Johan hadn't used the carriage since the beginning of their misfortune. The carriage was now standing in front of the house and a crowd had gathered around it.

Johan was upstairs in his room and his father in his. Johan hoped until the very last minute that his father would come to say goodbye. He did not appear. His eyes burned red and sore, his hands fragile and trembling, but he didn't dare let his emotions show with all the people milling around his very exceptional carriage.

He hurried down the dark stairwell, along the white downstairs corridor, past the old clock, into his carriage, and off he went. Brimming with resentment, he thought: 'All those people envy me, because they think I'm happy, because I have money and property. If only they knew how miserable and rejected I feel taking leave of my father, the man I love beyond every desire.'

Johan's exclusive carriage hurtled along the main country road out of Cuilemburg. The road was busy with Sunday walkers and

Johan had to control his tears. Everyone was staring at him, drawn by the rare appearance of his unusual carriage.

16

Johan wasn't alone on the train that day and he was relieved. It meant he would have to control his delicate, burning eyes and would not look as if he had wept all the way when he arrived in Haarlem.

Johan peered red-eyed through the window as the train crossed the river. He could see an entire stretch of water, tranquil and wind still, boats and barges bobbing motionless on the marbled silvery surface. He then caught sight of the river from bank to bank, and before long he was in the countryside to the north of the river, a landscape he did not know.

His train carriage chugged along, its wheels turning at speed.

PART TWO

For Herman Bang

Ho una ferita in cor che gette sangue
Che poco a poco me fara morir.
Trafitta dal dolor l'anima langue
Amo e il segreto mio non posso dir.

There's a wound in my heart that is spurting blood
Which slowly but surely will take my life
Pierced by pain, my soul languishes
Love is the secret I cannot tell.

LORENZO STECCHETTI

Chapter One

1

The first neighbourhood of Amsterdam Johan saw that day was the trading district on the outskirts of the city. It was particularly quiet, given the Sunday rest.

His train then trundled through some less-than-prominent neighbourhoods, offering a rear view of several unattractive houses. He saw nothing of the city's renowned canals, and only caught a fleeting glimpse of the city centre when a street ended perpendicular to the railway.

The fire of Johan's suffering still burned within, but he wanted to control himself in this new environment. He understood then and there that the extent to which a person is able to master his many disorders is what makes a man of him. He resolved to be extremely cautious and controlled among all these strangers, aware that the first part of his life, which had been peopled almost exclusively by his father, had ended in unspeakable misery. The terrible moment that heralded Johan's present unhappiness was when he shared the secret of his desires with his father. He had spoken only after long and careful thought, intent on improving his existence, yet doing so had triggered his downfall.

2

The countryside between Amsterdam and Haarlem differed little from the Gerderland landscape between Cuilemburg and Zalt-Bommel. And the sunshine that afternoon in vibrant Holland was as beautiful for Johan as it possibly could be.

He was approaching Haarlem and he looked around to see if this new city was as expansive and well-appointed as his father had told him. He first noticed a wide stretch of water trimmed with tall trees, then a few empty streets, then tranquil parks. Everything was awash with bright white sunlight.

Johan then arrived at the dark and gloomy train station and looked around for the clock where Mrs Riemersma had promised to meet him in her letter.

He found her, they said their greetings, and they headed off together into the city.

3

The first street they entered was narrow, quiet and sunny. Johan spotted a tall white house on a corner in the middle of the street and was taken by the special light shed by the sun on its facade.

Chatting together about this and that, Johan managed to take a good look at the woman as she escorted him through this strange city to his new home. His father had written that she was approaching sixty, but while Johan believed his father he was also convinced that she looked much younger. Her choice of clothing was simple but unique. Johan was already satisfied with what he saw and his expectations of their new upper-storey home were improving by the minute.

They passed the corner in the sun-drenched street where the white house stood and soon arrived at an arched gateway leading to a stone lock where Johan spotted a canal. He glanced to the right and to the left. The canal to the left was lined with young trees without shadow and new bright houses, all bathed in sunshine. A veritable haven of sunshine. The trees to the right were more substantial, casting shadow on the street and the dark water's edge. The houses were shaded and there was little white sunlight, a haven of shade, which Johan quickly decided was more beautiful than the haven of sunshine. His eye then fell on a dark grey house, a remarkable structure, which he immediately assigned to the most prominent man in Haarlem and perhaps even all of Holland.

They descended the other side of the bridge and Johan looked back to catch a glimpse of the sun-drenched canal and the haven of shade at one and the same time. Both views were different and each was beautiful in its own way.

'What a beautiful canal,' he said with a shiver.

'Indeed,' Mrs Riemersma confirmed. 'That's the New Canal . . . very beautiful, and home to the wealthiest folk in the city. The Bishop and the Governor . . . he lives in that big grey house . . . I wish I could offer the same where we live. Your father said you were particularly keen on beautiful houses with gardens . . . Unfortunately, we can't offer either.'

Johan was suddenly terrified at the thought of his new upper-floor home and convinced he was going to suffocate without space and without a garden. He was also tired from the intensity of witnessing both parts of the New Canal in a single moment. He said dejectedly:

'Is it far, Mrs Riemersma?'

'No, not far,' she said in a friendly tone, and then she thought: 'Such a haughty young man . . . nothing like René . . . it could well be a disappointment . . . but then again he has to settle in . . . and it's the first time he's been away from home and from his father . . . he clearly comes from good stock . . .'

<h2 style="text-align:center">4</h2>

The Lange Veerstraat was a narrow alley where the shops were closed for Sunday, but the warehouses where the Jews lived were open, full of clothing and the latest fashions. Johan found it wretched.

The stairs up to the Riemersmas' house were broad, well-lit and easy to climb. Johan was suddenly curious about Mrs Riemersma's blind husband and what he looked like. To his surprise, he had completely forgotten him.

They arrived in the living room where Johan was introduced to Dr Riemersma. His wife then left the room after announcing that her maid had the day off. She would have to take care of the household chores herself and had to change into her working clothes.

The blind Dr Riemersma offered his hand and Johan accepted it. It was a frail, elderly hand, thin and soft to the touch. It pleased him that the man with whom he would be lodging had such a delicate right hand. A person's hand could be very revealing, he thought.

Dr Riemersma asked if Johan was thirsty. Johan said no, but added that the change of city and lodgings had left him a little perplexed.

The conversation more or less ended there. Johan was curious about the man's blind condition and examined his face with interest. His eyes were deep, dark and open. They peered at Johan when the elderly doctor spoke to him, as if they could see. Johan found them strange yet beautiful. He knew two other blind people, both with shrivelled, vacant eyes. It pleased him that the face of the man with such a delicate right hand wasn't ruined by two ugly sores for eyes. Otherwise he would have found it impossible to grow fond of him.

There were long silences in the living room, broken only by the hurried tick-tock of a thinly shaped clock.

The hustle and bustle of the busy street below was audible but invisible. The windows in the room were too high and the street was little more than a narrow alley.

Mrs Riemersma reappeared and Johan was delighted to observe that she was still neat and tidy in her everyday working clothes.

'Here I am, ready for work . . . ' she said jovially.

Her blind husband cut her short:

'No, Marta, now's not the time . . . Hans is tired from the journey . . . and leaving his home and his father can't have been easy for him . . . best show him to his room.'

Johan thought in a panic: 'If only they knew what saying good-bye to my home and my father was really like.' But then he regained his composure: 'They know nothing of my desperately unhappy life and are sure to say things from time to time that sound harsh and callous, but I want to get used to that as soon as possible.'

5

Johan was pleasantly surprised by the room they had readied for him. It was spacious and quiet, and when he looked out of the window he was thrilled by the cheerful vista of a multitude of colourful gardens. The houses clearly weren't pressed together on this side of the building, and his quarters weren't squeezed into some colossal stack of overpopulated houses as he had feared.

His considerate landlady asked if the room was sufficient, adding that she was sure Hans would miss his garden.

'I surely will,' he said: 'I always miss the things I'm used to . . . but at least I have plenty of other gardens to look at.'

'The neighbours downstairs have a little courtyard and a bit of a garden,' said Mrs Riemersma, 'but the gardens round here are delightful . . . although the flowers are gone . . . I mean most of them . . . not all of them, I don't think they're ever all gone . . . maybe in the winter . . . I'm not really sure. But it's small here, I give you that . . . and if the rents weren't so high, I'd much rather be living on the ground floor.'

Johan thought: 'She speaks more or less as she writes, constantly explaining herself.'

Anxiety about the house and its inhabitants had left him, so his response was friendly:

'The room is quite sufficient . . . and if the city is attractive . . .'

'We live a very quiet life here. We never see young people . . . but your father said you much preferred to be alone and didn't want to be around young people. I hope you don't mind my husband . . . I don't know what it's like to be blind and all . . . my husband hasn't said a word about it for as long as I remember . . . he just sits there in his big chair and says nothing . . . probably better than complaining . . . or maybe not.'

Johan interjected:

'And Richell?'

'He and my husband get on well . . . no, he makes plenty of fuss . . . and they always side with each other against me when it comes to suffering in the world. Believe me, Hans, there's so much suffering in the world. You'll see it for yourself soon enough, when you take your first steps . . . and most of the time it's the people themselves to blame, let me tell you . . . we're each other's worst enemy.

'Anyone can have an accident, of course . . . nothing to be done about it . . . like my husband, for example, when he went blind. But people are the worst offenders for making other people unhappy . . . if people weren't so heartless there would be a lot less suffering in the world . . . but everyone is worried that everyone else is better off than they are. I don't mean to complain . . . we know our limits and we survive with what we have . . . although our life isn't what it was, and it often saddens me when I think back, but then I'm reminded about all the suffering around me . . . and my husband is always kind and modest . . . but with those eyes of his it could have been a lot different.'

Johan was impressed by his landlady's gentleness. He then thought about his father: 'If I manage to get over the sadness of leaving my father, life here might not be too bad after all.'

He agreed that there was a great deal of suffering in the world, but it made no sense, he added, to be concerned about it all at once.

'That's true,' said his elderly landlady, 'no one can carry all the burdens of the world, no one wants that, but there's a big difference between doing everything and doing nothing . . . sadly, most people aren't interested in helping each other, more the opposite . . . but if people were a little more tolerant there would be a lot less suffering in the world.'

'You could be right,' said Johan politely.

'My husband and R.R. laugh at me all the time, and I some-times get annoyed when my husband laughs . . . But it's R.R. who annoys me most . . . he should be careful . . . people who live in glass houses and all that . . . not that I have the least ill-will towards him, on the contrary, I wish him only the best . . . there's a lot of good in him and his work seems to be making its mark . . . but he's an abso-lute devil at times, and careless as a child.'

'Well . . . I'm looking forward to meeting him,' said Johan cautiously.

6

Mrs Riemersma left Johan alone in his room and he listened to her departing footsteps as she made her way downstairs. Then there was silence, quickly followed by an overwhelming and desperate sense of desolation.

Johan looked around. Nothing was familiar, neither the fur-nishings nor the decorations. Even the view was new to him, and the sight of so many strange things distressed him deeply.

At home he was familiar with everything, every shade of light and darkness throughout the house, all his life. He knew Den Bommel and Cuilemburg inside out, the sky and landscape between them. Johan was so deeply attached to the Senior Secondary School, which was once home to nobility, that it felt like his own home.

But his life had now been turned on its head, city and country-side, people and lodgings. Tomorrow he would attend a new school where he knew no one, and experience told him it would be a pain-ful process.

He lay down on the closet bed and closed his eyes to screen off the room, the sight of which still hurt him. He thought about his blind landlord and his aged right hand, delicate to the touch, like living white porcelain. He also thought about what was left inside his damaged eyes. He had only seen them fleetingly, but he would never forget how deep and dark they were.

His elderly landlady was genuinely kind. She spoke as she wrote, constantly contradicting herself, but she had a kind voice, mature, soft yet penetrating.

Johan almost fell asleep, until vivid images of his father suddenly startled him.

He closed his oversensitive eyes again and in waking dreams he imagined an old house surrounded by a halo of golden light. His heart shivered and he thought with delight: 'When I see light as gold, as something more precious than gold, arising from my own emotions, then I know that my soul will have peace, in spite of the storms all around.'

7

Johan slept a lot in those days.

His landlady's voice woke him up and he realized she must have called him several times. He no longer felt tired, and he wanted to make a good impression by dressing properly for dinner so he lit a lamp in his room for want of natural light.

Johan often took great pleasure in attending to every last detail of his appearance, but he knew that such delights were limited to his better days. Today was one of them, and it pleased him immensely.

Johan was particularly drawn to fragrances of every kind, his favourites including the soft smell of roses and, by contrast, melancholy violets. He remembered once filling a little room with so much perfume that the vapours had lulled him to sleep for several hours. He stood in front of his dark mirror, wrapped in thin golden light, and readied himself for his first meal with his new family. Gloomy thoughts no longer plagued him. In fact, he was in the best of spirits, without knowing why.

Johan had never been to any kind of festivity before, because he had always lived alone with his father and had no affection for anyone else. But he had read about such festivities and about their joys and sorrows. As he perfumed himself with fragrant violet he thought: 'I'm going to a party ... my heart is pounding ... and I'm thrilled.'

He tended to his pale unblemished hands, aware that they always had to be clean and spotless if he didn't want to disgust himself. He then arranged the folds of his blond hair. Everything as it should be.

Johan felt unusually happy and strong, a rare sensation. He thought, 'It's possible after all, here in this strange place without my father.' His heart told him he was on the mend, and he looked forward to seeing his blind landlord's dark exceptional eyes and to meeting René Richell, the artist, who was worse than the devil and careless as a child.

8

Johan made his way along a dark corridor, and when he opened the door to the light-filled room his eyes blinked and closed spontaneously, dizzy for a moment in the pale-yellow gloom. The lady of the house was not present. Johan said hello to his blind landlord for the second time and René Richell for the first time in his life. He asked if he was interrupting an agreeable or serious conversation.

'Never,' said Richell, 'we don't have agreeable or serious conversations here . . . we just bore each other . . . much more fun than being bored alone . . . and it's time for dinner.'

Johan didn't immediately understand what the painter had said, but when he thought about it he thought it was absurd, without rhyme or reason.

The meal started when Mrs Riemersma returned to the room.

Johan said little. He was used to being treated with polite deference and Richell's manners were annoying. Only moments earlier he had felt strong, but now he felt fragile again and unhappy. He longed for the home he had left behind and for the father he loved so much, the man he had made so unhappy. In his dejected state, he started to miss all the artistic objects that accompanied every meal in Cuilemburg. Everything he touched here pained him. He felt vulnerable, empty. And he had no idea what to say to any of the people sharing the table.

9

Johan stared at the blind doctor. The man's face was old, but without a single wrinkle, pale, but with a distinguished paleness. The eyes in his motionless face were bright and full of life, which Johan ascribed to a story Richell was telling. He wasn't following. He found it particularly difficult to comprehend that the eyes of a blind man could be dead on the inside yet alive on the outside. While they no longer admitted light, they still managed to radiate light from within.

Johan listened to Richell's voice. His words were hurried yet even and controlled, as if he wanted to be sure that no single word was louder or softer than any other.

As he listened to the voice, Johan also listened to the content of Richell's story, which was full of words that Johan was sure no one could possibly mean. He had to ask himself at times what Richell was talking about, especially when his words seemed literally nonsensical, which they often were. Johan didn't like it much, but the blind doctor seemed to enjoy it.

Richell suddenly turned to Johan and asked: 'Suffering in the world, Hans! Has our landlady been talking about it? Has she?' Johan's blue eyes recoiled.

'No,' said Johan.

Richell seemed determined: 'So, that explains why you're so terribly unhappy.'

Johan gasped and responded with conviction: 'I am not unhappy.'

He had to bite his lip to avoid bursting into tears. Mr Riemersma heard Johan's response and thought to himself: 'Perhaps Hans is unhappy after all, if a simple question from René can upset him so.'

'We don't think you're unhappy either, Hans,' he said. 'Pay no attention to René.'

'Of course,' said Richell, pretending to be upset and startling Johan. 'Whether Hans is unhappy or not is of no consequence to me . . . I only asked to see if it would irritate him . . . and I'm delighted it did.'

10

Richell then announced that he was going to Amsterdam.

'I'd prefer you stay here,' said Mrs Riemersma.

'Yes, that's what I thought too,' said René with a straight face, 'but I suddenly had this urge to go to Amsterdam, and you know how immoral and dangerous I think it is to avoid my sudden urges.'

'It's up to you, but you've said more than once that Amsterdam is a dangerous city.'

'That's precisely why I should go . . . and anyway, every city is dangerous . . . two people in one place is dangerous . . . never mind, I just had a sudden urge not to go to Amsterdam . . . then I'll go somewhere else . . . I'm not sure where . . . but tonight I will not be here.'

After Richell left the room, Mrs Riemersma asked Johan if he didn't mind her putting out the lamps. The evenings had been light and warm for quite some time, she said, and she preferred to do without them. She also didn't have to read the Haarlem newspaper for her husband, it being Sunday. She didn't mind doing it, of course, in spite of claims to the contrary, but it was no easy task and took its toll on her ageing voice, especially if there was a supplement. Johan sipped his tea from his own Sèvres porcelain. He had told his landlady that he preferred his own cups. Using unfamiliar objects was always an emotional struggle.

11

Johan noticed that the blind doctor had returned to the way he was when they met for the first time that afternoon. In other words, he was nothing like the man at the table during the midday meal, listening to the whimsical stories of René Richell. In a pleasant and level voice, the elderly doctor spoke emotionally about his loss of ability to use braille in recent years. He could no longer rely on the sensitivity of his ageing fingers. He told Johan how he would borrow books that were of interest to him from the library of the Dutch Association for the Blind. But the more the books were read by the fingers of fellow sufferers, the less legible they became. He also told him that it was better to lose one's sight at an early age. As an older man it was so much more difficult to learn how to recognize fine objects by touch alone.

The conversation that evening fell frequently still. Johan's thoughts wandered wearily. He listened. The street—or better, alley—below was dark and busy. A lamp burned opposite their house, filling the misty evening air around it with rays of golden light. He could hear the hustle and bustle below, but he was unable to see the people going about their business. The windows were set high in the dining-room wall, and the street far below was as narrow as an alley.

12

Johan pondered René Richell, who blurted all sorts of things when he spoke and seemed to contradict himself at times. It was hard to tell if he was speaking his mind or not.

He said, 'René isn't as old as I expected.'

'No,' Mr Riemersma responded in his defence, 'he's still quite young indeed . . . not even close to thirty . . . my wife forgets that sometimes, treating him as sixty or seventy . . . and she's also inclined to forget that he's an artist.'

'Is his work as good as they say?' asked Johan.

'Yes! I've never seen any of his work, of course, and I've no personal opinion . . . and if I did it wouldn't be worth much . . . but if the articles in the papers and magazines I've had read to me are anything to go by, it seems his work has made enormous progress in recent years . . . but my wife isn't an admirer . . . she thinks every-thing he does is ugly and bad.'

'You're absolutely right,' said Mrs Riemersma, with more res-olution than her usual self-contradiction, 'from start to finish, one after the other, everything he produces . . . he might be talented, but if he is it's a demonic talent . . . and I'd be very disappointed if Hans were to find his work beautiful . . . '

The blind doctor's gentle voice hardened: 'My wife doesn't like René because he's not interested in the suffering in the world . . . and because he says that everyone should live as they see fit.'

'Yes,' said Mrs Riemersma, 'thank you for reminding me. If you ask me, the way that man lives his life leaves a lot to be desired . . . although it's not for us to speak ill of him . . . but then again, he shouldn't be so public with his thoughts.'

Johan noticed that Mrs Riemersma had lapsed into her habit of self-contradiction. Whatever the case, René Richell seemed to exercise considerable influence in this household.

13

Mrs Riemersma accompanied Johan to his room when the time had come to go to bed, as the house was still unfamiliar to him.

She lingered a while, and talked about her husband and about his doctor's practice and how important it was. That was before the eye condition, when he lost his vision. Now they still looked normal and undamaged on the outside, shiny and sparkling, and even she found it difficult to understand his blindness.

She told Johan she'd gotten used to it all over the years, including her husband's blindness, although she was often reminded of the way she felt shortly after it happened, especially when she watched him make his way through the house, blind and cautious.

She insisted that Hans shouldn't think they argued all the time. That would be far from the truth. They only argued about René Richell. Her husband admired the man's foolish words and contradictions, yet didn't tolerate such things from others.

They continued to talk about the blind doctor, who had spent year after year indoors with never a breath of fresh air. He didn't want to go outside because he was afraid of drawing attention to himself. As a result, his health had deteriorated without anyone noticing. Even his hands suffered, slowly losing their sensitivity until it became impossible for him to read with any confidence. He lived such a withdrawn life that people started to forget about him. Many even thought he had died and had sent Mrs Riemersma letters of condolence as if she had been widowed.

Johan told his melancholic landlady that every life had its share of suffering. He was thinking about his own desperately unhappy life, of course, but he thought it might help her somehow. He was sure nevertheless that his own suffering was far greater than the suffering afflicting the Riemersma household. He signalled politely that he was tired and ready for bed.

14

Mrs Riemersma descended the stairs, the sound of her footsteps gradually fading until the house was completely silent. In the hush, Johan wrote a silent letter to his father:

My dear father, my first day in Haarlem is over. I will always be unhappy as long as I cannot be with you regularly, but for a family I did not know, I have to admit that my first day was not bad. I'm sure my first day at the new school tomorrow will also be fine.

I promise to control the desires that have brought us such unhappiness and never surrender to them. Perhaps they will waste away, as a body part wastes away when it is never used. Perhaps then we can resume our life together.

Kindest regards from your son, Hans.

As Johan concluded the letter he thought to himself: 'I've left my beautiful garden behind, *Vier-Heemskinderen* Lane and the market square, all of which I would see if I were back in Cuilemburg and making my way to the post office.'

His spirits were low, his emotions flat.

Outside his new house, the wind rustled upwards from the darkness of the garden, through the branches of a leafless tree that had reached up to his window and gently tapped the glass. The reedy wind sounded like a sinister torrential rain.

Chapter Two

1

Johan's father set off on his planned travels and he sent his son a letter about it. When Johan read the letter, he thought: 'Did father stay all those years in Cuilemburg just for me while he would have preferred to travel, or is he travelling and visiting different countries because he is empty and unhappy?'

Johan's life was made easier by his father's travels. It was good that he was out of the country and perhaps Johan's well-being was his motivation. Knowing that he could no longer reach his father helped ease the longing he had to be with him. He also approved of his father's new wayfaring existence, especially considering his new family and their likely difficulty in understanding why father and son had no plans to visit one another.

2

Life in Cuilemburg had changed. Sien, the elderly housekeeper, no longer worked there. She continued to live in the house as if she was a lodger, but the coachman Gerard and his wife now took care of the place in his father's absence.

Sien wrote frequently about her gratitude to Johan's father and his generosity to her, just as the good God had favoured her throughout her life. But she hoped she would be spared the offence of pride. She had not forgotten her origins. She also wrote that she hoped Johan would remember the many good words she had shared with him from heart to heart and think about them often.

Johan was very grateful that his father had not put up their house on the market square in Cuilemburg for sale or for rent to an unknown family. Perhaps he kept it because he too hoped, and indeed trusted, that he would one day return to it with Johan?

3

Life in Haarlem wasn't quite as bad as Johan had expected. The house may have been small, but it was peaceful.

The new city also had much to offer. It was more prominent than Cuilemburg, and Johan was convinced that his sense of beauty could only be reinforced in this new environment. There were many more streets at the heart of the city and its canals were wider. The suburbs were also extensive, with villa districts and parks. The river Spaarne flowed through the entire city, its banks quiet yet fully populated. The area behind the market square was the only exception. The Spaarne quayside was both busy and noisy, a bustling centre of trade. Beyond the city, the river broadened and seemed almost motionless between the fields on either side.

Johan enjoyed extensive walks in the countryside surrounding Haarlem. Most of the time he headed west, past Overveen, where the landscape was alive with colourful flowers in the early spring, or towards Elswout, with its dark woods and forests.

One sunny afternoon Johan caught sight of something new, the open sea.

He gazed at the distant sky and water and his heart pounded with anxiety, forcing him to close his eyes and drop breathless to his knees.

He opened his eyes. There was plenty of wind in the West. Johan imagined cities of white in the distance surrounded by green fields on a sea of dark water.

4

The crests and hollows of the dunes were the ideal place to learn about the mysteries of flowers, an alien world to Johan thus far in his life. Star clusters of stonecrop were scattered here and there on the warm white sand. The cooler, moist hollows were home to purple mint and dark ground-ivy. Johan also spotted some parasitic broomrape, which lives on more substantial plants.

The heavenly void arched high above a blissful planet Earth.

While he didn't forget his misfortune for a single moment, Johan experienced intense yet unfamiliar pleasures in those days, joys that made him tremble.

5

There wasn't a single person or house in Haarlem that Johan loved more than the Church of Saint Bavo. He beheld the magnificent towering edifice every morning and at noon, each time from a different perspective. For Johan's subtle and unguarded sensitivities, it was as if there were two churches.

Johan followed the same route to school every morning and returned by the same alternative route every afternoon. Familiar streets brought him tranquillity, and deviations only pain.

Every morning, Johan crossed the Old Groenmarkt, which was more of a narrow shaded street than a broad market square. This brought him close to the towering Saint Bavo's, but meant he couldn't see it in all its glory, only a gloomy, dilapidated wall incorporating a row of single-storey vergers' houses, each with white guttering and a dark blue door.

In the afternoons, Johan was able to observe the immense church from a different perspective when he crossed the main market square on his way home. Then he was able to take in the magnificent edifice from the top of its heavenly spire to the bustling street below. And what he saw was quite simply stunning.

There were dunes to the west of the Haarlem which offered a panoramic view of the city. From here the houses seemed so tiny and colourful, as if you could toss the motley mess in the air with one hand. But not the church, of course, not the church. Saint Bavo's generous and steady walls towered high above all the other buildings.

When Johan ventured into the lowlands to the east of Haarlem and turned to look back, the houses were no longer clearly visible but had been reduced to a thin strip of cloudy grey, shimmering on a bright horizon.

Only the church was spared this reduction. Saint Bavo's stood solitary on the horizon, specks of brilliant sunlight glistening on its shiny roof.

6

Johan spent most of his time alone, both inside and outside the city, and had little to do with his schoolmates. Physical desires returned, however, especially for some well-dressed boys in the early years of puberty. One young teacher with the voice and eyes of a student also attracted his attention. He had potent dreams in those days that had a tangible effect on his body, but neither his dreams nor his desires had anything to do with his father.

Johan understood then that his attractions were not of a transitory nature, but the thought did not worry him as it had before. Articles he read in those days encouraged him to ascribe as much legitimacy to his own emotional desires as to the desires of others. No more, but also no less. In that regard, he rejected the letters from his father without condition.

He completely understood the importance of being both modest and discrete about his emotional life, since the majority of people, those with social standing, were unwilling to tolerate expressions of such desire.

But Johan was also resolute and convinced that he had a right to feel what he felt in his heart, although it might differ from the feelings of the majority.

He started to reflect with care at that time on the difference between the words 'bad' and 'unsocial', a distinction his academically competent father had made in his letters.

Johan also reflected on the words of René Richell, that everyone had the right to his own opinion, and the only feelings that counted were one's own, words he now started to appreciate much more than he had at first.

7

The blind doctor never left the house, insisting that he didn't want to be a bother to anyone. But he was open to the idea of a walk with Hans, since the boy was always so careful and quiet.

His elderly landlady likewise never joined him on his excursions outside the city, especially where the dunes were steep. But they did walk together from time to time within the city and its outskirts.

René Richell made serious fun of Hans and his blustery, sun-drenched excursions, which often resulted in a bunch of highly perfumed and colourful flowers.

'Don't you like the smell of flowers?' Hans asked, inhaling deeply.

'No,' said René, 'flowers are not allowed in my room . . . roses smell particularly disgusting . . . but do you know what's a delicious smell? When *you* smell of roses . . . that's delicious.'

Johan quipped in response that he had no idea what René was talking about or thinking: 'If our landlady were to hear such talk, she would think he's as wicked as the devil.'

Johan made sure from then on that his body did not smell of flowers. His dealings with René proceeded in a regular manner, with mutual goodwill.

8

Johan had grown accustomed to his new home in Haarlem. He had encountered people, streets and houses in the city that thrilled him intensely. But now that little was new and exciting, his days were quieter and his delicate emotions calmer.

The desire to write a few pages of proper prose returned at this juncture. Satisfying his desire was just as wonderful as dreaming of a golden sky. When he wrote his emotions were particularly high and he had trouble controlling his hand and keeping his hand-writing stable. He composed refined and detailed descriptions of: a tea cup; the Nieuwe Gracht canal in the sun; the grey residence of the Governor of the Province of North Holland; the Church of Saint Bavo in the morning; the Church of Saint Bavo at noon; the motionless white hands of the blind doctor; the courtyard of

Teyler's Museum; a bunch of wild flowers; the Bakenessergracht; the sea and the sun; a Chinese altar lamp; the lamp in his room burning brightly.

He submitted all thirteen descriptions for publication to a journal run by a literary artist he greatly admired.

The letter he received in response was itself a work of literary art and style. It informed him that his admirable writings were a welcome contribution to the journal. The editor went on to declare Johan's detailed descriptions 'pure and exceptional'.

The tone of the letter gave the impression that its admirable author considered Johan to be no less than his equal. He sensed considerable advantage in preserving it and sharing it with others.

Johan hoped fervently that the gradual and meticulous development of his writing skills would help him to become a literary artist, and the equal of René Richell.

9

Johan often accompanied his elderly landlady when she visited her washer and bleacher. The man lived in Den Hout, deep in the last of the tributaries of the Spaarne, where there was an ample supply of clean water which he needed for his business. His old house was cobbled together from the crumbling remains of other houses.

Mrs Riemersma had a running feud with her washer, convinced that he was careless with her laundry. Sometimes he was late, other times items of clothing were missing or switched. The man paid no attention to the letters she sent, no matter how urgent, so she had reason for a personal visit and she was justifiably angry. She told Hans it was time to put an end to their arrangement. It was too much of a bother to be running back and forth all the time, checking on her own property. It was a pleasant walk if the weather was good, and if it wasn't they took a tram. A trip to the bleacher was no more difficult than any other. But why was he so careless with her laundry when she herself was so careful with it? Simple theft could hardly explain it. If he had returned everything in good order she wouldn't have to look for another washer, but this was the last straw. She felt sorry for Nelissen the washer and bleacher. The man had a big family to take care of and had a lot of trouble with his laundry girls. She also felt bad about depriving the man of his living. So many were struggling to make ends meet, and everyone suffered in their own way. It was always better to suffer much injustice than to perpetrate little.

The last house at the end of Den Hout Street by the Spaarne belonged to Nelissen. Mrs Riemersma told Johan that she was sorry to be visiting the man on a busy Saturday, but this was the last time. She could no longer ignore the constant neglect and disappearance of her laundry. He had to make up his mind. Improve his service or lose her custom.

The washer and bleacher knew well enough that he wouldn't lose her custom. It being Saturday he was short but polite, since Mrs Riemersma was always so kind: it wasn't his fault. He worked long and hard for his family, which had grown in size over the years. The laundry girls were to blame.

Johan gazed at the washer and bleacher's curiously shaped house by the broad, motionless waters, absorbing and reflecting the rays of the sun.

10

On their way back to the city and home, they stopped at a farm where the farmer sold the purest milk. Johan was a regular customer. White milk and red wine were both delicious and among his favourite drinks. Mrs Riemersma told him she was happy to have settled things with Nelissen. She was sure his work would improve, although it wasn't the first time he had promised to change his ways.

She talked about the absence of mutual respect in the world and then about R.R. and how frivolous he was. He had achieved so much for a man in his late twenties, probably more than she knew, but he had the habit of teasing people with frivolous sayings that often turned out to be cringingly painful.

But she was still happy to have him as a lodger. And in spite of all her own problems, she still felt a call in her heart to help steer René along the right path, no matter how often he laughed at her when she told him. 'Every path is excellent,' he would say, 'except the right path, which is far too narrow and troublesome.'

Everyone has their calling, she continued, but her husband didn't help her much. He was inclined to tolerate René and everything about him. A good artist needs room to breathe and do his work. He also insisted that she made life in their house difficult for René with all her talk about suffering in the world and how hard people can be.

She told Johan that René sometimes disappeared unannounced and without a trace, leaving her worried sick. Then he wasn't much help to either her or her husband. But he had been calm of late, so she hoped that something of her unfailing good counsel had rubbed off on him. He worked in his place on the Koudenhorn which was a good sign, although she was often convinced his creations were the work of the devil.

Johan said she was perhaps being a little too harsh. She had every right to disapprove of his work, of course, just as the majority had the right to praise him, and many among them were accustomed to evaluating paintings after years of experience. But R.R.

also had a right to work as he saw fit. She might not like it, but she shouldn't hold it against him.

Johan found René's work refined and colourful. He had grown more accustomed to the artist's ways and words, and was now quite fond of him.

Johan's affection for his elderly landlady was increasingly heart-felt. She worked hard and did her best, and she always tried to be as unobtrusive as she could.

11

Johan later freed his elderly landlady from the burden of having to read the Haarlem newspapers for her blind husband. She never refused to help when asked and as a result she was usually run off her feet, so her newfound freedom was a delight. She was also con-stantly busy with household chores, fearing otherwise that her maid would have too much to do.

Her blind husband took greater pleasure in listening to Johan's careful reading than to his wife's tired voice. He listened attentively, eager to learn what was going on in the city, the country, and the world, and determined not to miss anything. Johan never looked up when he was reading, but when he paused for a moment after reading at length he would gaze at the doctor's delicate face and extraordinary sightless eyes. He would happily have gazed much longer with affection and feeling, but he didn't want to remain silent for too long, fearing the doctor might think he was tiring him.

When Johan was reading he was thus prevented from gazing at the doctor's amazing eyes, and the unfulfilled desire to do so caused him pain.

The blind doctor sometimes lamented about the misfortune that had ruined his sight. An irreparable rupture of the delicate retinas had robbed him of his life's work. Being a doctor was so dear to him and he had studied so hard for it. Life now had no more value than death.

12

The blind doctor once spoke about the emptiness in which he lived. Johan had been working in the living room. The blind doctor had mentioned in passing that he enjoyed having him present even if they didn't speak and Johan didn't mind. The man sat unperturbed, deep in his ample armchair, staring as always into his endless night. His face was entirely motionless, as if the world meant nothing to him and he desired nothing.

Then he asked out of the blue:

'Hans, do you think I'm unhappy?'

Johan responded with caution:

'A strange question to ask . . . I mean, being blind must indeed be the greatest misfortune to overcome a person.'

'I rarely talk about it because I don't think it does me any good, but for once I want to, just to be sure you don't think I'm desperately unhappy. I've been blind for so long now and the changes took place only gradually. In the beginning I was restless . . . unable to sit still for a minute, and I spent the day wandering around the house . . . the moment I sat down I would start to brood about my troubles. But that slowly changed . . . I can now sit for hours without moving a muscle and without thinking about anything in particular . . . and I'm not unhappy. Life without sight is completely different. I'm now dependent on sound and touch. I recognize people by the sound of their voice and by the feel of their hands . . . and just as you might consider someone with an unpleasant face at first sight to be in a bad mood, so I can sense a person's mood by touching their hands or by the sound of their voice.'

The blind doctor's voice grew stronger as he took Johan by the hand: 'I'm telling you this because I don't want you to think I'm more deprived than I really am . . . I'm also very content to have you here and to know you're doing so well . . . I can feel it . . . it's undeniable.'

Johan thought how terrible it must be to be blind and dependent every day of one's life on the goodwill of others.

13

Johan started his summer vacation in good spirits. He looked forward to the freedom of sun-filled days, ideal for further forays into the Haarlem countryside.

He also visited Cuilemburg because Sien had asked, although he wasn't happy about it and feared the fierce emotions such a visit might bring. But nothing happened. He was quite calm when he saw their home, the white porch, the clock, the hallway, the stairwell. He thought: 'Have I forgotten so much . . . to feel as calm as I now do, or have I grown much stronger?'

His elderly maid Sien was so happy when he visited, and he was happy to oblige.

14

Summer that year was abundant in sublime and perfect days, with bright clear skies a constant. Johan wandered hour after hour across meadows and stacking dunes, the sand and soil warmed by the sun. And he returned each day with a wealth of wild-scented flowers, their perfume lingering on his clothing.

Richell told him he couldn't stand the smell of so many flowers, but found it wonderful when Johan was so fragrantly perfumed.

Johan's blue eyes darkened in the strong light of the sun, and likewise the pale skin on his face and hands. He looked half-Dutch, he thought, like Paul Mansfeld. The blind doctor helped him dry the flowers, his delicate fingertips quite familiar with their structure, their leaves and stems, silky or coarse. Hans told him all about his walks and the many sunny places he had to visit to gather so many flowers. He was often afraid to say too much about the amazing sun and sky. He felt sorry for the blind doctor and his housebound exist-ence. Johan suggested they go for a walk together to get him out of the house. Not through the undulating dunes, of course, but some-where level, Den Hout perhaps, which was so beautiful as evening fell and filled with the fragrance of trees and soil. It was often so quiet there, as if indoors.

The blind doctor turned him down, lamenting wearily that he had been feeling his age of late.

15

A restless discontent disrupted the tranquillity of Johan's new home, and all because of René Richell and his casual lifestyle. Just when everyone seemed content with the man, he disappeared with-out notice or trace.

Mrs Riemersma insisted that his troublesome disappearance was not her fault, pointing the finger rather at her husband who always dismissed her warnings and undermined her words.

The blind doctor retorted without irritation or ire that there was just as much chance that she was to blame. Constantly con-fronting him with all the suffering in the world and complaining about the way he chose to live his life were enough to drive anyone away.

A letter addressed to Mrs Riemersma arrived shortly thereafter from the Rue des Saints Pères in Paris.

Richell wrote:

Dear Mrs Riemersma, I was convinced I had discovered a new crime while in Haarlem. The inventor of a new crime must surely be considered a great benefactor to all humanity and that is my ambition. There is nothing more wonderful. I decided to go to Paris to put my new crime to the test among my friends. It transpired, however, that there is no such thing as a new crime. My friends were already familiar with it. But other friends told me of certain businesses here I knew nothing about, so I decided to stay in Paris and explore them. I plan to return to Haarlem at a later date to put what I learn into practice, and I would much appreciate your continued hospitality.

With kind regards to you, your esteemed husband and to Hans.

Sincerely,

R.R.

The blind doctor said nothing. His wife complained that she preferred not to have him back in her house, but she knew all too well that she would change her mind when he was standing at the door, bruised and tired, asking to be let in. She had done it before and would do it again. She still hoped the time would come when her efforts would be rewarded and René would change his ways. But not a single day went by when she did not have her doubts.

She wrote to Paris with urgency more than once, asking about his return. She admonished him at the same time, urging him to examine his excessive lifestyle and reconsider. She, her husband and

Hans were deeply concerned about his absence, afraid that he would lapse into a life of crime in Paris and be terribly unhappy.

Despite her many letters begging him to return, she received no response. She then started to fear that René had met his death in Paris in one or other criminal manner. Their anxiety evolved into mutual accusations and each tried to win Hans for their cause, making his life in the house almost unbearable.

16

Johan decided to write a harsh letter of his own to the belligerent artist. In a few words he condemned Richell's behaviour and assured him he would do everything he could to prevent his return to the Riemersma household if he didn't respond with a reassuring message within the next few days.

Two letters from Paris followed in quick succession. The letter to his elderly landlord and landlady was kind and simple. Richell informed them that he preferred to enjoy his freedom in Paris for the time being, where he had found many interesting subjects to paint. He was working at his best and was sure he would return to Holland and Haarlem with some excellent material. There was no reason to worry about him. He was doing well, and for someone like him, indulging in a bout of liberty was like rain to a thirsty meadow, the kind Hans loves so excessively. He was planning to return to Harlem in late autumn and was looking forward to quietly rejoining the Riemersma household.

Hans received a letter from René addressed to his school and it concerned him deeply.

Dear Hans, the letters from Mrs Riemersma were kind and heartfelt, so I decided not to answer them. She hasn't changed as far as I am concerned and I see no need to spare her.

Your letter was a different matter. It was unfriendly and threatening, and I fear you will manage to convince the Riemersmas not to have me back. But I need them to have me back because they are the only people I know with any certainty who are able to tolerate my continually unpleasant character. So, I want us to remain friends, and I have written to Mrs Riemersma since that is what you asked.

I enclose a small charcoal sketch for you, a detailed drawing of a couple of trees on the road near the well-known porcelain factory in Sèvres.

Kind regards

R.R.

Johan knew immediately that he could not share the content of this oddly unruffled and detailed letter with his landlord and landlady. He decided to tear it up but kept the Richell's charcoal sketch. That evening his feelings towards the artist softened. This time he wrote a well-intentioned letter to Paris, thanking René for the gift and advising him to avoid writing such peculiar letters and engaging in impassioned conversations in the future.

17

Autumn arrived unobtrusively that year, without the usual commotion of rain and wind. Johan sensed a greater tranquillity in his life, in contrast to the long and sun-drenched summer.

One afternoon as he sat with the blind doctor, his landlord said:

'I'm truly sorry I let the summer pass, Hans, and that your holidays are now over, but I'd really like to go outside with you after all, if it's not too much to ask.'

Johan was surprised at his landlord's words. He responded politely that it would be his pleasure and he did not mind at all. His landlord continued:

'You're probably asking yourself why I spent the entire summer indoors and now that autumn has arrived I want to go out. I haven't been outside for years, so I postponed an outing day after day while the weather was so good. But now the weather is still fine and not too warm . . . and I'd like to feel the outside air you spoke about so often, at least once before the winter sets in.'

18

Johan and the blind doctor left the house together one free afternoon as autumn darkness descended on the city and the surrounding countryside. Johan held his walking companion's left hand in his right. He had never done so before. It felt old and delicate.

They walked side by side through the streets of the city, through the noise people made with their feet and their voices. The hubbub inspired a vague sense of anxiety, making the blind doctor stop abruptly every now and then as if he had almost bumped into something. It reminded Johan of Paul Mansfeld in the darkness of their garden in Cuilemburg. Paul's hand was smaller than Johan's back then, but the blind doctor's left hand was thin, slender and delicate.

They made their way to quieter streets, walking side by side at an even pace. Johan noticed that some people stared at his distinguished companion, his eyes revealing his blindness as he was led through the silent streets.

They arrived in Den Hout, where the quiet day was already fading. Trees bowed in the gentle wind, blowing like a soft autumn rain. Johan could see his blind companion listening carefully, unable to see the waning light between the trees. He didn't dare describe what he could see, how beautiful the light was, for fear he would break the blind doctor's heart.

His walking companion's thin, delicate hand shuddered. Johan offered some words of comfort:

'Your first time outside for so long . . . you must be exhausted . . . but next time it'll be so much easier and more relaxing . . . you'll see.'

19

They sat at the edge of the woods where the trees were sparse, those behind them embracing in the wind, thicker and darker. Level fields stretched into the distance before them, the sky hanging low, like a blanket. The sky to the west was livelier, replete with light and wind, and grey clouds drifting against a background of deep sun-red.

'Hans,' said the blind doctor, deeply moved. 'Tell me what you see.'

Johan reported in the greatest detail, his words expressive yet restrained, as if he was writing prose. He described the contours and colours of the fields and the houses, and the shades of light and dark in the sky. He said nothing about the sounds he heard, aware that his blind companion could hear but not see.

The elderly doctor responded with loud lament, a voice Johan had never heard before, harried and fierce. He cursed life in no uncertain terms. It had broken him, defeated him, forced him to depend on the compassion of a young boy if he wanted to leave his house. The man howled from his confinement: 'It's so difficult, Hans, the darkness that surrounds me, and there's no escaping it. I'm doomed to live with it to the end of my days.'

Tiredness took hold of him and when Johan realized he rightly said:

'Let's go home.'

They headed back through the city as darkness fell. The streets and canals were now wrapped in mystery, as if more was going on than daylight could endure.

'Hans,' said the blind doctor, his voice humble and heartfelt, 'please say nothing to my wife about my improper outburst . . . it would only sadden her.'

Johan drew solace from the fact that someone like Dr Riemersma could also be prone to losing control from time to time.

Mrs Riemersma awaited them as they drew near to the house, not sure why she felt so terribly anxious. She embraced her elderly husband with uninhibited emotion, noisily kissing his mouth and eyes just as Johan had done with his father when he was still a boy.

The spectacle surprised him.

'They're such decent people,' he thought, 'and Richell takes such advantage of them. But René is an outstanding artist, and his charcoal drawing of the two trees is simply wonderful.'

20

As the days shortened and Johan returned to school, opportunities for walking were few and far between.

Winter's slow but steady grip engulfed the nations of the earth, and the cities of the earth grew tranquil under heavy skies.

But Johan and his blind friend profited from a mild and sunny afternoon to head off to the sea. They had both been looking forward to it.

They sat together, out of the wind behind the boardwalk, hand in hand like a couple of children. Only Johan could see the swell of the sea, wave after surf-tipped wave, and the faint horizon embracing the restless waters in a static, unbreakable ring of silver.

The sun set in the sea to the west, but without its autumn glow of red and orange. The waves swept across the beach, dark and contrary, foaming at the foot of the dunes. The absence of colour chilled Johan to the core and the fear of death made him tremble. But instead of getting up, he sat still in his anxiety, for fear he would disturb his oversensitive companion. His sight inexplicably severed, the blind doctor stared out over the grey groaning swell, picturing it all in his mind as if his powerless eyes could still register the abundance of light and life whenever he willed.

21

Late that evening Johan described the shades of sea and sky as if he were writing for the blind. He wrote nothing about sounds, which the blind could hear. It was an exceptional page of prose, Johan thought, the most important he had ever written.

22

Night followed evening and evening day and Johan dreamt beautiful dreams, abundant with light and soft sounds. He thought they would last till the break of morning. Johan woke in good spirits, for muted dreams of light and the softest sounds were a sure sign that peace, still as an autumn day, held sway in his soul.

As he walked through the hushed and weather-beaten autumn morning, he felt awake yet still in a dream. Both worlds shared the same frail autumn tenderness, fragile yet profound.

It was impossible to go to school in this exceptionally delicate state, so Johan yielded to his desire to go to the sea. That day he headed to Zandvoort and he spent the time strolling on the windy beach and between the tranquil autumn dunes. His special state survived the entire day.

The following day, autumn's thin and fragile light gave way to showers and wind. Johan sensed an inner change. He was happy to have enjoyed so much of the summer and early autumn, and that it had inspired him to compose page after page of the best prose. But too much pleasure was a dangerous thing, and he was content with the blustery squalls and the occasional storm.

Chapter 3

1

The winter wind drove rain from the skies and the winter firmament stretched high and cloudless above cities and countryside. The days filled with clean crisp air and light, hard on the eye, throat and mouth.

Johan observed that the subtleties of an autumn day differed from those of a winter day. Autumn's colours were gold and dark blue, in mid-winter they were white and thin, bright and blue, especially when chill and ice set in.

Winter's sounds were also different, as if transformed into white music in a chamber of frosty air. Winter's days unfolded from overcast mornings, but before becoming bright they folded once again, dimming unobserved into twilight evenings.

Some days failed to unfold, locked in by a melancholy mist hanging motionless between heaven and earth, dripping rain. Occasional gusts of wind shook heavier squalls from the dense fog, but the wind seemed powerless in face of the rain-filled mist, suspended like a dull-grey blanket between heaven's light and earth's lack.

2

As the days grew clearer and brighter, René Richell returned to Holland and to Haarlem. Early one free afternoon, Johan walked in on one of his conversations with the blind doctor, as if he had never been a source of unrest in their household. Johan sensed that René would resume his role as the doctor's best friend and that he would be relegated to second place. This saddened him and he realized how close he had become to the elderly blind man with the slender delicate hands. He was sure that his life would be easier and more balanced if there was no one to like or dislike.

Johan thus fell out with Richell, expressing his sense of inferiority in stony silence and scant, carefully selected words.

He continued to be kind to the elderly doctor and always polite, insofar as his mood permitted.

Mrs Riemersma told him she had had a long and serious conversation with Richell before allowing him back into the house. But she didn't dare leave him on the streets for fear he would succumb to wanton behaviour. She hoped that at least some of her good advice would make a difference sooner or later; she was willing to accept her calling and do whatever was necessary to keep René on the straight and narrow.

Johan felt sorry for his landlady, who always gave priority to the other residents in the house. For her and her alone he purchased a select bunch of flowers, each of them exquisite and rare in the winter months. His hands shivered with joy as he hurried them with care through the frozen streets. He gave them to Mrs Riemersma in a much-treasured porcelain vase, in the shape and colour of a white flower. Both the flowers and the vase, he said, itself a rare porcelain flower, were because she was so goodhearted.

When René saw the flowers that evening his words were kind and affable: 'It's a shame they have no scent . . . I don't like flowers without scent . . . I much prefer scented flowers, like roses . . . wonderful.'

Johan hadn't forgotten what Richell had said previously about scented flowers in general and the smell of roses in particular. Was this a subtle form of abuse?

3

Johan had never been to the house in Koudenhorn where René stored his curiosities and worked on his grander paintings, which were too large for his lodgings. He had once told Johan that his house was perfect in every way, like no other in Haarlem or indeed in Holland. Everything he owned was from overseas, assembled with care and creativity. The interior was subject to continuous improvement, less valuable objects making regular way for more worthy replacements. Johan thought: 'René is so proud of that house, and he also knows how much I appreciate beautiful things. Why has he never invited me to visit?'

He threw caution to the wind and asked:

'I would genuinely love to see that house of yours . . . if you don't mind.'

René's response was gracious, thoughtful, kind: 'I was just about to ask you for a visit, and it would have been such a pleasure . . . but now you've asked I have to say no. I always refuse when I'm asked. It's one of my principles.'

Johan was deeply offended by René's words and actions and thus refused his later requests to visit his unique house.

4

It was a Sunday. A lofty, white day of fragile-frozen, brittle silence. Johan had spent the morning deep in the grey, frost-covered countryside. He then spent some time with the blind doctor, reading him verses of poetry in a steady yet gentle voice. And in complete tranquillity, he had written a long and amiable letter to his father.

He was also planning to pay a visit to René's exceptional house, having accepted the artist's apology for offending him.

Johan was dressed for the occasion, but he took care not to use any floral perfumes in his blond hair and on his hands. His spirits were high, elevated all the more by the thought of seeing so many beautiful things at René's house. He crossed the modest Dirk van Bakenes canal with a skip in his step, tempted to whistle to give voice to his contentment. But he did not whistle. Via a bright cavernous lane, his footsteps echoing against its walls, Johan finally arrived at the house of the renowned artist René Richell.

5

It was clear that René had not been exaggerating. Every room in his house was furnished with perfect taste, in an artistic mixture of museum and comfortable home. Johan's restored respect for René set his heart pounding. He revered him as a great artist in those days. René had also changed. Conversations with him were much easier and his responses no longer the opposite of what Johan expected.

6

The sight of so much beauty left Johan breathless, but when his calm returned he selected five objects in René's house that stood out from the surrounding sophistication.

The first, second and third were batik paintings from the Indies. The first was a blend of deep blue, light blue, creamy yellow, white and bright red, a marvel of colours, all in perfect balance. Johan's hands trembled as he held it, and he gave it the name 'vibrant batik'.

The second was greyish-white and the deepest blue, making the white, grey cotton seem heavy as velvet.

The third was black and grey with a pattern reminiscent of butterfly wings, both colours dusted in delicate layers over the priceless cloth. René told him that the canvases were painted in a mental institution outside Batavia and that its residents were the happiest of artists.

7

The fourth object was tiny, but it drew Johan's attention like a spark from a fire.

It was a face in half-relief, vividly carved in ivory. Its stare was stern, alive, forbidding. The eyes were thin open slits, the corners of the mouth slanted downwards in perfect diagonal alignment with the narrow ruthless eyes. The sight of the ivory face with its sharply carved corners and lines genuinely pained him. René told him in the nicest terms that he was truly sorry Johan found the carving so beautiful. He always felt sorry when someone appeared to have a pure and broad appreciation of the beauty in art. He also said that the same regret was the reason he refused to spend time with other artists, in spite of his frequent desire to do so.

8

Johan asked after the artist who had created the unique object, and René replied: 'A Chinese coolie made it for me, in Deli . . . such fun to have a coolie make it . . . I could have redeemed him and offered him his freedom, but I didn't . . . If I had, he would have made more and more objects just like it, the one more beautiful than the other, and that would be intolerable . . . the very thought of someone making beautiful things . . . everyone is entitled to a good life in my view . . . all except artists . . . otherwise they would create beautiful things, more beautiful than my own creations.'

'Where is he now?'

'Hop-Ki? Dead . . . executed for a string of murders . . . I was very fond of him, you know, because of his wonderful creations, but for the same reason I was also happy to hear he was well and truly dead. Such a likeable killer, don't you think? If you ask me, murderers are all likeable people.'

René continued, his voice soft and calm. Johan was completely taken by his words:

'I quite like the idea of killing someone . . . it would be something different, a completely new experience . . . and new experiences are hard to come by . . . but I don't dare . . . I'm afraid of the punishment. Of course, I'm pretty sure I would be declared insane and unaccountable . . . I've been guilty of countless follies in my life . . . so I'd be safe enough . . . if you ask me . . . I'll consult a legal and medical expert when the opportunity arises . . . if they think I'm safe to do it then I'll do it.'

For Johan, René was in part a unique artist and in larger part a refined and dangerous lunatic. He said:

'But René, you shouldn't talk about all those criminal things . . . you don't mean any of it . . . you're your own worst enemy . . . people just think you're crazy, that's all.'

'No, no,' René laughed, 'they don't think that at all . . . they're not smart enough . . . they think I'm handsome and intelligent because I paint unusual paintings now and then, paintings that raise good money in Paris . . . and those criminal things, as you describe them, of course I don't mean any of it . . . I never say what I mean as a matter of principle. It's impolite to force your own opinion on others all the time. Much better to say things other people mean, and best of all to say things no one means . . . that's the only way to be sure you say something intelligent from time to time.'

<h1 style="text-align:center">9</h1>

The fifth exceptional object Johan selected was a painting of a river in two colours, cobalt purple and gold. There were four objects on the canvas: a tranquil river, a bridge arched over the tranquil river, a tense sky stretched above the bridge and the river, and a star the size of the sun in the tense sky. The river and the sky were cobalt purple, the bridge and the star gold.

Johan told René how much he admired the painting.

René answered: 'How wonderful that you find it so beautiful. I always think it's wonderful when someone has a pure and broad appreciation of the beauty in art.'

'But René, now you're contradicting yourself! Such a terrible habit!'

'I can change my mind, can't I? I always say exactly what I mean . . . lying is bad, unless it's necessary.'

<h1 style="text-align:center">10</h1>

'You're probably wondering who painted that magnificent work? Well . . . he was a good friend . . . a Rumanian boy I met in Paris . . . down on his luck . . . the Rumanian aristocracy have an extraordinary pedigree . . . they exploit their farmers and send their children to Paris. My friend's name was Hélénus Marie Golesco, and I loved him deeply . . . so much that I put up with almost everything, even his excellent paintings.'

'Is he also dead?'

'Yes, . . . and I was so pleased to hear it. I'm always delighted to hear about the death of people I love . . . it relieves me briefly of my perpetual fear that someone such as him will ultimately die. Heleen drowned himself in the Seine in Paris . . . dirty, don't you think? If he had asked me I would have advised him not to drown himself in the dirty city, but north of the city, or by cyanide . . . much more efficient . . . or not to do it at all. But he was determined. He was always talking about the magnificent things he had seen that were beyond his ability to paint.'

11

René was left speechless with emotion after talking about Golesco. Shivers ran down his slender spine and his brown eyes filled with tears. Johan was moved by René's public display of emotion and didn't know what to say. But René quickly pulled himself out of his morose disposition.

'Nonsense . . . as long as things can still get worse there's no reason to be sad . . . let me show you the portrait I painted of Golesco.'

Johan was excited at the prospect. The portrait was René's usual style, lacking definition in colour and line yet highly detailed.

The face of the young Rumanian nobleman was modest and unassuming, his eyes dark and anxious, the eyes of a man who would later drown himself in the river in Paris because life had become unbearable.

'You must have loved him very much . . . I can see it . . . am I right?'

René's voice was vague . . . hesitant:

'I honestly don't remember, Hans . . . it was all so long ago . . . but I can always ask people who knew us if I truly loved him . . . when I'm in London . . . they'll know for sure . . . it was more important for them than me . . . once I know I'll write to you . . . did I tell you already I'm leaving for London this evening?'

'No . . . you didn't.'

12

René's voice was grave, threatening:

'Well now you know, and I'm sure you'll want to tell our landlady that I'm off to London . . . at least that's my plan for now . . . I can always change my mind and go somewhere else . . . I might reconsider . . . no, tell them at home that I'm off to Rome . . . I'm sure of it . . . I'm going to Rome, if I don't change my mind.'

Johan was sure René had completely lost his mind and it worried him. Where would it all lead, for René himself and for others around him?

'René,' he said in a friendly tone, 'of course I don't mind telling the Riemersmas that you're going to Rome, or to London . . . but why not just stay here in Haarlem? It's peaceful here and quiet.'

René's response was curt and below the belt:

'No, I refuse to stay in Haarlem . . . and I'm leaving because of you.'

'Because of me?'

'Yes, you! Are you deaf? Are you deaf, Johan van Vere? There's nothing I'd prefer more than to stay in Haarlem . . . but I've made up my mind . . . I'm going to London and London makes me unhappy . . . and if I perish in London then it's not my fault . . . it's your fault!'

Johan was completely confused both mentally and emotionally. He couldn't tell if René meant what he was saying, and he was certain he wasn't guilty of some careless offence in the way he had treated him.

'You always say so many things you don't mean, so I'm sure this is just another example. If you want to go to London or somewhere else that's entirely up to you . . . but you have no right to say you're leaving because of me . . . I've done you no harm.'

René responded with genuine tenderness, confusing Johan even more.

'Forgive me,' he begged, 'I had no right to snap at you . . . but my sorrow is a great burden . . . try not to be insensitive to it . . . there are many profound secrets I want to share with you, but I simply can't right now . . . you're so haughty . . . can I write to you from London . . . I'm going to London.'

'If I'm honest I prefer you didn't write to me from London, certainly not the way you did to Mrs Riemersma from Paris,' said Johan arrogantly.

'No,' was René's humble reply. 'I promise not to write such letters to you . . . or to anyone else . . . go home now if you prefer . . . I need some time to think about the two of us . . . I'll write to you later.'

13

When Johan left the overexcitement of René's house, he felt that his life had changed. It was as if he had awoken from a complicated dream about perilous sophistication that had the power to drive him mad.

He was standing by the frozen-white river Spaarne at the beginning of a crystal-clear winter night. He wanted to calm down, so instead of going home he decided to take a long leisurely walk through the silent streets of the city and past its silent waters.

He had seen things of great prominence and magnificence that afternoon, beyond his imagination. And René was wealthier than Johan had thought. But that same afternoon he had said some very strange things. Johan thought: 'Crazy people don't make sense when they speak, but René does. His words make complete sense, they're just the opposite of what I would normally say.'

Now calm, Johan figured that René had given no indication whatsoever that he was planning to stay in Holland and Haarlem. On the contrary, he felt driven to go to England and London, and feared by his own admission that he would perish there.

14

Johan told his elderly landlord and landlady that René had gone to London. Mrs Riemersma was alarmed by the news and lamented that Richell was beyond redemption. If she hadn't been convinced that it was her life's calling to do her utmost to keep René on the straight and narrow, she would never have tolerated so much of his idle chatter. She asked Johan a question that took him aback: 'Did something happen between you? You were with him the entire afternoon and now he's scuttled off to London . . . if it's true, of course . . . I had no idea he had plans to go anywhere.'

'You're right,' said Johan, now back on solid ground, 'I was indeed with him the entire afternoon, and appreciate only now how great an artist he is . . . so many magnificent objects. And René was quite calm. Of course, he said some incredible and irritating things with the same composed politeness as he did reasonable things . . . but he does that all the time . . . it's nothing unusual.'

15

At table that evening, the Riemersmas were gloomy and quiet. Johan profited from their silence to muse on the five or six matchless objects he had seen at René's exceptional house. He then went to his room. In spite of the warmth Johan shivered to his core, but it wasn't the kind of shiver his room usually triggered when it was ice cold.

He wrote page after page of passionate prose about the objects: 'vibrant batik', 'ivory carving', 'painting in cobalt purple and gold', 'portrait of a young Rumanian nobleman'.

Writing about these fine objects lifted his spirits enormously. He was grateful to René and inspired to be the best literary artist possible in his life, as fully developed in his own art as Richell was in his.

René's tormenting words and deeds were far from his thoughts.

16

Johan treated himself to a splash of his melancholy cologne, which smelled of violets, frail as purple velvet. He then went downstairs to sit with the blind doctor and read for him. As he read, he reflected on the afternoon's peculiar course of events. René's foolishness was at the front of his mind, especially the accusation that Johan was the reason for his forced departure from Haarlem and Holland. But reading for his blind landlord distracted him and he was afraid the man would notice something in his voice. He also struggled to look at him for any length of time although he wanted to. In the past, when reading brought him rest, Johan would gaze at his blind land-lord at length and felt very attached to him. He considered telling him what René had said about moving to England and London on his account. But Johan remembered that life with his father had become impossible because he had shared an important and serious matter with him out of a sense of trust and affection, a matter that was to spell unconditional disaster for their relationship. Johan thus felt insecure, and he continued reading without discussion.

The blind yet highly sensitive doctor later remarked:

'Your reading seems a little confused, Hans. Is your mind on René . . . is something wrong?'

'No,' said Johan, still insecure and thus polite: 'René isn't so important to me.'

He stopped reading at that point, but continued to listen to the silver tones of Saint Bavo's Bells of Damietta ringing out with great clarity through the brittle winter air. He shivered. He sensed that his life was unstable and precarious but had no idea why.

Chapter Four

The winter days drew in, low and silent, and the darkness deepened. Winter was yet to reach its deepest point.

Johan did what he had to do for school with regularity and uniformity. And he continued to live with the blind doctor and his wife. With the greatest of care, he worked his way through numerous articles exploring the moral and social value of his experience of love, which differed from that of the majority of people. He was more and more convinced that his feelings had their own legitimacy and he decided it was time to tell his father.

Dear Father, more than once you were inclined to reject my special feelings, describing them as 'unconditionally immoral' and 'socially intolerable'. I have never tried to contradict you in my letters, firstly because I find it unpleasant, and secondly because my opinion was as yet uninformed and incomplete. I have struggled hard to arrive at this juncture.

I fully understand what socially intolerable means, but not unconditionally immoral. I am of the opinion that my particular feelings have a legitimacy of their own, for the simple reason that they exist. I have a right to this opinion as you have a right to the opposite. You agree with the majority of people and thus your opinion is socially tolerated and mine is not.

It goes without saying that people should be careful with their feelings and not indulge them at every turn. It seems likely that I too will have to be careful with my feelings for as long as I live. But I have to say that caution is not the most important social value.

I'm also convinced that there is no such thing as unconditional immorality, but rather a very conditional morality that does not differ from social intolerability in any appreciable way.

Perhaps my opinions have no scholarly or ethical value for you, but for me they do.

I shared the secret of my emotional life with you out of deep affection, and the result, I need not remind you, was bitter ruin. I have no idea if this present letter will facilitate a reunion and restore my happiness. But I prefer you know where I stand in this important matter. If you refuse to see me again as a result, I will learn to live with it. But it would be wrong to reunite under the guise of a fundamental lie.

I have avoided writing about other matters in this letter because I consider this to be the most important by far.

Your son, Hans.

2

When Johan mailed his letter, his father was in North America, in the state of New York, studying the peculiarities of prison life there. His father evidently responded as quickly as his circumstances would allow:

My dear son Hans, I'm replying to your letter as promptly as I am able.

Broadly speaking, I don't think your opinions concerning your emotional life are especially important. But when they relate to you

in particular, I think they are extremely dangerous. I remain con-
vinced that immoral is not the same as unsocial, but I don't have the
time to argue about it. Ruskin says that most immoral people generally
consider themselves vindicated in such semantic disputes, and he is
probably correct.

Your desire to be socially cautious is positive.

I appreciate your honesty and openness towards me.

On the question of us living together in Cuilemburg? Certainly
not before you are a student.

Your letter has opened the door to a potential reunion, but the
extent of its influence remains to be seen. It would be reckless of me to
offer an opinion at this juncture.

Keep me sufficiently informed about your life.

I read your prose regularly, but I can't say it's always a pleasure.
Orchids are not my favourite flower, however uncommon they may
be. I feel the same about your prose. I stay in touch with developments
in Dutch literature, without having a particular opinion about it.

Kind regards, Hans,
Father.

3

Johan now maintained his own opinions in contrast to those of his
father, and he realized how much this independence pleased him.

4

René Richell started to irritate Johan and weary him. Very few
letters arrived from London, and none of them were addressed to
him. Mrs Riemersma wrote René constantly about his return but

he didn't answer, or rather he did but only to tell her that a return to Holland and Haarlem was impossible. He also wrote that the situation in which he now found himself was very troubling.

Such statements generated great anxiety among the inhabitants of the house in Haarlem. Johan fretted over René's accusation that he was the reason he couldn't stay in Haarlem. He couldn't imagine what he had done to pain René, and he regretted not asking for a precise explanation of his accusatory words that Sunday afternoon in his sophisticated house. By blaming himself in this way, Johan felt trivial and worthless, while René seemed to him entirely selfless and unblemished. Anxiety and self-blame affected his health. He first noticed this disturbance in his dreams, and shortly thereafter in his usually more balanced waking thoughts.

As time went on, René's words became increasingly disturbing: 'If something bad happens to me in London it won't me my fault . . . it will be your fault, pure and simple.' These words pursued him day and night and confused him terribly.

5

Johan was also conscious of another of René's statements: 'There are many profound secrets I want to share with you, but I simply can't right now.'

He now blamed his own misplaced arrogance for preventing René from saying what he wanted to say. He dreamt more than once to his horror that he found René dead, floating in London's dark river. His face was white, the river cobalt blue, and tall houses were stacked to infinity on either side of the river in London's urban dullness and yellow city lights. René did not write, yet the letters Johan wrote to him were at first not returned. But later they did return, marked 'undeliverable', and that left Johan distraught, even out of his mind. He wanted to travel to London and bring René back home.

The confusion in Johan's head made it impossible to go to school. He couldn't bear the thought of lessons. But the anxious atmosphere made staying home just as bad as going to school. He told his teachers he was sick and needed to stay home, but he then pretended to the Riemersmas that he was going to school. He spent the time wandering the streets outside the city and his disquiet was unrelenting.

He later forced himself to go back to school, afraid his life would become as much a lie in Haarlem as it had become in Cuilemburg, where his final days had been utter misery.

6

Johan remembered that on that Sunday afternoon, René had spoken about 'profound secrets' he had wanted to share with him if the opportunity arose.

The only profound secrets Johan could think of had to do with his personal affections and their development. He then thought: 'Is that what René meant? Perhaps his attractions are the same as mine? Perhaps he's attracted to me? René doesn't know I'm familiar with such attractions, from experience and from reading. He was probably afraid he would go too far. So, he left for London because he feared he would say something inappropriate or act towards me in a manner he might later regret both in private and in public.'

While Johan's daytime thoughts were thus preoccupied, René was also prominent in his nocturnal dreams and his presence stirred his physical passions. He knew that changes in mind and body often manifested themselves first in the less restricted world of dreams before making their way into the more measured assembly of day-time thoughts. He thus assumed that he had developed strong feelings for René and that René felt the same. This inspired him to reflect on everything he knew about René's life and work. And his new perspective did indeed shed considerable light on some of René's peculiarities.

Johan feared that René might be miserable in London, in part because of his general emotional state and in part because of his feelings for Johan. He wanted to write to him, to ask if he was correct about the 'profound secrets', but he resisted the urge. What if he were wrong? Then any such exchange with René would be a step too far.

7

One fine morning in spring, when the flowers were abundant and the sky was clear, Johan received a letter from René in London delivered to his school. He jumped with joy and thought: 'Nothing's wrong after all . . . we've been such idiots, the three of us, getting ourselves so worked up . . . absurd.'

Johan stood in the shadow in a remote corner of the school grounds. The letter from René made all his anxiety seem ridiculous. René had written:

Hans, I have postponed writing this letter time after time because I want to tell you what I feel for you and I have struggled to find the words. Our relationship has become profoundly important and deeply serious. But my life here in London, which is darker and more miserable than Paris, is so wretched that I must decide. I am now certain that I left Holland and Haarlem because of you alone, and the possibility of my return depends on you alone.

I wanted to say these words that Sunday when you visited my atelier. And had I succeeded, there would probably have been no need for me to leave Holland for the misery in which I now find myself these last months. But I didn't have the courage.

Hans, it's important that you remain calm when you read this letter and only reply when you are ready. Do not concede to my desires because I ask it, out of compassion, but only because you share them. If you cannot reciprocate my feelings, then any return to Holland will be impossible. Then I must stay here in London or move further afield.

I love you, Hans, I love you so much. I knew it the first time I set eyes on you at the Riemersmas. You probably didn't notice, of course, but I remember your arrival to the last detail, and every other detail since. Great affection is always a great burden, and my affection for you has been a source of terrible suffering, although I have done my best not to let it show. I left for Paris that first evening, and the sole reason was you.

Hans, will you be my friend?

When I say friend, I don't mean just ordinary friendship, I mean love. A very special kind of love, unfamiliar to most, a kind of love they deeply despise.

Speak with no one about this, I beg you. Do not speak about this letter, even with Dr Riemersma who trusts you completely. You would otherwise do me a great and potentially dangerous disservice, and I'm sure that's not what you want.

Hans, I beg you, be my best friend. Then you'll see how wonderful my work will become under your good influence. With the exception of Heleen Golesco, I have never loved someone as much as I love you.

Again Hans, keep this letter to yourself, and if you don't understand it, pretend it was never written, or ask me to explain.

Farewell, dear Hans. I bought some handsome earthenware for
Mrs Riemersma. I will write to them.
  R.R.

<h1 style="text-align:center">8</h1>

After reading René's letter, Johan knew that the profound secrets
he had longed to know about had been revealed.

He sat down in an empty room, weary from all the emotion.
His irrational fear that René would die had left him, but in its place,
he felt anger and spite towards René for distressing the three of them
without necessity. Johan also sensed a trace of perversion in René's
character, and he feared for emotional confrontations and conflict
should he return to Holland. But he also thought: 'He is a great
artist and I love him dearly. I'm sure I can do something about those
wilfully wicked statements of his. And if I refuse to be his friend,
he will not return to Holland and Haarlem. Then Mrs Riemersma's
anxieties would never end, and her blind husband, whose life is as
dull and dark as death itself, would lose one of his few companions.
And If I reject him and leave him wretched and miserable, then it
would surely be my fault. And when all is said and done, I love
him dearly.'

Johan read René's letter once again and it cheered him greatly
that it was free of foolish and cutting rhetoric. He started his reply,
taking his time and weighing his words:

René, I just received your letter and I am answering by return.

I deeply resent the fact that you gave the impression you were plan-
ning to kill yourself, and even after you changed your mind we heard
nothing from you. Your silence caused much unnecessary sadness to
two elderly and well-intentioned people.

I am delighted nonetheless that your letter was free of wilful statements.

When you speak of friendship as love I understand you more or less. But for that reason, I cannot make a decision without taking time to think about it. Am I able to give you such friendship and can I expect it in return from you? Great friendships generally lead to great happiness.

Let me conclude by saying how pleased I am that you plan to write to Mrs Riemersma. It is important and you should have done it already.

Kind regards, Hans.

Johan wasn't sure if his letter said what he wanted to say, so he added:

I'm willing to write to you this coming Sunday about what I consider best for our relationship.

Hans.

9

No one asked Johan why he was late getting home. Mrs Riemersma was busy and clearly happy with the letter she had received from René. He had also sent the English earthenware, a slender, brightly coloured, pottery milk jug, with a pair of matching beakers, all artistically decorated with strutting chickens in a grassy meadow. Three vivid colours had been included in the decoration: black, red and green. Johan usually disliked such combinations, but here they went exceptionally well together. He admired René's choice of objects and his affections towards him thus became more accommodating and gentler. The lady of the house was delighted with her elegant gifts and named the 'chicken jug' and 'chicken beakers' her 'chicken set'. She also said that it would probably be better not to use them too much to avoid erasing the finely formed colours. She knew that the colouring was sturdy enough beneath its glaze and thus protected from water, but she still thought it best that such difficult-to-replace objects be spared.

Johan described the intensity and form of the colours to the blind doctor. The elderly man carefully caressed them and sensed their simplicity, running his delicate fingers over the glazed upper lip of the slender earthenware jug.

This was what he always did with newly acquired objects: ask about the colours then explore the shapes with his fingers. He didn't want to be a stranger among his family's objects.

René filled Johan's thoughts that day and increasingly so in the days that followed. He was no longer worried that René would take his own life and this lifted his spirits. His eyes seemed to radiate light, a golden glow, like the light of a blissful dream. And when he read for the blind doctor he noticed that his voice was lighter, more cheerful.

The home he shared shook off its deep anxiety and happiness took its place. Johan saw that René's impact on his home was profound. He wanted to spend the days until Sunday reflecting on his relationship with him and defining it precisely. He thought: 'If I do what René asks, then I'll be in trouble with the blind doctor. I'll have to pretend that I trust him completely while keeping an enormous secret from him. But if I don't do what René asks, then he'll never come back, and that would be a great shame for the Riemersmas. And who knows what dangerous things René might do, for which I would then share the blame.'

'And if I welcome him after all?'

The thought both pleased him and scared him. He loved René for his qualities as an artist. But he hesitated at the thought of living in a relationship, which he had only read about in biographies. He also thought of his father, who utterly condemned such friendships, such relationships of love. If he were to move in with René he would want to tell his father about it, but he knew that this would put an end to any possibility of a reunion.

Johan's father no longer featured in his longings by day or his dreams by night. He had deep feelings for his father, which still made his heart flutter, but he was able to distinguish them from erotic desires. He thought back to his earlier feelings with bitter aversion. They were a scourge from his youth that now weakened his self-esteem.

10

That Sunday, the weather outside unsettled and blustery, Johan wrote to René in London:

René, I've thought long and hard about your proposal of friendship. It would make me very happy if you returned to Haarlem. My answer is Yes.

Hans.

11

Johan had planned to write to his father and tell him he was moving in with René, but after writing his letter to London he realized that he simply could not tell his father about it. He thought: 'I have followed my insights as best I can . . . I can't write to my father, I simply can't . . . my life would be so much easier if my attractions didn't deviate from the norm.'

The remains of that Sunday were particularly burdensome. Johan spent much of the day with the blind doctor and was constantly aware that he was engaging in secretive things he could not share. His elderly landlord and landlady did nothing but talk about René all day long.

12

A couple of days later, Johan received a letter from Richell addressed to his school:

Hans, now we are companions and you have my gratitude. I am looking forward to a wonderful, creative life together. Have I asked too much of you? I plan to return to Holland and Haarlem as soon as possible.

Farewell, dear boy,

R.R.

13

The following afternoon, Johan found René in the living room in a serious yet friendly conversation with the blind doctor. He trembled when their eyes met and had trouble speaking:

'Greetings René . . . welcome home . . . how are you?'

'I'm fine, thank you, exceptionally fine.'

His voice was deep and sonorous, but Johan was startled by it and thought about the blind doctor. He struggled to find the right words:

'Your English earthenware was beautiful, indeed it was . . . I'm going up to my room.'

Once in his sun-filled room, Johan thought: 'René is back and I'm afraid . . . I feel humiliated, as if I'm totally dependent on him and no longer free.'

Later he heard René's footsteps on the corridor. The sinister man's every step seemed to press on his heart making it pound in his throat. 'He's coming to humiliate me for my arrogance,' he thought as he positioned himself for defence.

René entered the room, wrapped both hands around Johan's head, tilted back his neck, and kissed him twice on the mouth and then twice more. Johan's body was limp, as were his arms and lips. All he felt was humiliation. When René sensed there was no passion and said dejectedly:

'Is something wrong?'

'No,' said Johan, flat and insecure, 'it's just this sense of humiliation . . . I'm sure it will pass . . . '

They stood at a distance from one another. Johan's heart was still pounding in his throat, but now it was irregular, with anxious moments of stasis. He thought of his father and the blind doctor as his head started to spin.

'René,' said Johan, 'I know you expected a different reaction . . . don't be angry or disappointed . . . I've always been used to people treating me politely . . . but you just marched in and kissed me on the lips and it feels like an insult.'

'From me?'

'Yes, from you.' Johan's words were now stable and clear: 'In the past I only ever treated my father as my equal . . . and at this moment I have the feeling you think you are my superior.'

'So, you never longed for me as I longed for you?'

'I don't know . . . I'm just being honest . . . this is exactly what I feel . . . but I also hope things will go well between us.'

'So, if I understand you correctly, I might as well have stayed in London and my misery?'

'No . . . In due course I'll be happy that you're here . . . '

'Good . . . good . . . in due course . . . in due course . . . I'll have to be patient. But it's already clear that I can't be close to you now . . . here in the house . . . I feel it . . . I'll go to Amsterdam, then, or further afield . . . is that what you want?'

'No,' said Johan, his voice calm and high-pitched, the sense of humiliation gone, 'I want you to stay more than anything . . . it would be the best for all of us . . . but if you can't stay then there's no point in further discussion.'

'Fine . . . I'll go to Amsterdam and come back this evening . . . or perhaps not.'

14

Mrs Riemersma stated calmly and without complaint that René had gone to Amsterdam because Amsterdam was now more depraved than Paris and he knew it. She was no longer concerned, she said, and he was now responsible for his own safety. Dinner that day was dull.

Johan read for the blind doctor as usual, but his mind was elsewhere and he struggled to pay attention. His thoughts and desires were with the dark, artistic René.

15

Alone in his room, his lamp's gilded flame hissed thinly and cast its light like a shadow of gold. It's hissing wearied his ears, its shadowy gold light wearied his eyes. His body grew warm from the light, quivering like a delicate flame. His dark blue eyes tensed. The evening hours passed in a chain of golden light, golden pages in the book of Johan's life. Surges of bliss made his pale fingers tingle. He felt slightly tipsy, as if he had drunk some pale-yellow wine.

16

René and Johan were together. Johan's room was filled with light. They approached one another. Johan moved first, embracing René with passion, unrestrained . . . he was conscious for a moment but then his mind emptied. He kissed René's panting lips.

René's body was of golden light. Johan felt his own body was also of golden light. The room had grown dark.

17

They stayed together until morning. It was spring.

Chapter Five

1

It was spring on earth and in the heavens. The earth was awash with beautiful flowers, everywhere, in the meadows as much as the warm sunny dunes. The heavens were aglow with sunlight by day and filled by night with golden starlight, twinkling in the firmament.

Johan felt strong, and awake to the passions of spring smouldering within. He took long walks as often as he could, enjoying the golden sunlight, all around and day after day, like the golden lamplight in his room that evening when he and René were first united.

Johan now preferred to be alone than with the blind doctor. He sensed that the man was aware of it and that it saddened him. But his days were full of cheer and light and the sadness of his sensitive landlord was not his priority.

He often thought about his father, but he didn't write to him about his relationship with René. He preferred to spare him needless consternation. With spring's warm light and gladness, he accepted everything that came his way with ease. He thought back to the time when a restoration of his relationship with his father would have been his greatest joy. But now he thought: 'I still want to return to our house in Cuilemburg and live with my father, but only if my father agrees to accept my principles and not insist on his own.' Johan sensed he had changed profoundly, and for the first time in his life it pleased him.

His blissful existence lasted two months.

2

It was still summer in the heavens and on earth when Johan noticed that the golden bliss of spring was dwindling. René, unsurprisingly, was being difficult.

Johan only wanted intimate relations when they both desired them, while René insisted on relations even when he alone desired them. Johan told René that his demands were hurtful and humiliating. He wasn't his slave and he refused to concede. René first begged him, then showered him with vile and inappropriate curses.

Johan said: 'I refuse to give in . . . if I did, I'd be no better than some whore you picked up on the street. What others think of me is unimportant, but what I think of myself is . . . and I'm not doing it.'

Johan used his personal pride to restrain René: 'The more you oppose me, the more you force me to retreat from you . . . that's all you stand to gain from your unreasonable demands.'

3

What Johan liked, René hated. He lived an idle existence between his lodgings and his atelier. He had an appetite for absinth and opium, and wanted Johan to share the experience. He always refused to leave the house and the city with Johan, and he stated more than once that Johan should save his love for *him* alone and not share it with a church, two branches of a canal, yet another canal, and a string of gardens.

Johan decided to write to René. His letter was a restrained yet detailed presentation of his grievances:

My dear friend René, when I try to explain some of my grievances with you, you either listen with obvious reluctance or you don't listen at all. That is why I'm writing to you with a serious request that you read what I have taken the trouble to write, carefully and to the last detail. After spending close to two happy months with you in the spring, my more recent experience has been very saddening.

You're now saying that my soul lacks passion and depth and that everything I do remains shallow and flat, but such words have no real meaning. I admit that I tend to be cautious around you, to be sure I do not become a slave to your bodily desires. That is not going to happen, so do not count on it.

René, you are making my life so difficult. I have struggled long and hard, and against my father's best judgement, to acquire my own opinions and to see our love as entirely equal to the love my parents had for one another. But I consider the way you live your life to be inferior and you will not succeed in forcing it upon me.

The only reason we are now living together is because I happen to be the most handsome boy in your social circle. If a prettier boy were to enter that circle tomorrow and make himself available to you, then you would drop me, in spite of the suffering you know it would cause. Your love for me is completely lacking in emotional depth, and the most unfortunate thing is that you prefer it that way.

I have had to endure a dressing-down from you on two occasions, as if it was your sacred right. And the only reason you haven't repeated your outbursts is because, for the moment, you are still afraid of me. But the time will come when you no longer fear me, and then I can expect an even choicer tirade.

I am writing this because I love you. I love you deeply, René, and I still hope I can change your ways for the better.

When you wrote to me from London at the end of the winter ask-ing me to be your friend, I had several reasons to say yes, but affection for you was not at the top of my list. It's only fair that you should know this, and I am sure it was evident to you the afternoon of your return. I believe my fondness for you at the time was less than your fondness for me. But your fondness has waned, or better said has become inferior, while mine continues to grow stronger. And it is here that I sense danger. I wrote to you before that great friendships can bring great happiness, but now I want to add that great friendships can bring great danger.

You also ask so much of me, but you do nothing in return. Yet one-sided love and friendship can often be of the highest calibre, so my grievance here is less important.

I have asked you to stop drinking absinth and opium, yet you con-tinue to do so unabated. You want to have rights over me, but you refuse to accept the responsibilities they bring.

There can be no doubt whatsoever that your artistic qualities are better than my literary skills, but why do you refuse to cultivate your gifts? I believe my prose writing has improved greatly since we met and other trusted writers share this conviction. Since we became friends you have hardly worked at all, and the little you have has been under par.

I had hoped you would be more like our blind landlord in your thoughts and feelings. When I leave the house and go to the sea and the dunes, you never come with me. The dunes are too far from the Quartier and the sea is less important than your Parisian piss-pot. That is the extent of your interest in nature.

I sometimes think that your ways are superior to mine and that you do and think more than I am allowed to know.

I have written this long letter at my leisure, yet another sign in your eyes of my tepidity.

If only you knew how much I love you, René, and how much I feel that my life is under threat. Do not make us unhappy,

Hans.

4

René didn't respond to the letter or speak about it, so Johan asked him if he had received it and considered its content. René's reaction was vague:

'I get so many letters . . . I don't read them all . . . certainly not if I recognized the handwriting . . . and I never reflect on their content.'

Johan felt deeply humiliated but did his best to maintain his composure:

'Did you read my letter . . . yes or no?'

'I'm not sure . . . was it a long letter? . . . Well mannered? . . . yes, now I remember . . . but it was a few days ago and who knows what I've been up to since then . . . Do you know what your problem is? You're far too cautious. Take it from me, cautious men and incautious women never succeed in this life.'

5

Johan decided it was time to leave René. If there was no other option, he was prepared to leave his home and Haarlem and find alternative accommodation in a different city in spite of the pain he knew he would suffer.

But at that point René changed for the better, most clearly reflected in the lines and colours of his paintings. Johan spent a great deal of time in his company in those days. René abstained from absinth and opium and he assured Johan that he also abstained when they were not together. It dawned on Johan that he no longer believed René. But he was happy nonetheless that he didn't have to leave his home and Haarlem.

6

It didn't take long for René to relapse. Brasher, more aggressive, and all too often drunk and debauched, Johan was sickened by the smell of his drunken breath. And the belittling resumed in both word and deed.

Johan confronted him:

'I'd rather be without you, René, if you can't change your ways . . . you make me sick.'

'That's possible,' said René, 'but it isn't important. I need you to be sick so that I can be healthy . . . healthy in my own way . . . isn't the Devil as healthy in Hell as God is in Heaven?'

'If you continue to treat me badly, I'll leave you.'

'Even you don't believe that . . . you can't leave me any more . . . imagine what it would do to you. Do you know what your problem is? You're too attached to some people, and you trust yourself too much . . . obsessive affection is a mortal wound . . . it's time you realized that.'

7

Johan drew some conclusions on reflection:

'Whenever I do something with prudence and caution to better my life, the same prudent and cautious deeds seem only to make things worse. That's what happened with my father, and that's what's happening now with René.

'There are so many reasons why I can't leave René. First, because I love him too much. Second, because I'm terrified he'll put himself in some grave danger without me. Third, because I would probably have to leave this house and Haarlem. Fourth, because the Riemersmas would suffer greatly if I did.

'While René believed I was capable of leaving him he was manageable and moderate, but now that he's convinced I can't he's become a danger.'

It was autumn when Johan came to these conclusions and melancholy engulfed him.

8

In the summer preceding this eventful autumn, Johan's simple shared existence with his blind landlord got mired in complications and obstructions. Whenever they were together, Johan could sense the man's genuine goodness. 'Why is this man so caring and good,' he thought, 'while my René is so bad?' He was also disturbed by his deception, living with the man as if he was the first in his affections while he was secretly in love with René. He wondered if the time had come to make changes in their shared routine. He withdrew from the blind doctor and at times was markedly unpleasant to both him and his wife. The Riemersmas remained kind and obliging, and didn't understand the significance of Johan's change of attitude. But Johan interpreted their obliging behaviour as grovelling humility and questioned their good intentions. He belittled them because they belittled themselves and felt justified in doing so.

When autumn arrived and Johan's troubled relationship with René made him unhappy and melancholic, he realized how badly he had treated his elderly landlord and landlady. He was quick to better his attitude towards them, but the turbulence now confronting him was hard to bear.

<h1 style="text-align:center">9</h1>

As autumn progressed, he allowed René to keep him away from school and even let him violate him in his house in Koudenhorn.

He knew that René would not have dared to do such things when they were first together.

Johan now understood that he was no longer able to control René, nor could he walk away. René was making all the decisions and Johan simply complied. Their life together was as René wanted it and he no longer had a say. René was in charge. He had lost himself.

<h1 style="text-align:center">10</h1>

Johan knew that René would follow him wherever he went. He considered writing to his father, telling him his life was in danger and asking if they could resume their life together in the familiarity of their home in Cuilemburg. He was sure that René would not dare to follow him to his father's house.

This was the only way out, he thought. He would miss Haarlem, of course, but he would win back Cuilemburg . . . the Riemersmas would understand that he preferred to live with his father and his departure wouldn't sadden them. He then thought: 'Can I live without René . . . what if my anxieties about him return and I leave my father to go back to him?'

11

Johan penned a cautious and provisional letter to his father:

My dear father, there is a possibility that my unhappiness might become a permanent reality if I do not receive your permission to return to Cuilemburg and resume our life together. Should this possibility present itself, may I count on your permission? I shall do my best, of course, not to let it come so far.

Your son Hans.

12

Johan's father replied:

My dear Hans, should the possibility present itself—which you allude to in your letter but do not specify—you can count on my permission as you request.

I hope you don't imagine that it is easy for me to be constantly separated from you. I am confronted day after day with the thought that some great misfortune will overcome you on account of your affections and in spite of your intellectual qualities and many virtuous gifts. I am left to conclude, nonetheless, that you would have been deeply unhappy had we decided to stay together as before.

But I still have hope that we will be reunited. Hans, my boy, heed my warning: be moderate in all you do. If you struggle with my understanding of immorality, at least try to avoid living an unsocial life. If you can't be moral, at least be smart.

I work hard, and I see a lot, but I have not forgotten a single day of the happiness we shared in Cuilemburg.

Father.

13

In the days between the evening Johan wrote to his father and the morning he received his reply, René continued to live in conflict with Johan and his overbearing ways persisted. Johan thought: 'I can return to my father . . . I'm leaving René.'

He still felt that René was his superior and his heart pounded fast then slow as he made his way to René's room to tell him about his decision to leave him.

'René,' he said, 'I just received a letter from my father . . . I can return to Cuilemburg to live with him . . . I'm leaving Haarlem.'

René's response was kind and his words well chosen:

'How nice for you, and how wise of your father . . . you know I never approved of the way he treated you . . . let me have his address . . . then I can write to him. I'm sure he won't mind me moving in with you both . . . there's room enough in that house of yours.'

The shock in Johan's eyes betrayed his immediate reaction. He wasn't yet rid of René. He responded with courage and without emotion:

'You can forget that idea . . . you know exactly what my father thinks about relationships like ours.'

'Fine,' said René, obliging and friendly. 'Then I won't ask . . . so humiliating after all . . . I'll just arrive unannounced . . . much more fun that way.'

'And I don't want you to come either . . . you know that well enough.'

René was in good cheer, but he expressed it with restraint:

'I'll come anyway,' he said. 'I've always been adventurous, and this is such a wonderful opportunity . . . to live in a house where I rule the roost against the will of its owner and where I continue our relationship under your respected father's nose . . . how exciting!'

'So, you're determined to prevent me from returning to my father?'

'Of course not . . . preventing someone from doing what they want is the height of immorality . . . I just don't want to lose you, that's all.'

'Even if I tell you I've decided to leave you, because of the way you humiliate me?'

'Even then,' said René with stubborn determination. 'There's no way out of a relationship like ours . . . you have to keep going . . . to the bitter end. And what that end will look like depends on me, not you.'

Johan felt like a servant being told off and degraded. He also knew that René was right. René continued:

'I'm pleased we've been able to speak our minds so spontaneously . . . I'm in charge, you know that well enough . . . and I've struggled enough and been forced to restrain myself enough to get to where I now am . . . and now you think I should let you go back to your father? You want to be safe from me? Good! The best way to be safe from me is to stay with me and do what you're told.'

Johan was motionless, paralysed. René kissed him.

'Hans,' he said with affection, 'I love you, in spite of your excessive prudence . . . and you know I don't have time for prudent friends . . . and to be brutally honest I wouldn't like to be in your shoes . . . you've had your best days in this relationship, but mine are yet to come.'

14

René unexpectedly changed his ways at this point. He worked with diligence, abstained from absinth and opium, and no longer treated Johan as an inferior deserving of humiliation.

Johan wrote to his father:

My dear father, thank you kindly for your willingness to have me back in Cuilemburg should necessity require it. At this juncture, however, I don't think it will be necessary. It's better for me to learn to live independently and rely on myself. I prefer to stay in Haarlem this year, at least until I go to university. Otherwise I would have to change schools again.

Your son, Hans.

He was calm as he wrote, in spite of his subdued anguish. He no longer had control over his own life. René was in charge.

When he told René he wanted to return to his father, he responded:

'Of course you can, it's up to you . . . but if you leave before I think it's time, I'll tell everyone about our life together and then I'll kill myself . . . and rest assured, Johan, you might as well do the same after that. Society will reject you completely.'

What hurt Johan most was the sense of humiliation, the idea of being subordinate to the power of another.

Johan was happy that René was leading a better life. He thought: 'René would never admit to doing anything at the behest of another or on behalf of another, but I'm convinced he has organized and improved his life because of me.'

For Johan these were the best days of their life together.

15

In those excellent days, René painted a portrait of Johan, more handsome than the portrait he had painted of H. M. Golesco. Had he been able, Johan would have painted a portrait of René, and of equal beauty.

The painting was a work of excellence, its contours and colours finished to perfection, delicately flawless, without exaggerated intensity.

Johan started to think that René must be a deeply sensitive artist after all, and his nature much better than one might suspect from his words and deeds.

Johan wrote a detailed description of the exquisite portrait on the same day René gave it to him. He was emotional as he wrote, and after filling a full page and reading it through he thought: 'It's been a long time since I wrote like this.'

16

After a few days, René announced without agitation that he had decided they would both leave the Riemersmas' home and settle in his acclaimed residence in Koudenhorn. Johan was terrified. Their life together had greatly improved, but he was still afraid of René and his power over him. The thought filled him with shame. He responded, cautiously unassuming:

'Yes, if that's what you want, then I'll go with you . . . but I don't think it is a wise idea . . . certainly not for the Riemersmas . . . it will sadden them enormously.'

'That's precisely why I'm doing it.'

'That's what you say, but you don't mean it.'

'Indeed, I don't mean it . . . but as you know, I never do the things I mean, only the things I say . . . and I say that the Riemersmas mean nothing to me . . . a man without a future and a woman without a past . . . not my cup of tea.'

René continued, unruffled and serene:

'Hans, I probably didn't mean what I just said about moving house . . . but I'm happy you didn't dare to say no . . . if you had, I would likely have insisted on moving . . . but now it's no longer necessary.'

Johan felt humiliated yet again. In his desperation he thought: 'I'll go to my father in the state of New York.' But he knew right away that he wouldn't be going to his father in New York for fear of the consequences.

His only emotions were despair and shame. He neglected his school work and the critique he received as a result only deepened his humiliation.

17

Johan's contentment was restored in the days that followed. René kept himself busy, was kind towards him, and modest in his demands. They did almost nothing together at that juncture beyond sharing at length about their pasts. Johan spoke about his affection for his father, which had remained the same although its nature had changed. René told Johan about his life in the urban abyss. His words were simple and clear, without exaggeration. For Johan these were good times. Much that had once been unbearable was now bearable. He was confident of a solid recovery, and he loved René.

18

In the silence of the evening, in the light of the lamp, René said:

'Hans, do you know what makes me so happy? The fact that I now know all about you and I now have you completely in my power.'

Johan was startled. René hadn't spoken like this for such a long time. René continued, his voice gentle:

'Honestly, Hannie, a relationship like ours would be impossible for me if I wasn't the boss . . . otherwise I'd have to control myself, and that would be unhealthy and immoral . . . but that's no longer necessary . . . now I know all about you and you are completely in my power.'

'You forget that I also know so much about your life that you wouldn't want me to share with others.'

'You know nothing about my life . . . those stories I told? If memory serves, not a word of truth in them . . . write them down on paper for me and I'll check with my friends in Paris and London if there's any truth in them . . . none, I imagine.'

Johan felt deeply humiliated by René's cruelty. Barely able to raise his voice, he said, 'That makes you indescribably immoral.'

'Oh yes indeed,' said René, 'that's exactly what I am . . . and the best thing is . . . I'm proud of it. It's the best possible immorality, but that's something you will never understand.'

PART THREE

FOR OSCAR WILDE

Lugete, o, Veneres Cupidinesque
Et quantumst hominum venustiorum.

Mourn, O Venuses and Cupids
and pleasing people one and all.

(Q. VALERII CATULLI)

Chapter One

1

The brittle winter firmament cracked open that year in a sudden deluge of rain. Johan woke to find his frosty winter world completely drenched, and ominous clouds hanging low above the gardens and houses. Still drowsy from sleep, the entire city was dripping and wet. The square behind the Church of Saint Bavo was without shadow or light, dark in the morning as if it was night. Light was wanting in those winter days, in school, in the city and at home. After a while, the incessant rain started to weigh on Johan's spirits, leaving him unhealthily melancholic. René's comings and goings were a tyranny without end in which Johan had lost his way.

2

René appeared at Johan's school one day during the midday break and in the middle of a downpour. He was clearly agitated.

'Hans, I've come to take you out of school . . . I just had a great idea . . . we're heading out for the afternoon.'

'I'm not going anywhere . . . I have school.'

'You don't have school . . . I decided that this morning . . . we're going to Zandvoort . . . it's beautiful there at this time of year.'

'I have school, so I'm not going to Zandvoort . . . I don't mind going on Sunday.'

'I don't want to go on Sunday . . . I never want to do what others suggest . . . I only want to do what others deny me . . . but I understand . . . you don't want to give in to me because you want to prove you're not afraid of my threats . . . good, I never do what I threaten to do anyway . . . so you can expect even worse!'

'René . . . don't make my life such a misery.'

'Aha . . . is that what you want? I can't think of anything more glorious than a miserable life . . . if it's someone else's life . . . if you had agreed to go with me to Zandvoort, I would have changed my mind and told you to stay in school. But now you want to be so arbitrary and refuse my request I'm left with no other option . . . we're going to Zandvoort . . . and if not, I'll make you even more unhappy.'

'Fine, do what you have to do . . . my life can't get much worse than it is . . . I don't have a say in anything.'

René grimaced and walked away. Hans ran after him and said:

'What are you planning?'

René was now even more agitated:

'Have you lost your mind? Well . . . I suppose it makes sense that you've slowly cracked under my superior tutelage . . . but do you really think I know what I'm going to do? Shopkeepers and politicians know what they're going to do . . . I follow my sudden whims . . . and the wonderful thing is that my sudden whims are always more delicious and cruel than my plans.'

It was already two o'clock and the other boys had returned to class. The rain had tempered his rage, but it simmered under the surface.

'Come on, Hannie,' René wheedled, 'it's already past two and you can't go back to school . . . and you know how miserable it makes me when you say yes to another or say no to me . . . go on . . . !'

'It was you who made me miss the end of break . . . but all right, I'll demonstrate my love for you yet again . . . I'll go with you to Zandvoort, although I know full well that giving in to you is far from safe.'

3

Johan withdrew into a troubled silence filled with regret. They made their way through the quiet streets of the city, drying slowly under a grey-white watery sun. The train to the seaside town attracted few passengers at that time of year and they travelled alone. They did not speak. Johan thought: 'I always give in to René . . . driven by fondness and fear . . . René is fond of no one and fears no one . . . he knows I'll do whatever he wants . . . and here we are again . . . I've lost my independence . . . I should try to say no to him . . . but I don't dare.'

Johan tried to think about something else. He listened to the clickety-clack of the wheels under the juddering coach. A desolate, wailing winter wind circled the speeding train. Johan shuddered. He looked outside. The rainclouds had gathered over the dark dunes. Noon was dark as night.

4

They walked far beyond the town and past the empty beach, left dark brown and desolate by the capricious weather. A stormy wind churned up the murky waves that crashed on land sending mountains of sea foam in every direction. Johan said:

'It's so beautiful here . . . I'm glad I came after all.'

René was quite affable:

'Me too . . . if you weren't such a cautious friend, and if you weren't convinced that everything I say is true, we could be quite happy together.'

They walked hand in hand into the wind, close to the sea as it heaved and laboured. A layer of trembling sea foam fringed the entire length of the coast. Johan felt René's hand in his own. He loved the man more than life itself, and he knew he could never leave him, of that he was sure.

He said:

'It's good we came out to Zandvoort, but let's not stay too late, otherwise Mrs Riemersma will worry.'

René responded as a teacher to his pupil:

'You must never do that, Hans, worry about others . . . but you should always make sure that others worry about you . . . let's walk on to Ijmuiden, then we can take the train back.'

'No, I refuse . . . absolutely not.'

Johan's heart stopped for a moment, then pounded in his throat. He feared René would force him to keep on walking until they reached Ijmuiden, and giving in to René's demands yet again would only reinforce his power over him.

René's response was friendly and unassuming:

'Good, then we'll head back right away. Forcing someone to do something they don't want would be against my wicked nature.'

Johan was pleased at first that René had so readily conceded, but it wasn't long before his fear returned. What had inspired René's readiness?

René continued to be kind and polite:

'Hans, I've been struggling this last while with the idea that you want to leave me and go back to your father . . . so I want to warn you against any such decision . . . it would force me to do what I said I would . . . first publicly expose you . . . then kill myself . . . and that would make your life impossible.'

He continued broodingly:

'I would miss the pleasure of reading your death notice, of course, and what an excitement that would have been.'

5

Johan was shocked to the core by this confrontation with death:

'That's nonsense . . . you're only saying it to scare me . . . you don't trust me.'

'Of course, I don't . . . I don't even trust myself, except when I'm suddenly inspired.'

'You said we should go back, so let's just go.'

They were standing by the sea, far from the dunes, on the open beach, where the sea wind was lord and master. The open space and the sound that filled it tired Johan.

At that moment René grabbed Johan, wrestled him to the ground and violated him without the least shame. René kissed Johan, bit his lip, and groped everywhere in a wild frenzy. Johan fought back, gasped and panted, his screams drowned by the wind and the sea. He freed himself from René's grip and raced towards Zandvoort and civilization.

He heard René yelling behind him:

'Hans . . . Hans . . . Hans.'

Johan listened and was moved. His anxious flight came to a sudden stop and he fell to the sand, hurting himself in the process.

René was suddenly by his side:

'Did you hurt yourself?'

'That too . . . and I'm so tired of this . . . that you're so wicked . . . you're so wicked.'

Broken inside, Johan wept. René tried to console him

'I couldn't help it . . . it just took hold of me and I gave in.'

'Shut up . . . stay away from me . . . it's better that we go home each on our own.'

'No,' René roared, 'I'm staying right here . . . you're so exhausted I could do whatever I want with you. It's wonderful to see that you can't control your emotions . . . I've never seen you like this before.'

And with those words, René grabbed Johan and violated his defenceless body a second time.

6

They travelled back to Haarlem together that day because René insisted and Johan had nothing to say about it.

The trains were rarely used in the quiet winter period and their carriage was empty. René had violated Johan, whose shame was deep. The thought of René's loud and uncontrolled passion only made it worse. He didn't want René to speak to him.

'You shouldn't take every little thing so personally.'

'Shut up.'

Johan's mind was empty and his spirit drained. He slept, and his only thought was 'I'm asleep.'

He later thought that the only way to survive would be to send René away. But he knew he couldn't do it. He also knew he was unlikely to survive. The commotion inside left him trembling with fear. He spoke his mind:

'My life's a misery with you, René . . . I can't go on like this.'

'I can see that,' said René with a smile, 'and watching your collapse is such an exceptional experience.'

'I wish I was dead.'

'Indeed, that seems like your only way out, if it's peace and quiet that you want . . . I'll slip you some poison when the time comes . . . in the meantime you can consider your options.'

7

The city of Haarlem had barely recovered from a hefty downpour and a menacing storm was on the horizon. Only those with good reason were out and about, so the streets between the station and the Riemersmas' house were more or less empty. Johan felt humiliated and said nothing. René, on the other hand, was friendly and talkative:

'Hans, try to come up with some amusing lie for the old lady when we get back. I don't want to lie . . . I'm against every lie. You could tell her the truth, of course, if that's what you want.'

He continued in a quiet, brooding voice:

'I'm also against the truth, otherwise I would tell Mrs Riemersma exactly what happened between us this afternoon . . . it's the first entertaining truth of my life.'

8

Exhausted from stifled anxiety, Mrs Riemersma was dressed and ready to head out into the city in search of her lodgers. In the end she didn't dare. Dangerous fires and burning lamps in the neighbouring houses held her back.

Her relief was palpable and she sobbed with joy:

'They're here . . . they're . . . heavens above . . . where have you been?'

Hans was ready with a lie to save the day. His voice was cheerful, indifferent, with a hint of irritation:

'A good question . . . René's to blame, of course . . . he appeared at school this afternoon at four and announced that a four-master had run aground on the beach at Zandvoort . . . so we headed off to take a look.'

'But you should have sent us a message . . . I've been so worried . . . and what a state you're in . . . you look terrible.'

'I fell . . . you can give these clothes away . . . I won't be using them again.'

Tired despair took hold of him once more. René had already gone up to his room.

'I should get changed,' said Johan.

Neither Johan nor René said a word to the blind doctor. His wife was no longer sobbing out loud, but her thin, delicate face trembled unrestrained. She said:

'Hans, let me tell you why I was so worried . . . I have a feeling that there's more going on between you and René than we know, and I'm terrified that René will take you with him, I don't know where, to make you unhappy . . . I wish René would leave us alone.'

Johan was shocked at his landlady's words and responded with arrogant calm:

'You're free to feel what you want and think what you want . . . but let me warn you: if you force René to leave this house, you can be sure I'll be right behind him.'

9

René was waiting upstairs in the doorway of his room. He called to Johan as he passed. His voice was stern:

'Hans, next time you lie try to make it a little more amusing, otherwise I'll be sorely tempted to tell the truth, and I know that's not what you want.'

Johan didn't respond. René continued:

'Why don't you change in my room . . . you look so delicious . . . try not to be such a cautious friend for once.'

Johan refused and went to his own room. He was emotionally empty.

He carefully groomed himself from top to toe, washing himself with mildly fragrant cologne and avoiding anything that smelled of violets or roses. He was now determined to do nothing that might please René, certain that he would use the least opportunity to humiliate him. But he realized for the first time that he had dared to say no. Johan knew well and good that René would say nothing to anyone about their love affair and he was also convinced that he wouldn't take his own life because death terrified him.

Johan arrived at dinner that night and before he had time to sit he grunted aggressively at René:

'What a sight you are! You look like you've been out in a storm! You could have taken a little more trouble.'

René was taken aback by Johan's unexpected hostility. Johan noticed, and he smiled inside, but only moments later he felt ashamed of himself for taking pleasure in another person's suffering. This was the first time in his life. He thought: 'René has made me a different person . . . a lesser person . . . someone who gloats at the suffering of others . . . I'm ashamed of myself, yet I'd do it again.'

Johan said:

'I can't bear to sit at a table with such an unkempt person. I'll find somewhere to eat in the city.'

10

Later that day, Johan found himself in an excellent restaurant surrounded by flowers and light. His sense of joy at having defied René was immense. 'If I can hold my ground,' he thought, 'then I might survive this after all . . . as long as I don't weaken out of love, or fear, or compassion for the sadness he must feel because he no longer has power over me.'

He took his time in the restaurant, enjoying the light and the flowers, then he went outside at his leisure and made his way along the quiet streets and canals that surround the city. The weather had settled and so had the wind. The city was much brighter and more people had ventured out onto the streets. Johan even enjoyed the hustle and bustle of some of the busier thoroughfares as he made his way home.

At home in the living room, the sense that he had regained control from René was still strong.

The evening was tedious and depressingly quiet. The blind doctor made no mention of the day's disquiet, although Johan would have welcomed a complaint from him and thought he had every reason to lament. He sensed the doctor's silence was more like servility. The lady of the house was still agitated after all the stress and commotion. Johan was listless. He wrote a short letter to the headmaster explaining that he had felt unwell that afternoon after the school break and had decided to go home. He also planned to stay at home the following day. He wasn't happy: 'Yet another lie,' he thought. Then he felt indifferent: 'It goes without saying that I have to lie . . . my relationship with René has dominated my entire existence of late, but I have to keep it a secret.'

As Johan sat with his elderly hosts, he couldn't help but think that their relationship was also full of lies.

René had spent the evening with the doctor and his wife and Johan used the opportunity to taunt and make fun of him, something he would never have dared before.

René understood that his power over Johan had suddenly dissolved. He feared he might lose him completely and that was the last thing he wanted. He felt humiliated and anxiety got the better of him. He ran outside, and when Johan knew that he had won, he laughed at René. It felt as if a young man with a cruel, calm yet focused face was laughing in his soul, laughing without facial movement. This feeling was tangible, like any other observation. He thought: 'I'm taking pleasure in René's suffering and that can't be good.'

<h2 style="text-align:center">11</h2>

That night was a muddle of morbid dreams that haunted Johan's sleep and woke him with a start again and again as if someone was stabbing him and drawing blood.

His eyes tight shut and tense in the yellow lamplight, Johan tossed and turned throughout the night, weakened by exhaustion, his dizzy head pressed into a pit in his pillow. But to his surprise he felt refreshed and happy the next morning. Yesterday his life was a complete misery, but today he was modestly cheerful and in good spirits. He decided to go to school after all, in spite of the note he had sent the day before announcing his absence. School now made perfect sense.

The weather outside was mild that morning, without rain, without wind, the silent streets sprinkled with sunshine. The shadowy alley behind Saint Bavo's was like a vaulted structure and inclined to reverberate. Johan would certainly have whistled with good cheer had he not decided to refrain from whistling in that particular street in the early morning stillness.

Happy days followed, during which René stayed away from him and the Riemersmas. Johan no longer desired René, and he no longer wallowed in the pain René was suffering at having lost his power over him. He was content with the tranquillity and absence of passion.

12

Johan received a letter from René before he left for school one day:

Hans, my dear friend, how are you? I have stayed away. Do you resent what I did in a sudden moment of uncontrollable passion? I tried, but I couldn't help myself. Can you forgive me? If you continue to hate me then I can't be with you, and if I can't be with you I might as well drown myself in the indescribable depths of London or Paris. Do not abandon me. You are so young and so admirably handsome, but your stern indifference towards me is driving me crazy.

I beg you to write to me, and above all not abandon me.

R.R.

13

Johan took no satisfaction in René's humiliation and that pleased him so much that he was inclined to be generous.

He now felt stronger than René and able to keep him at bay. He also knew that he loved René too much to live without him. Separation kindled powerful anxieties, like the fear of death. Hans also remembered that he had accepted his relationship with René the year before. He now had to live with that decision.

14

The evening was quiet, enhanced by warmth and light, when Johan penned his response to René's letter:

René, the letter you sent grieves me because it would seem to be the best you have to offer. But I consider it utterly insufficient.

My feelings, which are entirely genuine, are not to blame for the rupture between us. The problem lies in your nature, which is depraved and corrupted by excessive cruelty. Your cruelty is not a necessary part of our love as some people claim. Cruel thoughts are new to me, and I have done my best to eliminate them out of shame. It remains for me a bitter pill that the man I love has such depraved sexual inclinations. If I did not know myself, I would be tempted to doubt the moral equality of our inclinations and lapse into despair.

You speak of forgiveness, that what you did cannot be forgiven but rather be understood. But for anyone who knows the true nature of your wicked abuses, it must be clear that being in a relationship with you is a dangerous thing. I may not have the right to judge; you are who you are. But I do have the right to avoid you and I claim that right.

I used to be terrified by your threats, so terrified that I became completely dependent on you. For my own self-esteem, this was intolerable, but I no longer fear you.

If your wickedness inspires you to make it difficult for me to live and work among the people I choose, then it's up to you to justify yourself. I can tell you nevertheless that I have enough money to live outside the country if you make it socially impossible for me to remain.

If you want to kill yourself, that is your right. But using the threat of suicide as a means to humiliate me and force me to accept and do things I deplore is simply wicked. Such threats have lost their power over me.

We could have lived an exceptional life together, with mutual happiness, each intensely engaged with his own art. How wonderful that would have been! But you can only be happy if I am unhappy. And you insist that I remain inferior to you, which I cannot bear.

In spite of everything that has happened between us, I still love you. I feel it in my heart and my heart never lies. But if you cannot better yourself, then our love has no future.

Let me repeat that I do not regret my affections for you, only the fear I experienced at the impurity of your affections for me.

You are free to return to me if you are willing to do so on my terms. My friend, I pray you for friendship's sake, come to your senses and mend your ways.

Come back, but with good intentions.

Hans.

15

Three days later René returned to the house. For the first time in a long while, the conversation at table that evening was cheerful and easy-going. When Mrs Riemersma left the room for a moment, René slipped Johan a note, careful not to make a sound:

Hans: my desire is great and my health so poorly. Let me come to your room this evening. I promise to control myself and not be rough, even if you insist on being a cautious friend.

R.R.

Johan nodded inaudibly. René was welcome.

16

Johan was tired late that evening, but he waited for René, his lamp a gentle background whisper. That golden evening was soon transformed into a golden dream. Johan's thoughts were particularly refined. He was convinced that he could manage René to their mutual advantage and he drew solace from it.

His mind now sharper, as if he had emerged from his golden dream, he reflected on the merging of his life with René's, a union that remained a secret. Not even the blind doctor knew. The relationship of trust and friendship between the doctor and his wife was certainly admirable, but his love for René was more precious, beyond estimation.

17

Johan let go of his drowsy dreams and prepared himself for the night with his usual diligence. But since he was expecting René, he chose a melancholy cologne that smelled of violets. He was half asleep and half awake.

He gazed at himself in the mirror, his face veiled in golden light and shade. His eyes glistened, wide with anticipation. The room filled with golden, living light, finer than any light and a delight to soul and senses. He thought: 'My love for René makes me feel so wonderful . . . if his love for me was the same, how happy we would be.'

18

Johan's blue eyes opened wide in the golden light. They radiated a deep, robust glow, blue under a quivering veil of gold. His words were soft yet intense, as if he could taste them, more a feeling than a taste. His lamp whistled thinly, his head in a spin. He felt agreeably tense, brittle. This was the height of happiness, scarcer than gold.

He said:

'René, I'm so happy . . . I don't know how to say it . . . I don't have the words to describe such happiness . . . but leave me be . . . if you continue to treat me with such restraint, you will ruin my happiness.'

'Good,' said René, 'I'll go if that's what you want . . . I don't want to force you.'

The blissful state of Johan's body dissolved at René's words. Pain invaded him. The lamp hissed loudly, and his own voice was hard and abrasive when he said:

'Fine! You've no idea what makes me happy. You only listened to me because you were afraid I wouldn't do what you want . . . please, just leave me alone.'

René shuddered. The light flickered in his dark eyes.

Johan looked up at him, unable to see if he was about to embrace him or strangle him. He continued unabated yet anxious:

'You've nothing to say? Fine! But what's on the tip of your tongue? A reproach? I should keep my promises? I know . . . I should never have promised . . . but that's the way it is with promises . . . you either keep them or you don't . . . '

René was a broken man. He collapsed into a low chair as he said, 'I'm so afraid you'll leave me, but I can't live without you.'

Johan wrapped his thin steady fingers around René's heavy head. He looked him in the eye and kissed him twice on the lips.

'I can't live without you, René,' he said. 'I wish I could but I can't . . . you can be sure of it.'

Johan felt cold without his warm, golden sense of bliss. He had second thoughts:

'Should I have said what I said? Have I exposed myself too much?'

He continued without emotion:

'Let's be calm and go to sleep.'

René got to his feet and reluctantly made his way to the door.

'So . . . I'll be going then . . . '

René's words and their tone of resignation were extremely unpleasant to Johan's ear. He lay down on his bed, but sleep eluded him.

19

Spring replaced winter in the blink of an eye that year, the dull, dark skies transforming overnight into a crisp, clear spring morning. All the trees suddenly sprouted and the sky lifted and opened high above the church and the city. Johan and his blind landlord resumed

their harvest of colourful flowers far from the house. As they nego-
tiated the peaks and valleys of the tumbling dunes, Johan felt the
pain of René's absence and the derisive and sometimes profane language of his refusal to join him. It was a struggle to be kind with the
good doctor.

René had minimized the value of their love once again.

20

Johan returned to his room with an abundance of flowers and a
heart full of joy. On the table he found a new portrait, promised
him by René, and an accompanying letter.

*Dear Hans, here is your portrait as promised. It's not the same as the
first portrait, rather it expresses to perfection the way I see you now. I'm
sure you understand. You express your opinion in words, I mine with
lines and colours. Lines and colours are often exquisitely expressive.*

   R.R.

Johan turned to the portrait. There were no colours, only lines
drawn with prefect precision. It presented him as a fool, his eyes
weak, his mouth bland and quivering, timidly begging. He looked
depraved, a nervous wreck.

Johan was furious: 'How dare René write such a letter. Does
he still think he has power over me after all we've been through?'

21

Hans replied when René was residing outside the city:

*Thank you for the portrait, René. Hmm . . . it's your work, of course,
so it's not a complete disaster. But what is the point in portraying me*

as a gibbering fool? Have you forgotten already who is the stronger between us? It was clear enough not so long ago, and it certainly wasn't you. As soon as that honour reverts to you it will be the end of me, and you can be sure I will remind you of the poison you so obligingly offered me at the time.

The portrait and letter tell me all I need to know about the value of your plans for the future. I would pay a fortune for our relationship to endure without one of us having to be superior to the other. I have to control or be controlled. Under normal circumstances I would have opted for the latter, but in our case, it would put my life at risk. Our life together could be better than any other couple the world over. But because of you we are doomed to be the unhappiest of couples.

I repeat, René, that my love for you remains in spite of everything. Otherwise I would not have been able to do so much for you or put up with so much from you. It's probably dangerous to speak this way, knowing that you can't live without being in control of me. And I know you will never give up until we have ended our relationship once and for all.

Hans.

22

Johan thought to himself as he wrote: 'I love René too much . . . that's why I can't leave him . . . neither fear nor love suffice . . . I have to leave him if I'm to survive, but I can't leave him.'

23

René said nothing about the portrait or the letter when he returned to Haarlem. He remained calm in their romantic relations, leaving Johan confused and unable to understand him. The unremitting fear that René was stronger than him left him exhausted.

One particular evening in Johan's life at that time was wonderfully restful. His lamp glowed like a fountain of gold. He found himself in a liminal space, neither awake nor dreaming, yet more exquisite than both. He was not alone. René's affection towards his friend was intense. He had to control himself and avoid sudden physical expressions of his fondness.

24

They were about to take leave of one another. René asked Johan not to go and said with a light-hearted voice:

'Long may it last, dear boy . . . the two of us . . . we still have years of happiness ahead, don't you think?'

'I hope so,' said Johan with conviction.

'Do you still love me?' René shrieked insanely. He lifted Johan up in a fit of shameful rage and threw him on the bed. He kissed him without restraint, bit him, ripped off his clothes and underwear, burrowed his fingers deep inside his body.

They wormed over the bed, panting and heaving, up and down. Johan was conscious of the blind doctor and his wife who lived and slept in the room below. He struggled not to scream as the full weight of René's body pressed down on him. Fortified by misery, he grabbed René's throat and pressed as hard as he could while René punched him and bit him to the point of bleeding.

Johan felt the full weight of René's body slump on his own. René let him go, and he loosened his grip on René's throat.

'Bastard,' said Johan.

René responded with complete self-control and without the slightest hesitation:

'Indeed, I am a bastard . . . so glorious don't you think? . . . bastards get to experience things their cautious friends will never understand.'

René left him alone, careful not to make a sound, opening and closing doors in silence to be sure the elderly doctor and his wife would not be disturbed.

25

Johan got up from his bed and stood in front of the mirror in the black-and-gold light of the lamp. He saw his wounds and was grateful they were hidden in places that were not usually visible. He was calm. René had done what he had done because it was in his nature. The only way to prevent any further threat to life and limb was complete separation from René, without love or fear. He now knew he could no longer put up with him. He prepared a short letter, each word formed with care.

René, I want you to leave me alone once and for all. I no longer have any feelings for you, nor do I fear you. I pity you, but my pity does not make me weak.

Hans.

26

Later that same night Johan felt completely at rest, and even cheerful in his light-filled room. He had a feeling that he owed someone a debt of gratitude for his freedom from René.

He remained awake until the morning softened the lamplight in his room. He doused the lamp and lay on his bed, staring at the ceiling as the misty dawn gave way to the light of day. He then fell into a light sleep, replete with dreams of light and sound. He went to school that afternoon, blessed with inner calm and in spite of feeling tired. He thought: 'Last night my life was a storm, but now the storm has passed and I am at peace.'

Now that he was independent of René, he could look forward to long stretches of tranquillity in his life and his relationship of trust with the blind doctor was restored.

27

Later that afternoon Mrs Riemersma told him that René had decided to leave Haarlem and Holland. She also told him that René's words and actions scared her. She had no idea where he had gone. She continued without her usual habit of self-contradiction:

'If you ask me . . . for the first time in my life I'm pleased that René has gone . . . intolerable things have been going on in this house.'

Her blind husband said nothing.

Cheered by his freedom and independence, Johan said: 'I'm happy you're pleased at René's departure . . . such wisdom will spare you much sadness.'

28

The days and nights that followed were marked by freedom, happiness and rest. His days were filled with sensible activities and his nights with dreams, and his dreams were days filled with light and the sound of gentle breezes. He looked forward to studying medicine in Leiden or Amsterdam which would allow him to stay in Haarlem. Utrecht was also a possibility if his father would let him stay in their empty house on the market square in Cuilemburg. He wrote to his father about his plans.

Since it was unusual to see Johan so happy in their home, the Riemersmas were assured that René had not harmed him and they were gratified.

Their little family was the picture of contentment. Johan himself was very strong.

Chapter Two

1

As time passed, a seed of decay was planted in the purity of Johan's strength and elation. At school one afternoon he thought: 'What might René be doing now? Would he be unhappy? . . . he hasn't written.'

These thoughts took Johan by surprise. They were evidence that he was still concerned about René and his interests deep in his unconscious mind. His independent vigour was broken. Before long René returned to his dreams. At first, they were vague and formless, cloaked in cobalt purple and golden light, the colours of Golesco's river painting, but they evolved into dreams of death. He dreamt of René's sombre face floating in cobalt purple water with a serpentine streak of bright red blood. The houses were black, their windows yellow in the night. The sky too was yellow like the light in the houses.

Johan feared that his anxious concern for René's well-being was resurfacing and that subjection would soon follow.

2

In those days, Mrs Riemersma dedicated her time to writing letters to René using all the addresses she knew outside of Holland. Her letters presumed his well-being and eventual return, but they came back one by one marked undeliverable.

Johan had an important but worrying conversation with the blind doctor about the extent of René's influence on their family. All three of them were now worried sick about René's life and liberty. Johan observed that his elderly landlords seemed to think that René had left their home, city and country on his account. This saddened him deeply and his sadness quickly turned to intense self-incrimination. The effects on both his mind and his body soon became evident.

He felt terrible for letting René go, the man he loved and enjoyed so much, just because he struggled to express his love with decency. He now recognized he should have helped René understand the depravity of some of his inclinations. He had failed René, but he had also been wise enough to consider his own safety. Wherever he was, in London or any other big city, René was in danger of abandoning every restraint and even dying as a result. There was also a danger he would succumb to the reckless insanity of the city and perish in some act of desperation.

Johan was convinced that whatever happened it would be his fault. The incessant self-incrimination left him feeling dark and miserable.

3

The tension in their home increased with every passing day. No one said a word about René, but each of them knew that the other two could not get him out of their mind.

After an entire day of dread and self-incrimination, Johan lay awake all night. His mind, his eyes, his hands, his spine were stricken with fever. He spent his evenings writing to all the addresses where he thought René might be staying. All but one were returned undelivered and his days remained anxiously silent. Going to school was no longer an option, nor was he inclined to leave the house. He felt helpless and hopeless, and lapsed into a restless, useless state. During the day he longed for the night and at night he longed for the day. Life *without* René was more miserable physically and mentally than life *with* René.

4

Johan finally received a letter from René addressed to his school. It confirmed that he was still alive and free and settled his mind to some extent, but he was still angry with René for the misery and fear he had caused. He tried to comprehend why he and his elderly landlords were always subject to such terrible anxiety on account of René and his regular disappearances, in spite of the fact that he always found his way home safe, sound and unperturbed. At first, he didn't want to read the letter and thought of returning it unopened to London from where it had come.

He changed his mind.

René wrote:

My dear boy, let me thank you for your very humble letter. It was a great pleasure to receive such a letter from such a haughty young man. Don't think I went to London because your little epistle announcing our separation saddened me in any way. Let it be clear once and for all that I am never really saddened, about others or myself. Such sadness does not exist, only deceptive joy at the most. I went to London because I was suddenly reminded of a boy who lives there whose downfall I want to witness for myself. And if I'm not mistaken, I've managed to do plenty of terrible, heartless things during my stay here.

But what about you, dear boy, dear Hans? I wish you would make life easier for the two of us. Simply give in to my desires when I want you to and not when you want to. What I can have makes me sick, but what is refused me restores me to health.

It's also time to face the fact that you're not so wholesome and distinguished as you think you are, just because you manage to pen the occasional page of decent prose. If you keep it up, you might achieve immortality, until you die, and then you'll be a world-famous artist in Haarlem and Cuilemburg.

But when all is said and done, you're nothing more than a slutty little poof, no better than the whores who walk the streets of the big cities. The only difference is your pretence. You contain your attractions and your debauched desires and live a dull existence with an inconspicuous elderly couple. It's a good thing I'm here. I don't pretend to be better than anyone else. That would be a bad idea. But I don't brag like you and I don't share your narcissism. I know exactly who I am: a decent artist with a depraved mind. I revel in being an artist, but I revel even more in the knowledge that I'm depraved, and of that I am completely certain.

Your foolish words and fictions are so incessant that my reluctant memory has learned them by heart: 'rigorous study, stylish and distinguished, good and correct, pure insights, successful outcomes' et cetera, et cetera. All of it nonsense, and enough to make me uncontrollably angry.

Why can't you just be my boy and write the prose that no one likes, otherwise I'd have to forbid it. Your odious conceit makes you think you're too good for me, although it's evidence of love, I'll give you that. There's nothing criminal to do here in London, or in Paris for that matter. I inquired. So, I'm coming back to Holland in the sincere hope that my absence has done me good and you the opposite.

Ta-ta dear chum.

R.R.

6

Now that Johan was no longer worried about René's well-being and freedom, his feelings towards him were reduced to little more than suppressed rage, unexpressed rage, rage that resolved itself in a determination to confront René and accuse him of committing a crime against him. Days of fear and trembling made way for renewed strength.

Without a sign of life from René, Mrs Riemersma had nothing to announce when Johan returned home that day. He thought: 'Shall I leave her in distress, or shall I tell her about his letter, aware that she might insist on reading it or having details of its contents?' He decided to say nothing about the letter, although leaving his elderly landlords in needless anxiety disturbed him.

After three days, Mrs Riemersma received her own letter from René and it bothered her to read: 'I already wrote to dear Hans a week ago . . .'. She invited Johan to read her letter in spite of his silence about the letter René had mentioned. She now knew that he had a secret relationship with René, but her seeming lack of interest worried him. He was convinced that this was just another of René's subtle cruelties.

7

Johan longed for René's return because he longed to attack his torturer with all the energy he could muster. He was miserable in those days. He readied himself each time he returned to the house, hoping that René would be home and he could lash out at him. But René had not returned and his readiness often turned into deep sadness, leaving him emotionally drained, empty and weak.

One Wednesday afternoon Johan found René in the living room. The sight of him filled him with joy. He felt strong and ready to defy him, to give him a piece of his mind.

René greeted Johan as he would a stranger and Johan did the same. René continued his conversation with the blind doctor. Johan didn't know what to do in this situation. He felt indifferent and decided to go to his room. He thought: 'What is it about René that we welcome him back so often and forgive him so much? All three of us? Mrs Riemersma sees it as her calling in life . . . I have my secret . . . but what inspires the white-haired doctor to tolerate him as he does?'

Johan was tired and anxious: 'I hope René doesn't think he can indulge his aggression, verbal or physical. I felt strong when I walked through the front door, but now I feel dizzy, tired and weak.'

8

On the day of his return and their reunion, and the days that followed, René kept to himself. He and Johan behaved like polite strangers sharing the same space. The silence tired and frustrated Johan. His anger was aroused, but he couldn't express it. He worried about the secrets René's silence concealed and it wore him out. Restless and trembling, he thought to himself: 'What does that man want . . . this silence is not in his nature . . . why isn't he making a fuss . . . his usual abrasiveness is easier to bear than this . . . he's driving me crazy!'

Johan broke the bizarre silence one day as he passed René in the corridor between their rooms:

'Don't you owe me an explanation?'

René wasted neither word nor gesture on a response. He maintained his silence to the point of absurdity. Johan lost weight as a result, a lot of weight, and quickly. School was out of the question. He simply shut himself up in his room, miserable, wasting away. In the middle of a night of light and despair, he decided to write René a letter demanding a clarification of his missive from London and his present silence. He tiptoed towards the door and opened it without a sound, aware that the rest of the house was asleep. His intention was to leave the letter at René's door, but in the end, shame prevented him.

9

After days of exhausting silence, René handed Johan a note at table when Mrs Riemersma was busy in the kitchen. It read: 'Hans, I'm expecting you tonight.'

Johan was thrilled. The note was the perfect opportunity to defy René. He pencilled a reply: 'You can wait if you like . . . but I won't be there.'

Mrs Riemersma returned from the kitchen and they continued their meal. Johan was pleased that something had happened after so many days of systematic harassment. After dinner he read for the blind doctor with a gentle yet firm voice. They then shared an intimate conversation about Johan's father, the city's canals, the peaks and troughs of the dunes, and about blindness.

10

Johan lay on his bed in the late-evening quiet, the Veerstraat and neighbouring streets hushed for the day. He was determined not to give in to René's demands. His heart was strong and his gaze resolute, and he was more than ready to resist René if he dared enter his room. He listened carefully for the sound of René's hand on the front door and his feet on the stairs. Waiting didn't tire him, it made him stronger.

He heard René, first at the door and then on the stairs. What if he used violence? Johan readied himself to resist. Body and mind were alert and unyielding.

René didn't try to enter Johan's room. He passed the door and went to his own room. The release of physical and mental tension left him paralysed, especially in his eyes and hands. His lips were cloying and sickly, as if he had just eaten something inedible.

He listened as René prepared himself for bed. Familiar sounds: water trickling, tinkling and splashing in porcelain. Then tense but undisturbed silence throughout the night. Johan was completely deflated. He had readied himself to resist with all his might but to no end. He felt flat and exhausted. René was waiting until his exhaustion was complete, then he was sure to come to dominate and humiliate him.

The following two days René showed no interest in Johan and reserved himself to obligatory politenesses.

On the third day he received a note at school before the beginning of the first period:

My dear boy, I'm beyond infuriated with you and my patience is running very thin. These are exceptional feelings I have never experienced before and I'm pleased to make their acquaintance. But now I've had enough. This evening, when I get home early, I expect you to be ready and waiting in my room. Otherwise I will come and get you.

Your friend, R.R.

Johan quickly perked up, excited by a renewed sense of resistance. Anything was better than the creeping exhaustion brought on by René's silence. He was in the best of spirits and still resolute, a feeling that kept him going throughout the morning.

After school Johan took a different route home, avoiding his usual path across the sunny market square and opting instead for the narrow shadowy lane behind Saint Bavo's. He stopped and read René's note again and again. He stared at it, his eyes bulging . . . how dare he, how dare he write such a note. In a fit of rage, he tore the note to pieces. He was ready to resist and reclaim his independence, even if René were to try the soft approach.

11

That afternoon his thoughts turned to René once again, but this time with a clear change of perspective: 'What difference does it make if I resist? René is in charge and I can't walk away.'

These thoughts appeared and disappeared in his mind with measured clarity, as if they were spoken statements rather than thoughts. They thus broke Johan's resolve and perpetuated his decline. He was terrified of such thoughts. They seemed profound, almost like proverbs, and could easily be a signal of looming insanity. Streaks of pain flashed through his head and his temples tingled and throbbed.

He felt sick to the core. He knew he couldn't stay at school, and was certain he would faint if anyone saw him, so he decided to leave during the midday break. He first had to ask permission from his teacher and then the head master. He hated doing it but he did it nonetheless.

He knew he was sick, horribly sick, and he had to go home.

In this feeble-minded state, Johan abandoned every thought of resolve and resistance. He was completely worn out. His feet staggered as he walked and his arms shook as if he had been forced to subject his fragile body to a burden it could not carry.

12

Johan crossed the sunny market square and passed Saint Bavo's in all its glory, but his mind was elsewhere, his spirit was waning, and he was unable to bear the light, the open space and the bright sunshine. The canals in his inner ear that support balance and a sense of location seemed to be under attack. The houses round him on the market and adjacent streets started to move, to tilt in every direction. The normally solid facades melted before his eyes and Johan reeled in a white misty blindness. He fell to the ground, badly, painfully. His head was adrift in a whirlwind, his eyes rolling in a crackling fire. The people on the streets surrounded him and stared at him.

With all the energy he could muster, Johan sought shelter on a bench carved into the stone of the church and out of the light. Trembling, terrified, elbows bent, his heavy head in his hands, he didn't dare to move. He waited and waited, weak and wary, until he had the strength to get up.

The sonorous golden bells of Saint Bavo's resounded loud and clear above his quivering head, their last echo petering thinly into silence.

Johan knew he was sick. He got to his feet and continued on his way, clinging to the houses until he reached the safety of his lodgings.

He crashed onto his bed and was soon in the cruel grasp of a troubling nightmare. He awoke to a sense of defeat and crippling fear. Terrified to go outside and expose his deterioration, he joined the Riemersmas for dinner. René had left unexpectedly for Nijmegen and nothing was said at table.

Johan thought: 'René's unstable extremes have driven me insane . . . this afternoon, for the first time ever, I appear to have fallen.'

He conceded defeat.

13

The atmosphere after dinner was dull and dreary. Johan read for the blind doctor, unable to be alone. His voice was listless, tired and anxious, but he didn't dare stop for fear he would be left alone, and because his anxiety was increasing with every passing, tedious hour. So, he continued to read, certain that the blind doctor would show no signs of tiredness or surprise, or say anything at all when it was time to stop.

But his reading came to an abrupt end and he hurried upstairs to his room.

14

Johan readied himself for the night, his lamp unlit, the moon his only light. But he didn't go to bed. Instead, and without thinking much about it, he slipped into a nocturnal vigil. The moon cast its light over the enchanted gardens. Johan gazed at them and the pale, moonlit clouds. He felt himself descend motionless into a bottom-less pit of yellow light. The hours of night glided past unnoticed. Church towers rang out their golden song high above the hushed city.

In his dreamlike state, Johan sensed a longing for René, for the man he loved so much, the man who could only love him in return by abusing and humiliating him. He shuddered, dispersing the fragile sheath of pale moonlight covering the gardens and unlit houses. Johan felt stronger.

15

Johan listened to the many familiar sounds of René arriving home. He checked the mailbox first, then the place on the stairs where letters and newspapers were usually left. He quietly climbed the stairs, which creaked in the usual three places.

René made his way to his room. Johan heard the movement of porcelain and René washing himself with water. He feared that René would not come to his room. Would he resume his gruelling, inane silence? Completely ignore Johan's written threats and admonitions? He listened intently but heard nothing more. Surely, he would come. Johan longed for him to come to his room, to burst in with his usual hostility, creating the opportunity to resist, the necessity to resist.

16

René left his room and opened Johan's door. He was carrying a lamp in his hand and its light dazzled Johan, hurting his eyes. But Johan was not afraid. René spoke with a whisper, aware that the Riemersmas were asleep downstairs.

'Why didn't you come?' said René, their faces almost touching.

'The way you asked . . . your impertinence.'

René put his lamp on the table, smiling amiably:

'That's almost as good an answer as I would have given . . . I love it when you resist me . . . I hate it when things are too easy.'

He continued:

'Well, you didn't come to me . . . fine, then I've come to you . . . what a thrill that must be for you . . . watching me beg . . . '

'No,' Johan snapped: 'that's precisely what I hate . . . why does one of us always have to dominate the other?'

'So, you've decided to leave me? You still love me . . . you know that.'

'I don't want to be abused and humiliated . . . but you can't help yourself . . . I've lost my faith in you, and for me that's a major loss.'

'Leave me then . . . move out of the house . . . go back to your father.'

'You know I can't move back . . . that's what's so confusing . . . when I'm with you and you humiliate me I'm deeply unhappy . . . but when I'm away from you I don't feel any better . . . I'm at a complete loss . . . would you be able to stay with me without the abuse?'

17

That night was tender and pure. Johan had extinguished René's lamp. The stationary moon was the only source of light. Night made way for morning, dawning slowly, without getting lighter.

Johan and René lay side by side, motionless, without desires, framed in white on Johan's bed. René asked Johan what he was thinking, why so still? Johan's response came from the heart:

'I feel happy . . . deeply happy . . . happier than I've ever been if I'm not mistaken.'

'And unhappiness is just around the corner,' said René.

Johan turned to look at René, but René had turned away and was staring through the window. The moon was a pale sun, the night a pale, stagnant day. Johan shuddered.

18

René was restless and got out of bed. He kissed Johan on the mouth and eyes.

He said:

'Your unhappiness has returned . . . you have my sympathy, although I consider sympathy an inferior emotion.'

'Don't think you can abuse me again . . . I warn you . . . I won't let you.'

'I wish I could be sure of that . . . but that's the problem between us . . . I'm the stronger one . . . and if you were the stronger then I would be unhappy . . . would you rather I leave?'

'If you're planning to abuse me then yes, I'd rather you leave.'

René continued in a mildly sad voice:

'Don't worry, Hans. If a good person and a bad person live together, the good person is always the loser . . . in the long run your love for me will be your ruin . . . that's the way life is, and it's to my advantage.'

René left the room without touching Johan again.

Johan couldn't sleep. He stared at the pale moonlit night as it changed into morning. He had no idea why René, the cause of his downfall, had come into his life.

19

The days that followed were filled with abuse after abuse. Johan's once-unblemished body was now covered in wounds. He was emotionally exhausted. Johan had become René's plaything, without resistance.

Chapter Three

1

René wrote Johan the following letter as the abuse and brutalization continued unabated:

My dear boy, my dearest Hans, I can no longer trust you. Perhaps you think differently and consider yourself to be completely dependent on me, but if you do, then you are mistaken, just as everything you think is mistaken.

You've tolerated all the pain I've inflicted on you of late, it's true. Indeed, on occasion you've been a little too submissive. I've missed the thrill of your attempts to resist me.

By the way: you may have suffered much from me, but you've also had your fun. A life of extreme joy and deep sadness is better than a bland uneventful life. Perhaps you think differently, but it's time you realized that whatever you think is mistaken. In any event, you're no longer able to live as you see fit, only as I see fit.

I fear, nevertheless, that the sadness I bring you will ultimately exceed the pleasure you take from me. As my desires intensify, your increasing fatigue has become an obstacle.

But now let me warn you in my own interest not to think about leaving me. I'm now certain that I would drown myself or poison myself with cyanide if you did. I have enough in my possession. What do you think your life would be like after that?

But perhaps I won't drown or poison myself after all. To tell the truth, I'm convinced you will die by suicide, and that's an experience I wouldn't want to miss.

If you do try to leave I will simply expose all the details of our remarkable relationship to public scrutiny, including all your letters. I will begin by informing your father. You know exactly what he thinks about our relationship, and you also know how much this information will lift his spirits and indeed how much it will favour a family reunion and a return to your home on the market square in Cuilemburg.

I don't intend this as a threat, but simply as a warning. I need your caution. Cautious friends are just as dangerous as incautious enemies.

Of course, if I expose you I will also expose myself. But at present that doesn't bother me much. Some of my relationships will change significantly as a result, and every change is an improvement.

What can people do to me? I'm free to leave the country for a foreign land where I can work freely, and the world is full of boys to love and abuse. I could also become a monk and forever break my vows, all three.

But what are your options? You want to be a doctor. That's your plan if I'm not mistaken, and your academic qualities would seem to be enough, although I've noticed some deterioration of late, much to my personal satisfaction.

But let's be honest. Do you think you would be able to work as a doctor once people are aware of your inclinations? You wouldn't even get to finish your studies. Your fellow students would take care of that.

You have seen how your father reacted to the knowledge of your deviant attractions? Do you think other people will be any different?

Your darling blind landlord will be first to mock you, followed in quick succession by his darling wife. Perhaps Mrs Riemersma will be first? I'm curious!

Hans: think very carefully. If you want to do something stupid, which in my opinion is the smart thing to do, then choose someone else as your target and not me.

Perhaps I'll grow sick and tired of you in the near future and set you free. But only time will tell.

I love you very much, Hans, without the slightest doubt, although neither of us believes it. You shouldn't preserve my letters and read them over and over again. It only makes you sad. No, you're not a happy boy, Hans, on account of the burden of your love for me. It's an unfortunate thing when two people love each other, because then they stay together and make each other wicked.

Bye-bye, dear Hans,

R.R.

2

Johan's response was subdued and resigned:

René, given all that has happened, your cruel letter neither surprises nor saddens me.

I'm fully aware that my inability to leave you is having a negative effect on me, due in part to my fears concerning your personal well-being, and in part to my fear of what you might do in retaliation. So now you know what I feel.

I've also stopped asking you to restrain yourself and change your ways. You can express your love as you please, sullied or unsullied.

Fate brought us together. I have tried to free myself from you time and again, but the harder I try the more entwined I become.

Regards,

Hans.

3

Johan's physical and emotional state deteriorated further. Whenever he thought about his future he was inevitably confronted with closed boundaries and personal limits: 'I can't leave René . . . if I do, terrible things will happen . . . but I can't stay with him . . . if I do, terrible things will also happen.'

Johan understood that his personal future was no longer determined by his own thoughts and actions but by the intensification of René's whims and caprices. He was deeply ashamed of the extent of his dependence.

4

Johan thought it strange that his mind was more preoccupied with his life in Cuilemburg in this period of breakdown than with his life in Haarlem. He longed to be with his father who was now living and working in Turin in Italy. They corresponded regularly and their letters were usually warm and affectionate, but then this letter arrived:

My dear boy, dear Hans, finish your final exams this year then come and join me here. Italy is just as beautiful as Holland, and so many of Tuscany's towns and cities are a veritable universe of treasures.

You are now an adult, and your feelings will have stabilized for the rest of your life. My presence or absence will no longer have the profound influence I had feared in Cuilemburg.

We will return to Holland in October in time for university. Would you like to stay with me in our home in Cuilemburg and follow classes in Utrecht?

Father.

5

Johan replied:

My dear father, it would please me greatly if I could join you in Italy and live with you again in the old house, which we both love so much.

These last two years of separation have been necessary in spite of everything. It has been a very difficult time for me on account of my nature and inclinations. My convictions remain the same in this regard, as do yours I assume, but it delights me to know that even this difference of opinion cannot keep us apart.

Father, I sent my last prose piece to you quite some time ago and I haven't been writing of late.

Please let me know when you think it right for us to meet again.

I hope we can fill the short time between now and then with a multitude of letters.

Your son,

Hans.

6

Johan didn't think it appropriate to reply to his father's affectionate letters with words that revealed his deeply depressed state. His troubles were beyond lament and beyond tears. His eyes were burning red from endless, helpless sobbing.

Johan pictured the horrors ahead. René would prevent him from travelling to Italy, to Tuscany's little towns with their universe of treasures. Or he would insist on coming with him. And later in Gelderland, at home with his father in Cuilemburg, René would not grant him a moment's rest.

Johan realized it would have been much better if his father hadn't written about travelling together in Italy or living together again in Holland. His life had been turned on its head by René. Happiness was beyond his reach, and misery was being forced upon him.

7

Johan had dreams in those days of intimacy with his half-Dutch schoolfriend Paul Mansfeld. He decided to write to him, to tell him he had reason to be in the neighbourhood and that he planned to visit him in Breda. He travelled from Haarlem to Breda in a state of mental collapse, the only thing keeping him upright being his desire to be with Paul.

But his desire was soon replaced with disappointment. The darkly quiet young boy of memory had grown into a noisy, unkempt loudmouth, with a taste for alcohol and profanity. Johan was crushed.

8

On his way back to Haarlem, Johan spent a day and a night in his old home in Cuilemburg. So many of the town's sights and sounds reminded him of his happy boyhood: the inner gate, the city hall, the market square, the quay and the river. He savoured the exterior of the house, the exclusive stairwell, the white downstairs hallways, the dark upstairs, the tall antique clock, and the garden with the lane and the grass at the back. He listened with delight to the bell hung high in its tower, the clang of the doorbell, and the two different chimes of the corridor clock.

That evening Johan felt happy. An incredible bliss took hold of him, inspiring him to write a few pages of prose.

9

Johan's elderly housekeeper Sientje told him how grateful she was to have reached the twilight of her life with its brightness and tranquillity. She thanked God and Johan's father for these gifts. She also insisted that God was always there for us when our need was greatest and that Johan should have faith in him when he returned to Haarlem, to the Godless house where his commandments were ignored.

It seemed to Johan that his exceptionally insightful housekeeper somehow knew that his life was in jeopardy. Her words were unexpectedly appropriate and moving.

That night Johan dreamt of the heavens above, a vibrant dream of gold, bright red and blue, mixed with gentle music, like the deep sound of a southern wind.

When he woke he sensed contentment in body and soul.

But as he continued his journey to Haarlem, René darkened his thoughts. He was never more certain that without René his happiness would be complete.

10

A frenzy of nocturnal abuses awaited him in Haarlem. René tortured him with high-spirited jibes, alternating with slow, concentrated sombreness. He wrenched the nails from Johan's pale toes, which bled profusely. He was unable to sleep that night for fear he would stain his sheets, so he endured a night of agony sitting upright with his hideous feet in a basin of cool, soothing water. René paid him no attention during the day. There was no affection or even a hint of spiritual communion. There was only torture.

11

René tortured Johan in the still of the night when all was hush in the house. He couldn't scream to relieve the pain for fear of waking his elderly landlords. He was reduced to a twisted ball of agony. All he could do was groan deep in his throat as René bit, kicked and scratched. René suggested with affection that it might be better for them to leave the Riemersmas and move in together:

'Hans, I don't want to force you, and if you want to stay here I will too . . . but fate has decided that I cannot be without you . . . much to your dismay . . . but wouldn't it better if we found our own house . . . then you would be free to scream and shout as much as you want . . . when I inflict the occasional inadvertent pain.'

Johan's silence was callous and scathing, but he was terrified to contradict René. He was completely dependent on him and knew he would have to leave the Riemersmas if René so decided.

At times René declared in a sad and lamenting voice how much he loved Johan and how much he enjoyed torturing him.

12

René had a quantity of concentrated acetic acid in his possession. On occasion he would strip Johan naked, as naked as the day he was born, and smear the heated solution over his skin with a brush as if he was painting a work of art. The solution then crystallized as it cooled, generating a heat that gently seared Johan's skin and the underlying flesh. Such tortures lasted for hours. René would sit and watch, mumbling wistfully that he somehow shared Johan's every wince of pain and that there was nothing more thrilling than the deepest sadness.

Johan's skin was so badly damaged that he couldn't even bear wearing his everyday clothes. He spent his nights shrunk on the floor, beside himself with pain.

René said: 'You probably think I can do whatever I want with you. But you'd be wrong . . . I would love to mutilate your face and hands, for example, but I refrain because I love you so much . . . and I don't want you wandering around with such wonderful wounds attracting everyone's attention.'

13

Johan considered suicide. 'Death,' he thought, 'must be better than living like this and the shame I feel.' After his final exams, the dangers increased. René informed him that he could not permit him to join his father in Tuscany without him. He insisted that Johan inform him immediately of his father's return to Holland. He planned to tell him everything about their life together, their love life with all its ups and downs. René told him he was wrong to hide such important things from his dear father. Indeed, he felt a moral responsibility to put an end to this unfortunate situation.

14

Johan didn't dare to show his face on the market square on those bright, sunny days for fear he would have another spell of dizziness. There was no opportunity to enjoy the sight of Saint Bavo's in all its glory. Instead, he followed the dark, shadowy lane behind the high church wall, in silence and with great caution. He feared he might fall.

He rarely left the house, only when it was absolutely necessary. Visits to the countryside were out of the question. He missed the meadows, the dunes and the sea. His body was close to its limits, and so was his mind.

15

Johan's disintegration was open for all to see and didn't require special attention. His fragile facial colours were pallid and lifeless, as if illness had confined him to bed for months. His bright penetrating eyes were dim and pale. His hands trembled nervously, like the hands of an old man wearied by the years. The blind doctor recognized his deterioration from the hesitation in his voice, which was once perfect and a delight to hear. He finally questioned Johan with caution, begging to know what had happened. Johan assured him that nothing had happened that anyone needed to know about. Aware that people were now conscious of his decline, Johan withdrew even further into himself. His only contact was René, and his dependence on him grew stronger by the minute.

16

René had rendered him incompetent and his schoolwork quickly deteriorated. His enfeebled mind emptied itself of what he had learned, entire books he once knew from cover to cover, as if he had never seen them before. His teachers observed and remarked, but it was a struggle to tolerate anything from anyone, except from René. He often stayed home, missing lesson after lesson. He thought: 'All the other boys hope they'll pass their exams, but I hope I'll fail. That way I can avoid a confrontation between my father, René and myself for another year.'

17

The school's elderly headmaster summoned Johan to his gloomy office and gave him a dressing down, convinced that this was the best way to regain control of the stubborn young man in front of him. He reminded Johan Van Vere de With that he used to be the best boy in the school, but his deterioration of late had left him at the bottom of the pile. He saw no reason for this decline and it angered him. Even the way he addressed the teachers was unpleasant. Given these new circumstances, and to avoid any damage to the school's reputation, he was obliged to refuse him access to the final exams. And if he was unable to change his ways, it would be better for everyone if he left the school.

Johan felt he was being humiliated and insisted in response that he would do the final exams whenever he saw fit. He didn't need anyone's permission. He also asked the headmaster if he thought perhaps that he had fallen behind through lack of personal diligence.

Johan blurted unrestrained that he was seriously ill and that his life was a misery. The headmaster's voice softened. This explained a great deal, he said. What had happened, he inquired, to bring about such a decline. Everyone was talking about it.

Johan was shocked by his own lack of restraint and immediately regretted having spoken about his sickness and misery. He told the headmaster he would try to improve, and if he failed he would leave the school according to his wishes. He concluded their conversation with a stiff nod and left the room.

18

The only way Johan could imagine improving his situation was for René to agree to separate of his own accord. He no longer dared suggest the idea in conversation, so he wrote a modest and cautious letter to René, thoroughly ashamed at his helpless diffidence:

René, my life has become more and more difficult because of you and it seems to me that it would be so much easier if you were to leave me. I am turning to you therefore with this urgent appeal: please leave me.

In a few months I will have taken my final exams. Perhaps you could spend the time until then in one of Europe's great cities you enjoy so much? In August I will travel to Italy and in October my father and I will return to our home in Cuilemburg. After that you can return to Haarlem whenever it suits you.

You have brought an ever-increasing confusion into my life these past two years. I see no future if you do not leave me in peace,

Hans.

19

René's wasted no time in responding:

Dear Hans, to an even greater degree you share my unpleasant habit of not being able to listen calmly when someone is speaking to you. Hence this prompt and written response to your letter.

I have indeed spent time with pleasure in many of Europe's great cities. Great cities, Hans, are great human miracles. The capital of a great empire attracts the worst and the best of people and I thoroughly enjoy the tensions this creates. I usually object to doing things that please others, but since your request is so kind and simple I gladly agree to it. I will leave Haarlem and Holland on one clear condition: that you go with me. Think about it, dear Hans, and let me know.

Both of us know well enough that you will not be travelling to Italy in August. When your father returns to Holland, I will give him a detailed and accurate report of our involvement. He has a right to know, and I often feel terribly guilty that I did not inform your dear father already.

Let me repeat: you must stay with me until I say otherwise and you must tolerate whatever I want to do with you. Otherwise I will publicly expose both of us and then take my own life. If you don't believe I will do what I say, feel free to test me. I usually delight in giving others bad advice, but because of my affection for you, let me give you some good advice: 'Don't try to resist, it will do you no good.'

Your life is far from confused, dear Hans. On the contrary, it is quite simple: a life of shame and dependence.

R.R.

20

René's constant and determined suicide threats kept Johan tame. So, he complied with his savage and intensely deviant sexual life. The possibility to resist and find relief steeply diminished as time passed because his body was lame and his will unhinged. But the misery of his life was nothing compared with the suffering he would face if he was prevented from travelling to Tuscany, and the very thought of his father coming to Holland and Haarlem only made things worse.

His blind landlord was sensitive to Johan's inner deterioration. He tried with caution to regain his confidence, gently appealing to the discretion of their former friendship: 'Tell me what's making you so miserable?' he asked. 'Is it René? Your father?'

The realization that his deterioration was so visible and that everyone could see it shocked Johan. He responded with selfish indifference that there was nothing going on that was of any importance to outsiders.

21

In fear he wrote another letter to René, a letter of supplication.

René, I beg you to leave me alone. I am so sick that everyone in the house, in the city, and in school can see it. I can't cope with you and your repeated suicide threats. I don't know if you are actually capable of suicide, but you know that your threats are what keep me under your power. And I feel your abuse of that power in my body and in my mind.

I beg you, leave me in peace.
Hans.

22

René didn't respond to the letter, nor did he make any spoken reference to having received it or given it any consideration.

He continued his abuses unabated. Johan complied, without struggle, worried only about his dear father who was soon to be confronted with a detailed and accurate report of the horrors of his life with René.

Johan completely ignored his schoolwork. He had too much pain and it rendered him incapable of studying and learning.

All his teachers could see was a boy who had once shown such promise succumb in silence to a deathly sickness. Johan attended lessons, his face pale, his eyes bulging, and while he was still aware of the sounds around him, it had been a long time since he was able to distinguish words.

The people at school struggled to understand how a boy with such an excellent disposition could deteriorate to such a degree in the space of just a few months.

23

René often kept Johan awake at night and granted him little if any opportunity to rest during the day. As a result, Johan's thoughts were jumbled and his mind dull and confused. When he did manage to sleep, it did him little good. His dreams were an unremitting hell of blood and abuse, interspersed with shameful images of Paul Mansfeld, his father, and Gerard the coachman. In the midst of this chaos of impossible dreams, Johan recognized a looming mental disorientation. 'I feel it coming,' he thought, desperate yet helpless. 'René is driving me insane and there's nothing I can do about it.'

He didn't dare visit a psychologist, partly out of shame, and partly out of affection for René.

24

He occasionally lost his sense of time and place in those days. His muddled mind was under constant pressure and some days even his knowledge of the city and its streets seemed to have disappeared. He would leave the house intent on going to school, but on the way his intentions would evaporate and he would wander the streets without purpose. Then he would suddenly come to his senses, and his thoughts would return to his much-neglected school.

When the tensions subsided and his mind cleared, the fear of impending insanity was all that remained.

25

One afternoon at school Johan completely lost consciousness. It happened during a stressful classroom exercise under the supervision of a particularly strict teacher. Johan was pale, his eyes bulging, drowsy from a sleepless night and an evening of abuse, but the teacher insisted he participate.

Johan felt a huge hand covering his eyes.

In a dreamlike state he raised his tiny, trembling hand to his eyes to remove the huge hand. The next thing he remembered was a dull blow to his head.

Johan fell backwards involuntarily with a half-uttered shriek. His face was pale green, the colour of death and decaying flesh.

26

Later that day he was summoned to the headmaster's office for a serious if prudent conversation. The headmaster observed that Johan's condition was now clearly worse than anyone had imagined. But any repetition of that day's painful spectacle had to be avoided at every cost. Only if he regained his equilibrium would he be able to take his final exams. The elderly headmaster added that he would do his best to arrange for Johan to take the written and oral exams towards the end of the exam period.

Johan's affable response lacked any trace of wilful haughtiness. He would be happy to accept the headmaster's generous offer, but he didn't think it would be necessary. If the headmaster and the other teachers had no objection, he preferred to do his utmost to participate as scheduled. Following the rules was the best solution. The headmaster told Johan he would think about his request and consult the other teachers. Johan left his office with a friendly nod and headed into the city.

27

Sensing a substantial improvement, both mental and physical, Johan decided to walk past the front of Saint Bavo's, relaxed and cheerful for the first time in a while. The lofty and simply impeccable edifice gleamed dark yellow in the sun against a white–blue sky. He crossed the market square, no longer afraid of open spaces and blinding light. He didn't go home. His feet were pain-free so he took his time. He explored the city, visiting some of his favourite places, canals, streets, and houses he considered magnificent, places he hadn't seen in a long time. They included a sun-drenched segment of the Nieuwe Gracht, a shaded section then another sunny segment; the Koudenhorn and Teylers Hofje; the Bakenessergracht.

Johan thought: 'Am I on the mend?'

28

The house was quiet when he got back, but not dull and dismal as before. René had already announced his absence from lunch, leaving Johan free to talk about his father, their trip to Tuscany, and their planned return to their wonderful home on the market square in Cuilemburg in Gelderland. The blind doctor looked up when he started to speak, sensitive to the positive change in his voice. Johan noticed that his landlord was visibly cheered and said:

'I feel so much better today!'

Deep within himself he observed the danger of death in all its darkness, but he was somehow able to evade it. He shivered at this new sense of security and personal safety.

After lunch he read a selection of poems for the blind doctor, verses composed in the golden age of the Dutch School. Each composition was comprehensive and its choice of words immaculate. Johan and his blind landlord were both uplifted. Johan's voice was no longer dull and lifeless but clear, his intonation lively and unspoiled.

29

Johan wrote to René as the sun set and his room was hushed and dark:

René, today I sensed an unexpected improvement which prompted a sudden upsurge of shame at my dependence on you. You have made me so sick in body and mind that I simply broke down today at school in the middle of class. But now it's over. No one has the mental or physical strength to live with you, and you know it.

When you wrote to me from London two years ago, asking if I would give you my life and my love, I agreed in the fullest honesty and trust. My feelings for you have always been pure and genuine. But my affection for you has become a permanent danger to my life. You cannot love someone, myself included, with excessive abuse. I pity you, because you sully your own experience of love time after time. But my pity is also my weakness and your superiority, and it is destined to bend and break my mental equilibrium and my literary skills. I'm too good to be deformed by you, although I have been unable to maintain a sense of goodness in the face of your criminal malevolence.

You have succeeded time and again to make me submit to your intentions by threatening suicide. In the past I was afraid and took those threats seriously, but not any more.

You have also threatened to expose our love and our letters to public scrutiny, particularly the letters to my father. You are free to do so, but there would be little point because I plan to do so myself, either in Tuscany in August or at home in Cuilemburg in October. I know my story will shock my father to the core, but I also know that my father will do everything to protect me from you should that prove necessary.

If you decide to make our names a shameful byword, it will be your responsibility. If the worst comes to the worst, we will have to leave the country and live abroad.

As you can see, I am a different person,

Hans.

30

Johan lay on his bed, free of pain and irritation. He looked out at the night sky. It was bright as morning, only bluer, deeper, stiller.

He heard René open the front door and find his letter at the bottom of the stairs which he opened and read. Johan's heart was pounding. He feared suddenly that René would start another of his long and debilitating periods of silence and the thought made him shiver.

But René was quiet and retiring when he opened the door to Johan's room and came inside with the letter in his hand. He lit the lamp and sat down beside the bed. Johan was puzzled.

'Hannie,' said René with a quiver in his voice: 'I've read your letter . . . and you're right, I see that now . . . I'm prepared to go.'

'It's for the best,' said Johan.

René remained calm.

'We had some good times,' he said, his voice weary and sad.

'Of course we did . . . but I wasn't to blame for the bad times . . . and if we're apportioning guilt, that was entirely your fault.'

'You're right,' René confessed, his self-effacement touching Johan's heart, 'I treated you badly and I fully understand if you struggle to trust what I say . . . I say this not because I want to silence you, but because I want to state once and for all before I go . . . that I love you deeply, and it saddens me that I'll never have the opportunity to show you the gentle and untainted side of my love.'

But Johan was steadfast.

'No,' he said, 'I don't trust you . . . and what you now have to say is nothing more than pretence . . . to win my sympathy and subject me . . . I've lived with this for two years and I've had enough . . . I've taken my independence back. In August I will join my father in Tuscany, and in October we will return to our home in Cuilemburg . . . as far as I'm concerned, this is the end of our relationship.'

Johan closed his eyes and mouth.

31

René touched Johan. Johan stared into his dark shiftless eyes, unsure if he had cruel hatred in mind or genuine love.

'René,' he said, deeply uneasy, 'leave me be . . . it is over between us.'

René said:

'I don't understand you . . . every time I think you're weak and powerless, your incredible strength contradicts me . . . it didn't last as long with Golesco . . . would you like the purple-and-gold painting as a farewell gift . . . or the three batiks?'

'No . . . I just want you to leave.'

'Fine,' said René submissively, 'I'll go . . . but I'll stay in the country and here in the house until you leave, because I want to see you, because I love you so much . . . and when you join your father in Italy, I'll go to London or Liverpool, wherever I can live a life that will hasten my death.'

32

René left Johan alone in his room in the blue nocturnal light. He heard René wash himself and the water clattering in the ceramic basin.

Johan's anxiety dissolved into compassion for René who had to face a lonely future while he was looking forward to a reunion with his father. Johan sensed the strength of his affection for René and how impossible it was to hate him, but he was determined not to let his sympathy weaken him and expose him to further humiliation and abject dependence.

He heard René leave his room.

33

René burst into Johan's room, a long leather whip in one hand and a lamp swaying precariously in the other. He looked terrible.

'You're not using that on me . . . don't dare,' Johan snapped, but he was completely defenceless.

'I'll do what I want . . . shout for help if you dare . . . you want me to leave you, good . . . but before I do I want one final taste of what it's like when I inflict pain on you . . . and somehow feel that pain myself . . . in spite of my love for you.'

34

René had calmed down and his voice was steady. He said:

'I want us to talk first, I enjoy that so much . . . and there's nowhere to run . . . if you try you'll wake the Riemersmas and they'll be at your door in an instant. Let me warn you in advance that I plan to give your face and hands my special treatment this time . . . I've been too good with you up to now, avoiding the exposed parts of your body . . . but now I'm going to beat you so hard that people will be horrified at the sight of your face and will want to know what happened. Then you'll have to tell the truth, or lie, of course, but you don't want to do either . . . And what will you do then? I'm curious . . .'

René spoke with complete composure, as if he wanted to persuade Johan to join him in some subtle, incomprehensible duel. Johan was trembling and terrified. 'He's completely lost his mind,' he thought, 'but what can I do if he starts to beat me? Let him do what he wants? Or fight back and risk waking the Riemersmas?'

35

René beat Johan, not in a rage but with complete composure. He tore the blankets and night clothes from his passive body and set about his face and hands in a whistling whirlwind of blows, leaving them battered and bleeding. Johan writhed in pain but suppressed his groans for fear of wakening the Riemersmas.

René suddenly interrupted his assault. He stared at Johan, his eyes seemingly filled with admiration, and he left the room.

36

Johan lay on his bed, shattered by the pain. His face and one of his hands were covered with cuts and bleeding badly. The wounds on his feet, which had only recently healed, were now open again and bleeding.

The pain left him faint, his eyes burning yet tired and dull. He crawled from his bed and washed his wounds with cool, pain-relieving water. He was conscious and awake, but he feared he might collapse at any moment. Visible wounds, especially on his face, filled him with shame.

Johan still felt deeply sad and sorry for René. The man was so depraved that he could no longer live without abusing the people he loved the most. But he was determined not to let sympathy be a reason to prolong their relationship. Simple love between them had been impossible for more than a year, and René's intense and violent love was a danger to life and limb.

37

Johan wrote two letters. The first was to the headmaster, telling him that his condition had suddenly deteriorated, that he would soon have to leave Haarlem and would not return to school. He also told him that he would gratefully accept his offer to arrange for him to take the written and oral parts of the final exam together.

The second letter was addressed to acquaintances by the name of De Boer, millers living between Westzaan and Nauerna, villages located along the dyke to the north of Haarlem. He wrote that his holiday was about to begin and that he hoped to spend part of it outside Haarlem, but not too far from the city. He asked if it would be possible to lodge with them for a few weeks. Simple accommodation was all he needed, without any special preparations.

Johan thought: 'René has lost me forever . . . I'll stay in Westzaan until my final exams . . . then I travel to Tuscany . . . and then I'll go home to Cuilemburg.'

His compassion for René was harmful.

38

Johan lay awake and in pain on his bed, staring at the moonlit night. The new day was yet to dawn and the twilit night was clear and hushed as a motionless morning. He thought about the approaching morning with drowsy anxiety, about going downstairs, about the shame he would feel at Mrs Riemersma's reaction to his bruised and battered face, about what she would say to her blind husband.

39

Johan woke the following morning with a fever. He planned at first to stay in his room but decided to go downstairs after all. His elderly landlords would find out about his face soon enough. It was best to get the confrontation over with as quickly as possible. They would be shocked and full of anxious questions, which he did not intend to answer.

Mrs Riemersma was already ill-at-ease because Johan had not gone to school that morning. And she was certain that she had heard noises deep in the night and movement between René's room and Johan's room.

Johan entered the room, deeply ashamed at the state of his face.

Mrs Riemersma screamed, begging to be told what had happened under her roof. Johan's face was badly battered, and it could only have been René. But that was unthinkable. The man had to leave her house immediately. Her vocation to support and protect René was worthless in the face of such behaviour.

The blind doctor remained calm and said little. He did not want to pry, but he intended to ask René to move out. Such things were simply unsupportable. He did not suggest that Johan visit a doctor because he understood the sensitivity of the situation and how unpleasant it was. Instead he offered some good advice on tending his facial wounds and hastening their healing.

40

Johan was unable to leave the house until his battered face had healed, so he stayed at home, hoping for a speedy recovery, reading, working a little, but mostly too depressed to work or study. He received a letter from the house on the dyke between Westzaan and Nauerna informing him that their lodger had moved out and that the comfortable room he had left behind was now available for rent.

41

After witnessing what René had done to Johan's face and one of his hands, Mrs Riemersma told him she no longer wanted him in her house.

René was disgraced and his response spineless. He said he was so attached to living with the Riemersmas and that he would rather kill himself than move to another house. Why should he leave, he said, when he had given Johan precisely what he deserved? After all, the boy was leaving in a couple of days for Westzaan and then on to his father in Tuscany. After that they were planning to go home together to Cuilemburg.

42

Upset and confused, Mrs Riemersma told Johan that she had spoken to René and what she had said to him. Johan responded that René was well within his rights to want to stay, and that it must be extremely unpleasant for him to be told to leave the house in such a manner. He would surely miss it. He added that it wasn't necessary to insist that René go on his account, especially since he himself was soon to leave for Westzaan, and then Tuscany and Cuilemburg and was not planning to return.

43

René was thus able to stay in the house in Haarlem where Johan was resting until the wounds on his face had healed. The atmosphere in the house was gloomy and all four of its inhabitants roundly miserable.

Out of sympathy and affection, Johan kept a close eye on René and his general well-being. But it didn't take long for decay to set in and slowly accelerate. René ate little and drank a lot, mostly absinth, and was often to be seen wandering the streets of the city visibly drunk. One day he arrived home completely soused, trailed by a horde of spectators and the butt of their derision.

It pained Johan to see René like this. The memory of his own traumas helped him control his compassion and stay away from him, but it took all the energy his feeble spirit could muster. René's misery only added to his suffering, and the idea that it might lead to his untimely death was unbearable.

44

The battlefield of wounds and bruises on Johan's face had healed, and without visible injury he had no reason not to leave for Westzaan. But he didn't dare. Fear and compassion for René stopped him. Fear for his personal safety also prevented him from approaching René. 'I'll write to him,' he thought, 'tell him I can see what's happening to him, that I pity him, that I'm willing to give our relationship another chance.'

But fear prevented him from writing. Instead, René wrote to him:

Hans, please hear me out one last time, in spite of the pain I've inflicted. I don't need to tell you that I am sick in mind and body, you can see that for yourself. I cannot live and I cannot work without knowing that you love me. I am no longer the man I was, I'm nothing.

Hans, if you leave tomorrow it will be the end of me. I beg you to come to me one more time. You have no reason to fear. I promise not to humiliate or hurt you. I have conquered my rage. Let me prove it to you. I just need you to trust me. I beg you to trust me in spite of my many broken promises.

I can't live without you, all the more so now that I see how you are prospering without me.

R.R.

45

Johan read the letter again and again and reflected on their lives. He wrote to the people in Westzaan that unforeseen circumstances prevented him from leaving Haarlem as planned, but he would come a few days late. He took his letter to the post office in the best of spirits. On his way home, he visited some of his favourite neigh-bourhoods in Haarlem. He felt much better and ready to explore once again.

He later told Mrs Riemersma that the thought of leaving trou-bled him and he had decided to postpone his visit to Westzaan. His elderly landlady was delighted, but her blind husband was more insightful. He was convinced that Johan was staying because of René and that their problems would only resurface.

46

Johan wrote to René:

René, my respected friend, because you insisted on it, I agree to meet you. You can expect me in your room tomorrow evening. But don't assume I will give you any more than I would to anyone else.

I pity you greatly, René, but for that reason I have to be careful and avoid returning to a state of dependence on you. It would not take long for you to resume your abuse.

I'm sorry, but I don't believe that you've overcome your criminal inclinations. I suspect you said what you did against your better judge-ment in an effort to win me over. It's also possible that you are free of your brutal inclinations at this moment in time because you are weak. But a possible repetition of your cruelty remains and I won't be taking any chances.

Writing this letter is already a dangerous undertaking for me and I would not have written it if I did not still love you in spite of everything.

Let me repeat: my love for you has always been genuine and com-pletely unselfish. If your love for me had been the same, we would still be together and I would be happy beyond words. But you started to abuse me and my affection for you as soon as you realized you had me under your control with your threats of suicide and public exposure.

I intend to return to my father in Cuilemburg and study medicine at the University of Utrecht. And again, I'm convinced more than ever that our kind of love is not immoral, although society remains intolerant. But I'm equally convinced that your personal inclinations are thoroughly depraved.

René, I fully understand you might not be ready for a friendly conversation after reading this letter. But if you are, let me know and I'll come.

Regards,

Hans.

Chapter Four

1

René gave no indication that he had received Johan's letter. His deterioration continued unabated, fuelled by alcohol and undernourishment. Johan didn't want to ask about the letter for fear it might be taken as a sign of weakness. He was planning to go to Westzaan on the scheduled day, but then he realized he was unable. He wrote once again to the miller and his family explaining this new delay.

Johan announced at table that he had postponed his departure. Mrs Riemersma was delighted, but neither René nor the blind doctor reacted.

2

René's detached passivity and his own indecisiveness about Westzaan made Johan nervous and this took its toll on his resolve. René now looked worse than he himself had looked in the darkest days of his malaise. The very sight of René in such a state of unhappiness and decline moved Johan to the deepest pity. He thought: 'If only there was something I could do for him?' And later: 'Have I done enough? Is there still something I can do?' These thoughts were quickly followed by self-incrimination. He was now convinced that the letter he had written to René was arrogant and conceited. He was at a complete loss and didn't dare leave Haarlem for fear René would hurt himself.

3

He wrote another letter to René, this time unassuming and well intentioned:

Dear René, I now understand completely that an arrogant visit from me is the last thing you want, especially after my last letter. I wrote as I did because I felt happy and strong after so many months of misery and fragile dependence.

It saddens me so much to see you deteriorate day by day, as if you are at death's door. René: why can't we be happy together? If the problem lies with me, then be honest with me as I have been honest with you.

I'm leaving Haarlem tomorrow. I plan to return to the city for the week of my exams and expect to be very busy. So, I would like to visit you this evening in your room. René, my friend, if you could only find a way to change your life and save our relationship then I'm ready to welcome you back with all my heart.

But I've made up my mind, and I will not let you abuse me.

Good wishes,

Hans.

4

The sun was already setting that late summer evening when Johan entered René's room. The air was sweet with opium vapour.

Johan sat by the open window in the evening light. But René was sitting in a dark chair in a dark corner, with only his gaunt white face still visible. Johan was afraid. He knew he was in danger. René spoke with a steady voice:

'I'm so happy you're here with me and everything can now return to the way it was . . . it seems I was very far away . . . '

'You shouldn't smoke opium,' said Johan, confused and fearful at what he had just heard.

'I'll give it up today, now you're with me again, forever.'

But Johan's anxiety only increased:

'I'm not staying . . . I'm leaving tomorrow for Westzaan.'

'No . . . Hannie, you can't go . . . I can't live without you.'

'I *can* go, René, and I've made up my mind . . . I'm afraid to stay . . . I want to spend the next few weeks studying . . . then I leave for Tuscany.'

'You're going to Tuscany? And leaving me in this wretched state? You know it'll be the death of me? What kind of friend are you? You insist that I'm cruel and you are not. So, what are you doing here if you don't plan to stay? Are you just here to gloat at the depths of my misery?'

5

René begged Johan, touching him, grasping him:

'Please, Hans, trust me one more time . . . don't abandon me . . . I can't live without you in my life . . . '

'No,' said Johan, fearful and cautious, 'it's bad enough to see you beg me like this, but you're only doing it to regain control over me and abuse me.'

Now weak and helpless, René said nothing more. Johan was suddenly flushed with pride. The man who once held him in his power was now dependent and begging him for mercy. But his pride quickly made way for personal shame and pity for René, aware that he was ready to do anything for him in this state.

Johan was desperate and felt fragile and agitated. He wanted to stay with René out of affection and pity, but he knew it would spell his complete collapse if he did. Johan longed for his father.

He didn't know what to say or do.

6

Johan placed his hand at the back of René's head, knowing how much that meant to him. René relaxed. They had often sat together in silence like this, sometimes for hours, and René seemed to welcome the stillness and the absence of hostile words. Johan's thoughts were a battlefield. He feared for himself, that René's abuse would be the end of him; he feared for René, that he might take his own life; affection for René and longing for his father, to be with him.

Affection for René and fear that he would harm himself gained the upper hand. Johan hesitated: 'Staying with René means surrendering to his merciless control.'

7

René said glibly:

'Come on, Hans, don't be so moody . . . let me write to those people in Westzaan. I'll tell them you're not coming. Then we can live together in peace.'

But his words threw Johan into a spin.

'No,' he said, 'I've made up my mind. I'm leaving tomorrow.'

'So, you mean it?'

'I do . . . it's for my own good.'

'But not mine.'

Johan took his leave in spite of the struggle.

The next day he was living outside the city, in the countryside between Westzaan and Nauerna.

8

Life with the De Boers was calm and uneventful. They lived on the dyke, while their windmill and adjacent sheds stood solitary on a little island, surrounded by a watery landscape. The water was deep and clear and they used a little barge to connect the mill and the house. The barge was painted bright red and bright green. Johan used it often and enjoyed the abundance of water in this part of the country.

The unpretentious house was part of a hamlet on the dyke. Instead of the usual two rooms back to back, it had one large room taking up the entire floor, with a view both front and back. The front looked out over clay-packed fields used for farming, the back over low wetlands covered in grass. The wetlands were flooded with deep, clear water, with an abundance of tall windmills dotting the landscape. On clear summer nights they appeared much larger than on summer days. The fields were a waterless sea of bright yellow rapeseed and golden-brown grain, without a windmill in sight.

9

Johan gazed across the fields towards Amsterdam and Haarlem in the distance. On warm, steamy summer days these substantial cities were little more than grey blotches on a shimmering horizon. When the sun went down, he could see the light glisten on Saint Bavo's steep roof. It gave the impression that there was no city of Haarlem, just a solitary tall building. But Johan knew that this was *his* church and it was surrounded by broad city streets.

After sunset, when light had turned to darkness, the people of Amsterdam lit lamps in large numbers, many more than the population itself. The dark city seemed gilded with light, glowing golden yellow against a deep blue sky. For Johan, the sky appeared to burn with inner yellow light, as if it was shining on the dark earth below to cheer it up.

When the air between the earth and the heavens was filled with mist, the delicate gold expanse of light turned a dull red, as if the entire city was on fire.

10

Johan counted the long strings of light radiating from the low-lying villages in the wetlands around the river Zaan, all of them mirrored in the motionless wetland waters. The village lamps were dowsed earlier than the lights of the bustling city, and darkness thus came early to the wetlands. The windmills loomed large and dark, and when the winds were favourable they milled in silence, their giant shadowless sails whirling against the deep dark sky. Every now and then the voice of a log driver or sawmill worker echoed loudly in the silence.

11

Since the death of the elderly miller, the house was now occupied by three people. One of them was the miller's adult son who willingly laboured in his mother's service and bore much of the responsibility for running the mill.

His mother was also elderly and almost blind. She suffered from a bone disease that made it difficult to walk, so she spent most of her day in a chair in a dusky room below the dyke. Her hands shook incessantly, making it impossible to work. Her tired eyes peered into the murky distance, at the mill. She could tell if it was milling or standing still, but nothing more.

The third member of the family was a daughter, a sturdy woman who kept herself busy with the house.

12

The entire family was happy to have Johan in their home and Johan was happy to be there. He studied with consistency for his exams and often felt convinced that he was free of René for good.

His longing for his father was so intense it often made his heart race. But it also cheered him to think they would be together in just a few weeks, in a different country, in cities more wealthy than entire countries.

Johan wrote letter after letter to his father but made no mention of the horrors of his life with René. His father's replies were always cheerful.

He also received letters from Mrs Riemersma. She told him she had no idea what had happened between him and René, nor did her husband. She also wasn't sure if there was still something going on between them.

She wrote about René, that he had changed for the better after Johan's departure, that he wasn't drinking so much, that he had been working regularly, sometimes for days at a time.

Johan heard nothing from René himself and it left him uneasy and anxious. What if he wasn't free of him after all? According to

Mrs Riemersma, he was calm and hard at work. But that wasn't the René he knew, and the absence of details only confirmed his suspicions.

13

Johan's health and well-being improved so much that the desire to write returned, and he knew just how wonderful it would be if he satisfied it. He composed descriptions of the mill and the house, the water glistening in the sun, the wetlands during the day, the wetlands at night, the fields of rapeseed and corn, a view of Amsterdam in the evening, the dawn's early light, a boy playing on the dyke in the sun with flowers.

It cheered him to think that these eight descriptions were the best he had ever written.

He was also now convinced that he would be able to live with his father again, without disturbing feelings. He had grown out of them.

14

Johan planned to leave Westzaan the day before his final exams were scheduled to begin in Haarlem. On that same day he received a letter from René.

Dear Hans, my dear boy, I have not written or visited because I didn't want to disturb you.

When you are taking your final exams, I will be in London. My affection for you is undiminished as I imagine your affection is for me. That's why it makes sense for me to spend some time in London. Don't be afraid on my behalf. I won't overindulge myself. When the exams are over I'll come back to congratulate you on your success, which neither of us doubts. I look forward to chatting with you about certain matters important to both of us.

I've been working hard during your absence and the results are extremely satisfying.

Kind regards,

R.R.

Johan was overcome with fear as he read René's simple but resolute letter. He was no longer sure that René was out of his life. He wished he was already with his father in the small but prosperous towns of Tuscany.

15

Late in the evening on the last day of his exams, René appeared in Johan's room. They had met earlier in the day when the results were proclaimed and René had congratulated Johan on his success. His modest and friendly manner was unfamiliar, to say the least. The conversation at lunch was dry and uneventful. Johan said he was tired and that he was looking forward to joining his father in Tuscany.

16

Johan was alarmed at the cheerful glint in René's eyes as he slipped a neatly wrapped package under his hand.

'I've come to talk about our mutual plans,' he said. 'But do me a favour and spare me your usual laments . . . we both know you don't mean them.'

'René, don't interfere with my plans . . . enough is enough, more than enough . . . it's over between us . . . there's no going back.'

'Of course, that's what I thought you would say, but then I'm sure you'll understand when I say that it's not over between us . . . on the contrary.'

'Impossible . . . you made it impossible so stop fooling yourself . . . I'm going to my father in Italy.'

'Out of the question . . . unless we go together.'

'I'm going alone!'

'Oh, you can travel alone, of course, just as you did when you moved to Haarlem a couple of years ago . . . years of great discovery for you I might add . . . but you can't prevent me from following you, or meeting your father in Turin and telling him about everything that has happened between us.'

'I plan to do that myself,' said Johan stifling his rage and despair, fearing once again for his safety. He could see that René would go to any length to prevent him from leaving.

'Fine . . . not a very chaste conversation for a son to have with his father . . . but chastity was never one of your virtues . . . so feel free to tell your father everything . . . I'd rather have saved that particular honour for myself . . . you know how much I enjoy new experiences.'

Johan was at a complete loss. He was about to surrender to René once more.

17

René continued, his manner friendly but disconcerting:

'But that's not enough for me, you understand . . . you lie all the time . . . you're the only person in the entire world who admits to preferring lies to the truth . . . I've never caught you telling the truth . . . so I've had to take measures against your love of lies.'

'René,' Johan yelled, unable to contain his rage. 'I've had enough of your nonsense . . . get out . . . do what you have to do . . . just get out.'

'No,' was René's gentle response. 'In spite of the pain your outburst has caused me, I'll stay with you for your own good, and tell you exactly what I plan to do. I've never caught you telling the truth . . . nor myself telling a lie . . . so you can trust my every word.

Look at this.'

18

René handed Johan a book with a cobalt purple and dark gold binding.

'Feel free to open it,' said René, 'and if you like you can tear it apart . . . this is the story of our relationship, written by me in imitation of your now-renowned prose. And let there be no misunderstanding: if you leave me, many thousands of copies of this book will be circulated throughout the country. That's what I'm prepared to do to keep you in my power . . . so you don't have to ask how much I love you. Go on, take a look inside . . . it's beautifully made, the finest old Dutch paper . . . portraits of both of us painted by me . . . and drawings from memory of some of our racier moments together. Even Aubrey Beardsly's more obscure etchings pale in comparison.'

Johan's eyes filled with tears as he opened the book and saw page after page of René's drawings through a veil of white mist, portraying their most intimate moments and his most painful abuses.

19

René continued, his tone still friendly:

'I don't need to tell you how much such a precious book cost in time and money . . . lucky I'm convinced that the best way to spend one's time and money is in destroying others . . . and I must admit I've had help in this endeavour from someone very close to me, someone I've never abused . . . not yet . . . so he's in my debt . . . shall I read for you?'

'No . . . you're torturing me.'

'I don't doubt it . . . so, you don't think it's necessary for me to read to you?'

'No . . . '

'It's so wonderful to see how easily you believe that what I've written and sketched is the truth . . . indeed, the truth is sometimes equal in beauty to a lie . . . that's why I took so much trouble in preparing it, you see, because I want everyone who opens it to see immediately that it's not just another smutty book but a serious work of art . . . as I already mentioned, the drawings are mine and the text is a copy of your nonsensical prose, which I think is magnificent by the way . . . '

'Fine . . . ', said Johan, 'I can see you're determined to do whatever it takes to subject me to your criminal control . . . but haven't you thought about the damage you will be doing to your own good name?'

'No,' said René, his voice thinly apologetic: 'I've never been the selfish type and no, I didn't think about my own good name . . . how wicked of you to mention it.'

20

Johan and René sat together in the warm light, motionless and silent. Johan was convinced that this day was his last. He said:

'What do I have to do to make you destroy that dangerous and shameful book?'

'You've given me an idea,' said René. 'Let's deal with this like businessmen, then we can get back to our life together . . . but I refuse to destroy the books . . . I'd much rather destroy you, but I won't publish them if you promise to stay with me, somewhere outside the city, in a state of complete dependence.'

'But René,' said Johan, choked and desperate: 'I told you already, I'm going to Italy, to my father . . . you might as well ask me to kill myself.'

'I might do that later . . . I'm not sure yet. But for now, you have a choice: either you write to your father and tell him you're not coming to Italy or, and be sure of it, I'll start to distribute the books tomorrow.'

Johan sobbed:

'If only my father was here . . . you're heartless, René, heartless and cruel.'

'That's my intention . . . it that's precisely why you will sink and I will swim.'

21

'René,' Johan begged, 'please don't do this to me . . . how can I write to my father out of the blue and tell him I'm not coming to Italy? I can't do it, and if I did you can be sure he would return to Holland immediately . . . I beg you: don't ask me to do the impossible . . . and publish your book if you must.'

'Excellent,' said René, 'at least all my time and money won't have been wasted . . . I'm pretty sure its publication will make me famous as an artist and my name unforgettable . . . that would mean a lot to me . . . I love Holland . . . it's still the second colonial power in the world and the people here are spending a fortune in money on worthless American railroad bonds.'

22

Johan pulled himself together:

'I've had enough of your nonsense . . . listen good: the publication of a book guaranteed to make us both a laughing stock wherever we go is not part of my plan . . . and I also don't plan to write to my father to tell him I'm not coming to Italy and he shouldn't come to Holland . . . and if you don't leave me alone I'll kill myself.'

He added in haste:

'I've never used those words before because I couldn't bring myself . . . but I'm telling you, now I mean it.'

René was calm:

'It's up to you what you do . . . the last thing I want is to force you to live a life of misery . . . if memory serves, I've threatened to commit suicide before . . . but I don't think I meant it . . . I never say what I mean . . . and I'm afraid of death . . . but it's up to you.'

'You seem excited at the thought!'

René shrugged his shoulders: 'What can I say . . . Golesco drowned himself because of me . . . so it's not exactly something new to me . . . but I'm curious, I have to admit.'

23

The conversation ended there. René read from the extraordinary book he had written about his relationship with Johan. Johan stared at him, his thoughts a blur, unable to say a word or do anything to stop him.

'Hans,' René continued, his tone almost pleading, 'you have a choice: live as I want you to live, or die as you want to die. But I beg you, don't drown yourself. Do me this last favour . . . what if they don't find your body . . . or find it bruised and battered . . . I can't bear the thought . . . I want to remember you as sweet and beautiful. I'm not telling you to kill yourself, of course, but if you must, please use cyanide . . . it's instantaneous, and your body is untouched, dear Hans, as if you're resting or sleeping . . . as if you were still with your dear father and we had never met.'

René kissed Johan:

'Will you do that for me, Hans? Then let me fetch some cyanide.'

24

René handed over the poison in a beautiful golden box. Johan's thoughts had cleared.

'In God's name, René, why are you so determined that I kill myself?'

'I'm not . . . it's what you want . . . you can choose to live as I want you to live . . . don't dare point the finger at me . . . don't blame me for your suicide.'

'And this abysmal poison . . . delivered by hand . . . you're evil, René, evil to the core.'

'I hope so,' said René, 'I gave you the poison for your own good, and in such a pretty golden box which you can keep. You see how much I care . . . I've gone to extremes to satisfy your pretentious insistence on valuable and artistic things . . . and extremes, by the way, are what makes life so beautiful.'

25

René then spelled out exactly what he wanted:

'So, let it be clear . . . you write to your father and tell him you're not coming to Italy and he shouldn't come to Holland. If you prefer not to, and you don't agree to live with me as I see fit, then I'll publish my wonderful book. And if you can't live with that . . . make sure you're dead before it happens. In the latter instance, do me the favour of using cyanide . . . I can't force you, of course . . . the choice is entirely yours.'

René then left the room and the house.

26

Johan was alone, desolate, his mind a furnace of pain, his eyes bulging. His life passed in front of him . . . with his father, for whom he longed so much but could not reach . . . with the saintly Sien, whose words had once filled his dreams with heavenly visions . . . with Paul Mansfeld . . . with René . . . with his elderly landlady and her blind husband.

Johan sobbed. Life was so enticing, but the only way forward was death.

27

Johan made his decision and wrote to René:

René, you leave me no better choice than death.

    I beg you for the sake of my father, who I love more than life itself, do not publish your book, rather destroy it.

    Hans.

28

Johan opened the precious golden box to reveal its white poisonous content. His eyes bulged with fear and he was dizzy.

He tossed the powder into his mouth and throat.

He gasped, as if struck by an inner lightning, and fell dead.

Epilogue to *Pathologies*

Wim J. Simons

Jacob de Haan did not take the uproar surrounding the publication of his first novel *Pipelines* lying down, nor was that in his nature.[1] His dynamic and defiant mind needed the written word as a means of communication. The critique he encountered demanded rebuttal. By writing and publishing an 'Open Letter' to P. L. Tak in 1905, he drew a public line under the *Pipelines* affair, although for him this was not the end of the matter. He felt socially aggrieved—with justification—misunderstood by friends and betrayed and deceived by fellow writers. What bothered him most is hard to pinpoint, but to use one of his most typical expressions, he felt 'interfered with'. While a reworked second edition of *Pipelines* appeared in 1904, the second part of the novel was to remain unpublished. It would take until 1910 and 1913 before fragments of *Pipelines, Part II* were printed in [the literary periodical] *De Nieuwe Gids*, and even then, not without a struggle.

In 1904, however, a small collection of sketches entitled *Kanalje* [Scum] appeared with the 'author of *Pipelines*' under the author's name as a sort of recommendation. A reprint of this collection,

---

1 See my '*Pijpelijntjes, de geschiedenis van een "onzedelijk boek"*' [*Pipelines*: History of an 'Immoral Book'], included in the reissue of the first edition of *Pijpelijntjes* (The Hague: Kruseman's Uitgeversmaatschappij, 1974).

which was by no means important, appeared in 1911 under the title *Arbeidersvreugd* [Job Satisfaction]. This is probably a remnant of the first edition, with a new title page. The publisher also changed; G. J. Lankkamp–Deventer became D. Pach–Amsterdam. But the prose De Haan published in various magazines after *Pipelines* is more important than *Kanalje Scum*. 'Fijne fragmenten' [Pleasant Fragments], for instance, were printed in *Ontwaking* (1905, 1908), *De Amsterdammer* (1906), *Groot Nederland* (1907), *De XXe Eeuw* (1907) and *De Nieuwe Gids* (1907, 1908). 'Zwervers-schetsjes' [Sketches from the Diary of a Wanderer] also appeared in *Ontwaking* (1905, 1906) and *De Amsterdammer* (1906). 'Nerveuze vertellingen' [Nervous Tales] can be found in *Levensrecht* (1907) and *Groot Nederland* (1908). The aforementioned journals also included other sketches by De Haan. Special mention should be made of 'Besliste volzinnen' [Resolute Statements] which De Haan published in *De Amsterdammer* (1907, 1908, 1909, 1910) and *Ontwaking* (1908). The latter were published for the first time in collected form in 1954 by K. Lekkerkerker.

De Haan's second novel, *Pathologies: The Downfall of Johan van Vere de With*, was published in Rotterdam in 1908 by Meindert Boogaerdt. It was provided with a foreword by Georges Eekhoud, translated from French by De Haan himself, and a preface in which the author took the opportunity, as he writes, to 'clear up a mis-understanding concerning my earlier book *Pipelines*.' Besides the green linen-bound edition, a sewn edition also appeared with an anonymous drawing on the front, depicting a head looking at a rose held up by two hands. On the back of the book appeared another rose, placed between two horizontal bars.

A pre-publication excerpt from *Pathologies* appeared in *De Nieuwe Gids* in 1908 and was dedicated to [theatre director] Johan

Bendien. An excerpt was likewise included in *Ontwaking* that same year, corresponding to the second chapter of the second part of the book. In both cases, the novel was announced as appearing in the spring. On 1 March 1908, *De Amsterdammer* carried an excerpt 'from the soon-to-be-published novel *Pathologies*', corresponding to the fourth chapter of the first part of the book.

The author no longer referred to himself as Jacob de Haan, but as Jacob Israël de Haan, an addition he started using 1905 onwards. Both were Hebrew names he was given when he was circumcised in 1882.

The publication of *Pathologies* also marked the end of De Haan as a narrative prose writer. With the exception of an occasional magazine contribution, he ceased publishing stories and novels at this juncture. The narratives that can be gleaned here and there from the letters he wrote while travelling bear an entirely different character. The prose writer was to make way for the poet. It was primarily through his poetry, as a poet of Jewish verse, that Jacob Israël de Haan was to acquire a lasting place in Dutch literature.

His literary debut dates back in fact to the publication of verse in *Holland* and in *De Gids* in 1900 and 1901. This youthful work is, on the whole, of little significance and was rightly not included by K. Lekkerkerker in the two-volume edition of De Haan's *Collected Poems* published in 1952.

It was not until *circa* 1909 that De Haan's poetry began to find a readership. His *Liederen* [Songs] appeared in the fifth issue of the 1909 volume of *De Beweging*, after four years of knocking on its editor Albert Verwey's door asking to have his work published in his magazine. Broadly speaking, one can say that up to and including the appearance of *Pathologies*, De Haan was more important as a prose writer than as a poet. Why did De Haan choose poetry? Did he consider poetry to offer greater opportunity? Was verse better suited to him as a form of expression, or was he so engrossed in his scientific and journalistic work that he lacked the time for more extensive literary work, in this case, a novel? It certainly cannot have been a lack of ambition, since De Haan was clearly ambitious.

Whatever the reason for his transition to poetry, the issues De Haan raised in *Pipelines* and *Pathologies* were not abandoned. One need only read his verse, especially the collection *Een nieuw Carthago* [A New Carthage] (1919), to confirm this fact. Nevertheless, in a letter to Herman Robbers in 1907 he writes: 'I promised my wife-to-be, who is a doctor, not to write any more '*Pipelines*-like' literature, and I wanted to keep that promise.' He adds, however: 'Well, that made me so ill that she herself has already told me to write according to my needs.' In the same letter, he also characterizes his stories as 'atrocious and immoral' and states 'I cannot do otherwise. Even if it kills me.'

The comment about his wife's promise may seem a little odd considering that *Pathologies* was published a year later after all. But the novel had actually been written much earlier. While I have been unable to trace any details on this, I think I can assume that De Haan started work on *Pathologies* immediately after *Pipelines*. Evidence in support of this assumption can be found in his correspondence with Frederik van Eeden. From his time in Haarlem in 1899, where he attended the state-run teacher-training college, the young socialist Jacob de Haan sought contact with Van Eeden, impressed by his Walden experiment and his social commitment.[2]

---

2 [Inspired by Henry David Thoreau's *Walden*, Dutch writer and psychiatrist Frederik van Eeden (1860–1932) founded a community called Walden in Bussum in the province of North Holland. In this community, residents

From correspondence and later personal contact, a lifelong friendship evolved between the two, a friendship with many unsurprising ups and downs given their very different characters. When De Haan left for Palestine in 1919, he wrote about Van Eeden in his *Heengaan uit Holland* [Leaving Holland]:

> It has been twenty years since I, a boy fearful of life's dangers, sought and found support and friendship Many of those twenty years have been difficult. I have experienced everything a Jewish boy can experience of errors and setbacks in these years. But this friendship, this reverence has remained intact to the present day and has not been overshadowed. Such are the gifts of life, gifts that reconcile us with life. For that I am grateful. And it is right and just that I here express my thanks openly. I know of no poet or scholar for whom Holland has been less grateful than for these. Verwey and Van Eeden brought stability to my life, honesty and loyalty. This I remember as I take my leave.

Van Eeden must also have influenced De Haan's initial choice of studies. Like Van Eeden and Johanna van Maarseveen—whom he married in 1907—he wanted to become a doctor but ultimately chose to study law. The injustice he felt had been done to him in the *Pipelines* affair must have influenced this decision.

Van Eeden's friendship with De Haan did not prevent him from being dismissive of *Pipelines*. He noted in his diary on 25 June 1904: 'I read Jacob de Haan's dreadful book.' And on 8 June 1909

---

aimed to self-sustain as much as possible and shared all their resources. Van Eeden himself embraced a simpler lifestyle at Walden, markedly different from his previous habits, reflecting the socialist leanings of many of his Dutch contemporaries.—Ed.]

he characterized De Haan in the same diary as 'a poor, perverse and melancholic man', adding nevertheless that he is the only one who 'still writes me an occasional kind letter'.

It was thus Van Eeden whom De Haan asked to read the manuscript of *Pathologies* in 1905, expecting a favourable response and possible mediation with a publisher, perhaps the Amsterdam publisher Versluys, the publisher of much of Van Eeden's own work. His hopes were in vain. The manuscript was returned from Walden with a dismissive note:

> Dear de Haan!
>
> I am returning the book to you as I am unable to read it to the end. The beginning is reminiscent of *Cool Lakes*[3] but what follows is unreadable to me in terms of both style and essence.
>
> 'Art must be the expression of man's delight in God's work,' said Ruskin, and I agree with him. I cannot call a book such as this art. But since you insist on following your own path anyway and prefer to believe what the flatterers say, what I think will not be of much consequence to you. So please do not ask me to judge your work.
>
> Regards F. van Eeden

So, De Haan was unable to count on Van Eeden's support, nor was he able to turn to other authoritative literary figures of the day

---

3 From Van Eeden's own novel *The Cool Lakes of Death* (1900), the story of a woman who sought the cool lakes of death, where salvation is, and how she found it. According to Van Eeden, he wanted to 'depict the simple classical movements of a woman's life, driven to her limits by melancholy, sin, sensuality, madness and yet with the triumph of Death over Death.' According to Ch. M. van Deventer, the book is 'a medical tragedy'.

because of the *Pipelines* affair. In the meantime, however, he was fully occupied with his studies and was struggling to cope both socially and financially. He had even toyed with the idea of moving to Paris and simply ignoring what was going on in the Netherlands. As a result, the manuscript of *Pathologies* remained on hold. He finally found the Belgian novelist Georges Eekhoud (also spelt Eeckhoud) willing to write a preface. Eekhoud, who had founded the avant-garde journal *Le coq rouge* in 1895 and had made a name for himself with naturalistic novels such as *Kees Doornik* (1883) and *La nouvelle Carthage* (1888), was keenly interested in social conditions and had an outspoken sympathy for the deprived. He also recognized the influence of sexual urges on human behaviour. De Haan had come to the right place. It allowed him to write to Van Eeden to tell him that his novel would now be published, and in spite of Van Eeden's initial negativity, he appeals to him once more to mediate with a publisher in the conviction that his work would do better with Versluys.

> Dear Van Eeden,
>
> The typed drafts of my book *Pathologies* are ready. I will send a copy to Walden on Tuesday when the pages are bound together. I only have two copies, so I can't spare one for you. You, however, will receive a printed copy, which is natural, since you are my great and loyal friend.
>
> I know you will find little to love in my book, you have called this: divine wisdom. But I also hope you will enjoy at least some of its beautiful and endearing features. The vocabulary and phrasing might sometimes appear strange compared to everyday language, but there is not a single word or turn of phrase that I did not hear within me as I

carefully revised my work. Will you tell me honestly (well, that goes without saying) what you think of it?

Georges Eekhoud has already read it, and he praised it as a strong and flawless book. He will write a preface to it, and provide a translation.[4]

I'd much rather have you introduce the book to its readers. After all you have been my friend for so many years. In times of need I have always turned to you, and that should be proof enough that I care for you greatly and that I trust you as much as your patients trust doctor F.v.E.

Would you be willing to write an introduction after all? You did it for Adriaan van Oort.[5] I know you liked his *Irmenlo* and perhaps you don't feel the same about my work. But would you consider recommending its publication to Mr Versluys nonetheless? I have access to a publisher, but I don't like him, and besides I don't know any of these people. Would you do that even if you don't like the book? It will be published one way or another, but in a manner that pains me. You can tell V. precisely what you think about the book and that he would be doing you a favour to publish it if only to save your friend's book from lesser hands.

Van Eeden did not write an introduction, mediate with Versluys or write a review after publication. *Pathologies* may have been about to appear, but things were not going well for De Haan. At

---

4 A translation of *Pathologies* was never published.

5 Adriaan Willem van Oordt stayed at Walden from 1899 to 1901. Van Eeden had written a laudatory introduction for his historical novel *Irmenlo*, published in 1896.

the beginning of 1908, he was suddenly dismissed without notice from his job as a reserve municipal school teacher. He claimed in a letter to Lodewijk van Deyssel that his dismissal was 'entirely due to my writings'. Indeed, the newspapers were frequently critical of his journal contributions.

Things did not get much better when *Pathologies* appeared in the bookshops, despite Eekhoud's foreword. On 21 June 1908, Frits van Raalte published a stinging attack in the weekly *De Amsterdammer*, the magazine to which De Haan had been a regular contributor since 1905 and in which he would later publish many of his quatrains. A week later, De Haan responded in the same weekly with an article entitled 'A Lecture on Perverse Passion'.

Little has been written about *Pathologies*. The book, like *Pipelines*, was hushed up and forgotten. Many of the standard handbooks on the history of Dutch literature make no mention of either novel. Here too, De Haan the poet has eclipsed the prose writer, although a general lack of familiarity with De Haan's prose work may have contributed to this lacuna.

Like *Pipelines*, albeit to a lesser extent, *Pathologies* is not easy to comprehend. I do not wish to provide an analysis of *Pathologies* in the present epilogue, as I did not do so when commenting on the reissue of *Pipelines*. My intention, rather, is to inform readers about the author and the genesis of the book.

Comparisons between *Pipelines* and *Pathologies* are obvious. Both novels were written shortly after each other and both deal with an affair between two young men, a subject that rarely if ever featured in literary publications at that time in contrast to today. The latter already makes both novels unique in Dutch literature.

Although the subject matter in both novels is basically the same, there is a clear difference. Apart from the fact that *Pathologies* is, in my opinion, qualitatively more significant than *Pipelines* and is also written in a different, more impressionistic style, the premise in both novels is clearly different. Johan van Vere de With, whose 'downfall' is described in *Pathologies*, is presented as a victim in an entirely different way and with greater clarity than Joop in *Pipelines*. Moreover, Johan van Vere de With struggles with his otherness and suffers because of it. His father's rejection hurts him immeasurably, although he seems to understand his father's position. He sees his homosexual tendencies as wrong and he struggles not to give in to them with varying degrees of success. He is tormented by guilt and sinfulness. It is here that we find the voice of De Haan, who will later express himself in this sense with some frequency, especially as the author of the *Quatrains*. There is and remains a compulsion in De Haan 'to write according to my needs', as he observed in his letter to Robbers. Some examples from *Quatrains*:

> The Moment my senses seek
> And my Soul seeks Eternity.
> From the dawn of every day
> This struggle Tortures me.

Later in his life, De Haan's sense of guilt projects itself with increasing clarity on religious experiences, eternal doubt and constant turmoil.

> What awaits me in this evening hour,
> The City beset by sleep,
> Seated by the Temple wall:
> God or the Moroccan Lad?

> Men have separated lust and suffering.
> But God holds them together as night and day.

I know about lust—I know the intense suffering.
I praise God's One Name.

I suffered under my wanton urges,
Until I realized: sin too is of God.
My lust and my faltering prayers:
One single fate.

The renunciation of 'sin' makes *Pathologies* a fundamentally different book from *Pipelines*. Nevertheless, I cannot entirely agree with
the view of Dr Jaap Meijer whose study *De zoon van een gazzen*
[The Son of a Chazzan] (1967) claims that *Pathologies* formally pro-
claims the opposite of *Pipelines* and that, as a result, the second
novel was much less controversial than the first. But a different
approach need not imply an explicitly opposite one. The different
approach is related to a development that took place in De Haan
himself, although it did not mean he let go of his earlier feelings.
The fact that *Pathologies* was less controversial than *Pipelines* should
likewise not be explained on this basis. There was simply less reason
for uproar. For the reader, however, *Pathologies* must have been even
more shocking, because the sadism it portrays is much more explicit
than in *Pipelines*.

De Haan's growing sense of guilt and sin can also serve to
explain the title of his novel. Pathology refers to a symptom of disease, and this implies a position with regard to the relationships
described in the novel.

The story takes place partly in Culemborg (De Haan uses an
older spelling Cuilemburg), partly in Haarlem. De Haan had personal experience of both cities, having worked as a teacher in
Culemborg and attended teacher-training college in Haarlem. At
first, he lived in Haarlem with his aunts and uncle Gerson de Haan,

a mathematics teacher; later, he moved in with the blind Jewish doctor Koetser, where a somewhat extravagant figure by the name of Blok was also a lodger. The protagonist of *Pathologies* also moves in with a blind doctor in Haarlem, where he befriends his housemate René Richell.

The name Johan van Vere de With also has clear connections with De Haan. Indeed, J. A. Rispens observed a sound symbolism in this apparently deliberately chosen name. Using the pseudonym René de With, De Haan reviewed Wanda Sacher Masoch's *Confessions de ma vie* in *Den Gulden Winckel* (15 August 1911) under the title 'Literature and Pathology'. And under the same pseudonym, he published a review of the poetry collection *Lueurs et flammes* by Hélène Vacaresco in *De Amsterdammer* (16 August 1908). Hélène Vacaresco was an aristocratic Romanian writer who lived in exile in Paris where she died in 1947. Her name is found in *Pathologies* in a modified form where reference is made to Hélènus Marie Golesco, a painter who drowned in the Seine in Paris. De Haan used this name again in 1910 when he published *De Lupuslijder* [The Lupus Sufferer] in *Ontwaking* and *Nieuw Leven* with the subtitle *From the Life of Helenus Marie Golesco*. Incidentally, De Haan maintained contact with the Romanian writer, who was once destined by Romania's Queen Elisabeth to marry her adopted son Crown Prince Ferdinand. He visited her in Paris on his way to Palestine, and reported on the encounter in a letter published in the *Algemeen Handelsblad* (1 February 1919).

De Haan dedicated the three parts of *Pathologies* to three different writers. The first was to Georges Eekhoud who wrote the preface; the second, to the English writer Oscar Wilde (posthumously, as Wilde had already died in 1900), who had been sentenced to hard labour following a trial for homosexuality; the third, to the Danish writer Herman Bang, whose homosexuality was widely known. For each of these dedications, De Haan chose verses from Catullus.

Interest in the work of Jacob Israël de Haan has increased in recent years, after being largely overlooked in the period following his violent death in Jerusalem on 30 June 1924. The significance of his poetry is now widely recognized: De Haan is—and not only in my opinion—the most important Jewish-Dutch poet in Dutch literary history. His prose work, however, deserves reappraisal.

Pathologies is more than a novel. It is a constituent part of De Haan's life story, a life he once wrote about in relation to his *Quatrains*—although it should not be limited to this relationship:

> Those who come after me, who read my quatrains,
> > Will tremble, when they realize,
> > With what tormented heartache
> > I have gone through life singing.